MARK MANNOCK

LETHAL SCORE

A NICHOLAS SHARP THRILLER (2)

First published by Shotfire Books 2020

First edition

ISBN: 978-0-6489036-1-1

This book was professionally typeset on Reedsy.
Find out more at reedsy.com

For Sarah

Contents

Chapter 1

As the flames danced, they washed his eyes with fire. It was impossible to read him or see into his thoughts, but I could feel the dark inferno of his gaze.

"You have come here to pay respect, brother. I appreciate that." The voice was raspy, deep.

I waited for him to say more. He didn't.

The silence of the desert night was punctuated only by the sound of the fire between us, crackling like muted gunshots. I stared at him, transfixed. His long hair, thick and gray, matched an endless beard that framed his dark and weathered skin. A lifetime of wear.

I could feel the intensity as he drew me deeper into his soul.

Then he spoke again. "Your eyes speak of pain. I wonder if perhaps you live in the shadow of regret?"

I didn't answer. Back to the silence, the darkness, the flames.

He stood, I followed. He reached his hand over the fire for me to shake; his grip was firm.

"I think your music brings a calmness to your life," He said. "We appreciate you sharing it with our culture and our people."

The old man paused, as if deciding what to reveal. A flicker of confusion. "You live with hope, yet death walks beside you ... but of course, I think you know that." Another pause.

"Good luck, my brother."

With that, the Elder turned and left.

I looked around, seeking to regain some control, some normalcy. Several people sat around the campfire with us, but they had all retreated into silence when the Indigenous Elder had looked directly at me and spoken. Now the conversations slowly resumed. Out of the corner of my eye I saw Jack Greatrex, my oldest friend. He was smiling in the kind of way that said, "I told you."

Next to me, Patrick Jay leaned over and said, "We go now."

With those words we headed across the sand to our four-wheel drive. The Australian outback is unforgiving country. By day it can be exhilarating and powerful; by night, as we saw it, it was a theater of mystery. I climbed into the front passenger seat, took a deep breath, and closed my eyes.

My thoughts still focused on the Elder. How could a man I had only met for the first time, for just a few brief minutes, possibly sense so much about me?

It seemed I was to be a part of the desert's mystery.

From the back seat, Greatrex's voice broke through my thoughts.

"Nicholas, you were never going to sort this by running."

"What made you the keeper of all things wise?" I asked. He could tell there was no malice in my voice.

"Among other things, a bullet in my shoulder."

Jack had taken a hit when a situation we were involved in had ended badly on the Isle of Wight in Southern England. A world away from here. He had killed the man who shot him.

Greatrex continued: "Nicholas, people like you and me can't plan who we are. We don't choose which part of us is real and which isn't. That's decided by circumstance and the way we react ... in the moment."

Too damn wise for my taste, but despite my occasional fondness for reckless behavior, I knew he was right, as was the Elder. I knew I would have to learn to accept it. "The moment." A musician lives in the moment, a soldier lives in the moment. For that matter, so does a killer.

We would just have to see what "the moment" would bring.

Chapter 2

Six months later ...

The massive stone walls surrounding the room were covered by enormous tapestries, each capturing a moment from the estate's tumultuous past. We were shrouded in a rich cocoon of past conflicts. I looked up from the ten-foot black grand piano as rays of light from the high windows danced enchantingly, defying the room's shadows while my fingers caressed the keys.

The chamber already rumbled with the deep and haunting drone of Patrick Jay's didgeridoo, resonating through our bodies like a tremor from the earth's core. The piano's melodic lilt added another layer, softening the mood, infusing it with pathos. Then the final sonic brushstroke: Aislinn Byrne's voice soared high, bouncing from the tops of the cavernous walls, raising the emotional stakes. As her pitch climbed, her tone cried for all humanity. If hope was a sound, this was it. We were in the presence of an angel.

We were in the final rehearsals before our European tour began. The album I had recorded in Australia with New Age legends Aislinn Byrne and Patrick Jay Olden had been unexpectedly successful. Our music had somehow connected with an audience seeking to disconnect from an over-paced world. The record company had planned a tour, a different type of tour. Instead of playing the summer New Age and alternative festivals, we were to tour the great opera houses of Europe in winter. The plan was to let the acoustics of these buildings be our ally, and their magnificent history and architecture be our backdrop.

Rehearsing at Cuillin Castle, overlooking Loch Alsh in the Scottish Highlands, was a transcendent experience. The lake's tranquil waters were as calming as the high castle walls were imposing.

The castle belonged to Antonio Ascardi, the billionaire social media entrepreneur. Among his many interests, Ascardi owned Vittoria Records, the record company that had signed and recorded us. As the music subsided, I drew a deep breath and relaxed into the stillness of the moment.

"Bravo, bravo! Every time you three perform, it is different, a new exploration. I feel my pulse slow and my senses rise when I hear your spirited song. Bravo!" Our mellow silence had been shattered by Antonio Ascardi's booming voice and thundering handclaps echoing from the back of the room. We hadn't even heard our host walk in.

I glanced at him. The entrepreneur's straggly long dark hair surrounded a neatly trimmed goatee that gave him the look of an artist, a bohemian. He wore his dark suit casually, with a white open-necked shirt, informally formal. His tanned skin in the middle of a Scottish winter conceded a level of wealth that allowed him to travel anywhere in the world at any time. The formality of the man's language was a nod to generations past, the era of Cary Grant and the heyday of the

Riviera. Yet for Ascardi, his parlance sounded as natural as breathing. I was aware that underneath the mask was a brain with a technical prowess a world ahead of its time. Antonio Ascardi was an old-time raconteur thriving in a hi-tech world, a dichotomy that belied his relative youth.

I knew the man had a reputation as a maverick and an original thinker. Most of the world's media had labeled him a genius. Nearly a third of the planet used one of Ascardi's media platforms as their go-to social media site; unsurprisingly, the entrepreneur's success had seen him reach billionaire status by the age of thirty-five.

"Hello, Tony." Aislinn seemed slightly besotted whenever Antonio Ascardi was around. "It's lovely to see you."

Patrick Jay and I nodded.

"I've just returned from London. The final pieces are in place. This tour will be an innovative experience for these old opera houses and the audiences who fill them, a lavish musical banquet to be consumed, savored and remembered."

Antonio Ascardi was never short of a word.

Two hours later we were gathered in the castle's dining room. The wooden table before us had been scarred and scuffed by revelers who had feasted here for centuries. Ascardi was at the head of the table, holding court. I couldn't imagine Antonio Ascardi sitting anywhere but the head of the table. Aislinn and Patrick Jay were seated down one side, and Jack Greatrex and I sat down the other. There was space for twenty more. After two weeks of rehearsal, Greatrex had joined us to get the gear sorted and packed up for the tour crew arriving in the morning.

Spread before us were numerous bottles of ridiculously

expensive wine from Ascardi's cellar and an array of cordon bleu food prepared by his chefs.

"I will of course join you for some of the tour, Aislinn, but I fear other business commitments will tear me away soon enough." Coming from Ascardi, this was more like an announcement than a conversation.

"I do hope you can stay with the tour as long as possible. It's lovely having you with us." Aislinn, the besotted one.

"It must be difficult, Tony, to keep everything running smoothly with such a diverse business empire to oversee." I felt that I should make some contribution to the dinner talk.

Ascardi pursed his lips and stared down at the food on his plate before responding. "Yes, Nicholas, you're right. It can be taxing to have so many people clambering for your attention. It certainly wasn't the case when I began back in Rome as a simple programmer with the glimmer of an idea. Now I almost hunger for a world where there is less responsibility … and accountability."

I heard Greatrex grunt next to me. He had taken a dislike to Antonio Ascardi almost from the moment they met, several months ago. Nothing since had changed his mind.

Ascardi continued. "Nicholas, I believe you aren't traveling with the main group for the whole tour."

"No," I responded. "I'm looking for a little downtime. I'll be in each city for the performances well ahead of time."

"Ah, Nicholas Sharp, the lone wolf."

"Yes, I suppose so," I responded quietly.

The real reason for my forced independence was that I was perpetually restless and a mite conflicted. That night in the Australian desert, across the burning fire from the old Indigenous Elder, still troubled me. We had been there to launch the album in the most inspiring "New Age" atmosphere we could think of: Uluru and the desert outback. Among the celebrations, I hadn't counted on being spooked by such a confronting prophecy. I knew I should let it go.

My state of mind had also impacted my "on again, off again" relationship with a beautiful woman back in L.A. who deserved better. Currently, Kaitlin Reed and I were "off again." It was for the best.

Ascardi ignored my response and continued to hold court. "Well, as you know, we begin the tour at the Festival Theatre in Edinburgh. There will be plenty of media there to get the ball rolling. Due to pressing business commitments, I will have my helicopter fly me down to London while you folks do some interviews and then catch the train—first class, of course. Our second show will be at the London Opera House three days after you arrive."

Patrick Jay spoke for the first time. "I think we all appreciate the extended breaks between shows, Tony. This is so different compared to the music industry's usual 'time is everything' approach to touring."

We all nodded in agreement.

"As you know, Patrick, I spend a lot of effort and resources pursuing alternative solutions to the world's problems. Communication, of course, but also the environment, education, and medicine. I am a great fan of Carl Honoré's book *In Praise of Slow*. I believe the world is moving way too quickly and that we are rapidly losing our ability to take the time to appreciate our environment and the people around us."

Patrick Jay looked up in surprise. Greatrex let out a gurgling sound as he nearly choked on his food.

Ascardi took another moment to look around the table. His

face seemed etched in sincerity, while his broadening smile spoke of understanding. "I see you are all a little surprised, that a man who thrives in the world of technological media would have such a point of view. I began my career—I suppose you could almost call it an obsession—in social media in the hope of improving people's lives through stronger, more modern, and impartial channels of communication. The established media is biased and always with an agenda." Ascardi seemed to stumble for a moment, pausing reflectively. A second later he seemed to cast whatever he was thinking away with a casual wave of his hand. "I have in fact dedicated my life to challenging the populace to think about how we live and how we may extend the fading life of our planet."

Philanthropist for the greater good.

"My social media platforms, streaming services, recording companies, and other interests are all dedicated to this dream."

"Not to mention enjoying the billions of dollars you've made from 'promoting the dream,'" added Greatrex.

"Fair point, Jack," said Ascardi, ignoring the jibe. "I have been fortunate in that my aspirations for mankind have aligned with my ambitions in business."

Greatrex made no response.

At that moment Ascardi's butler, Harris, leaned over the entrepreneur's shoulder to replenish his wine glass.

"No, no, no," gesticulated our host as he held his hand over the top of his glass. He looked directly up at the butler and spoke in a quiet but firm voice. "I have told you, my friend, we do not move on to the 1982 Chateau Latour until we have completely finished the '90. To drink the '82 first, with its powerful and densely layered tone, would impede our ability to savor the beautiful subtlety and finesse of the '90. You must learn to get this level of detail correct."

Ascardi then looked up, shrugging his shoulders sheepishly.

"Please accept my apologies. I do tend to over-focus on detail—an occupational trait, I'm afraid."

I said nothing, but the reaction spoke of the man's character. Our host was obviously a complex individual.

In moments of deep thought, songs frequently popped into my head, as if to steer my thinking. Out of nowhere, while observing our host smiling across the table, Eric Clapton unexpectedly downloaded himself into my brain. The song: Strange Brew.

By midnight I was in bed. My eyes were closed, but the relief of sleep evaded me. Probably too much expensive wine and maybe even the company of some dogged ghosts from experiences past. As I dozed, a noise disturbed me—voices in the courtyard below. I was about to roll over and ignore the sound, but my inquisitive nature got the better of me. I got out of bed, padded over to the window, and looked down. The figure of Antonio Ascardi swaggered below. He spoke in an animated whisper, but I couldn't make out his words. The second person stood in shadow, but even in the half-light I was certain it was a woman. Her figure was too curvaceous and slender to be male. There were more words, a kiss on the cheek, and then the woman turned away and walked over to a sports car across the courtyard. I couldn't make out her face in the darkness, but as I watched her walk to the car and climb in, I was struck with a feeling of familiarity. I had seen that walk, that body language, somewhere before.

Nicholas Sharp, stupid man who'd had too much high-priced wine to drink. I laughed at myself as I climbed back into the luxurious four-poster bed.

Chapter 3

A clear blue winter sky framed the stark, snowcapped Scottish hills as we departed from the castle early the next morning. Aislinn and Patrick Jay joined Ascardi in his helicopter. They were flying directly to Edinburgh. Jack and I would go by car. Not only was there not enough room for us in the chopper, but also, after a recent experience with a helicopter that hadn't ended well, we now traveled by other means where possible.

The drive weaved past the tranquil waters of several highland lochs glistening in the morning sunlight, complemented by endless panoramic vistas. Glancing at the Google Maps display on the dash, I realized we weren't far from the Isle of Mull. You could almost hear the distinctive call of the bagpipes in Paul McCartney's "Mull of Kintyre" echo across the waters.

I had met McCartney once, backstage at one of his shows. It was an honor. He had just been rehearsing with a pipe band who were to perform with him that night. He told me that when he wrote that classic melody for Kintyre, he had invited a local piper up to his house to try it out. The bagpipes were so loud that the crockery on the kitchen shelves started shaking.

Powerful sound, powerful country.

CHAPTER 3

We were heading south, down the A82 through the Glencoe Valley. The sky had transitioned from a clear blue to an ominous gray. The hillsides on either side of the road were sparse and steep, towering up into the clouds. Our hired black Audi A5 was stripping back the miles as we flew down the bitumen. The bold Scottish countryside was as polarizing as the Californian desert. People seemed to either love it or hate it. It was in my blood on my mother's side.

Greatrex and I had been chatting about the upcoming tour.

"So really, don't hold back," I said to him. "Tell me what you honestly think of Antonio Ascardi."

He was silent for a few seconds. "I know you like him, Nick, but I see something darker underneath that altruistic image he likes to present."

"You don't think maybe you've just started to see the worst in people, becoming a little jaded perhaps?" I regretted the words as soon as they passed my lips. Before I could apologize, my friend answered.

"I understand what you mean, but no. I get the feeling there's something not quite right behind that welcoming smile. I also wonder if the man's bid to save the world from itself is genuine in light of his obsession with money. And of course, there's the wine thing. What the hell was that all about?"

"Ascardi is certainly a complicated personality," I responded. "But again, if you think of the new age of tech tycoons, they all seem quite complex. Their almost 'on the spectrum' way of thinking gets them started, allowing them to innovate and write code that others only dream of. The really successful ones seem to combine that with a flair for the entrepreneurial, the ability to build a successful business."

"Point taken," said the big fella. "I suppose the next thing you're going to tell me is they all have an altruistic streak as well?"

"Ambition and ego seem to be part of a billionaire's job description," I said. "But that doesn't mean they can't believe in something. Look at Zuckerberg, Gates, Sean Parker. They're all tech-successful philanthropists who have given millions if not billions to great causes. Parker's even on the board of the Obama Foundation, for Christ's sake. Is it so far removed to think Ascardi could be cut from the same cloth?"

Greatrex looked at me from the passenger seat. His face read like a book on skepticism.

"You see Richard Branson, I see Obadiah Stane," he said.

"You can't judge a man by his beard," I said, pointedly glancing at my friend's own manscaped exhibit.

The big fella chuckled and we drove on in silence.

A while later and farther down the road, my thoughts drifted to the woman I had seen in the castle's courtyard the night before. I'd been wrong to think I'd recognized her. Nothing sinister, nothing to see here. Maybe I was doing just what I had accused Jack Greatrex of—seeing the worst in a situation.

I tried to put the girl out of my mind.

The trouble was, she wouldn't go.

Chapter 4

Four days later, the tour had begun. The first show at the Edinburgh Festival Theatre had gone well. Better than well. The media had been there in droves and were glowing in their reviews. I wasn't used to the attention. In my musical career so far, I'd always been the sideman, the hired hand, living out of the public lens. It had been the same when I was a Marine Scout Sniper. A sniper's job, by definition, functions on the fringe of the group. Maybe Antonio Ascardi was right. Nicholas Sharp, lone wolf prowling the ridges.

I had to accept that, at least for now, things were going to be a little different in that regard. I didn't have to like it.

I'd done a few press interviews in the days after the show. I kept my story as simple as possible—love the music, love the people, etc. No one had mentioned my past life. I certainly wasn't going to bring it up.

After the attention, I needed some "lone wolf" time. The equipment had gone by truck, and Greatrex with it. The rest of the tour party had boarded a London North Eastern Railway service that afternoon. This created the perfect opportunity for the rented black Audi A5 and I to cruise the A1 down to London. I was enjoying the road and the car. No talk, just a little music and several speed limits to break.

Winter in the UK means darkness begins to set in around four in the afternoon. That took some adjustment for an Angeleno. It was still light, but the evening was making her overtures as the North Sea appeared beside the road. Storm clouds dominated the horizon. White foam topped the waves and a drubbing rain struck the windshield. I pressed my right foot down, the Audi clicked down a gear, and the road before me disappeared under the front wheels.

I had just seen a sign to the town of Skateraw when I came up behind a gleaming dark-blue sports car. I planned to take no prisoners today, so I pulled out to accelerate past. Even at that speed, I thought I could tell the driver was a woman by the shape of the hair. As I pulled out to overtake the vehicle, I recognized it. It was the same model BMW driven by the woman I saw at Antonio Ascardi's castle.

My curiosity was piqued. As I sped past, I turned to get a look at the driver's face. The shock was total and instantaneous. I couldn't believe what my eyes were telling me. A split second later I was fighting to regain control of myself and my car.

This couldn't be.

The BMW dominated my rearview mirror as we both hurtled along the A1. I didn't think she'd seen me, but I wasn't sure. I needed time to think, to pull this together in my head. I didn't want to lose sight of her car, so I matched her speed at about one hundred yards ahead.

I'd last seen Elena walking off into the glare of an L.A. sunrise after leaving only a bloodied note in my hand. It had been my blood.

An encounter in my favorite bar in Venice Beach had led to

a convoluted and painful night. I had been playing piano, we met, and we talked. She had known too much about me and my past, and I told her so, rejecting her pleas for some sort of help.

By sunrise three men who had abducted her outside the bar had been violently incapacitated, by my hand, despite my intent to stay uninvolved. The girl rewarded me by leaving. No explanation, just an obscure note. That was that.

The mystery of that night had bothered me for over a year. I didn't really understand what had happened or why. I had no idea. There were two things I did know. First, Elena was a dangerously unpredictable woman, and second, I wanted to understand what was behind the events of that brutal evening. Perhaps it was a fool's curiosity.

Elena, from the Republic of Georgia: stunning, beautiful, captivating, and quite possibly deadly.

As my thoughts cleared, I found myself working through a couple of hypothetical scenarios. Do I pull her over? Do I let her overtake me and then follow her? Two minutes later, the decision was taken out of my hands.

In my mirror I saw her indicator flash, and she turned off the A1 to a side road on her left. I stopped a couple of hundred yards down the road. Darkness was settling in. That would work to my advantage. I turned around and headed back to where Elena's car left the main road. No other cars had followed her, so I could see her taillights clearly over the distance that lay between us. I followed her along the side road but turned my own lights off. Until I had decided on a plan, there was no point in making my presence known.

After a couple of minutes, she passed through a small village.

When she turned right, I followed her. She was virtually on the water when she turned right again, pulling into a small car park a little way along the beachfront. I pulled up a discreet distance away, out of sight in the darkness.

As I looked on, the girl seemed to just be sitting in the BMW, waiting. I had no idea what or who she was waiting for. Through the dim light I could make out the road, the dirty white foam of the waves crashing on the beach, and a colossal edifice just a few hundred yards beyond her vehicle. The ominous structure's floodlights cast a mosaic of light and shadows on the surrounding landscape. Somehow it just didn't belong.

I had noticed the building from the main road, but I had no idea what it was. The more I studied it, the more it looked more like some sort of complex rather than a single building. I pulled out my phone and googled the location, trying to identify the building. As the image appeared on my screen, worry skewered my stomach. The ghostly white building looming out of the shadows was the Cinaed Nuclear Power Station.

What in God's name was Elena doing here?

The pain grew worse.

Chapter 5

Another ten minutes passed before there was any sign of movement from Elena's car. Then the cabin light went on as she opened the driver's door. I could see her face clearly. There was no doubt I was looking at the girl who had caused me so much grief in Los Angeles.

As she got out, I slunk a little lower in my seat. There was no need; she didn't even glance in my direction. I had wondered briefly whether she would have recognized my car from the castle courtyard when I passed her. I would have to assume there were enough black Audi A5s out there for it not to matter.

She walked a hundred yards or so along the shoreline toward the complex's fence, stopped, glanced over her shoulder, and then kept going. I took that opportunity to climb out of my own car and follow, staying in the darkness as much as possible.

I had made it to Elena's car by the time she reached the six-foot fence that surrounded the nuclear complex. She hesitated, and I ducked. Her next move surprised me. After looking around again she seemed to slip through a premade cut in the fence. Then, doing what I had just done, she used the shadows created by the complex's powerful security lights to move toward the closest building.

I had already been questioning how this girl was in some way connected to Antonio Ascardi. I had seen her with him in his castle's courtyard. Given my past with her, it was a hell of a coincidence. My first inclination was to warn Ascardi. He may not know anything about her. Then I wondered if he did. I put that thought aside.

Suddenly I didn't have the luxury of time to consider sorting through these apparent contradictions any longer. Elena was disappearing from view. I had to make a choice: act now or don't act at all.

Three seconds later I found myself running through the darkness after the girl. A moment later I slipped through the cut in the fence and followed her toward the building.

The car taillights of those working the dayshift at the station were disappearing along the entrance road in the distance. I assumed there would be fewer staff at night, but of course there would still be security personnel. It was a nuclear power station after all.

Ahead of me I saw Elena open an external door and head into what seemed like one of the outbuildings. I waited ten seconds and then followed her. The door led to an antiseptic white corridor that led to another door. No sign of the girl, so I went through the next door.

I found myself in some sort of external courtyard with buildings on every side. There was still no sign of Elena, but I was certain I saw a door across the yard swing close as I entered. My biggest problem was there was too much light on the area. If I crossed it, I would be very exposed.

Scratch that: I had a bigger problem. Muted gunfire rang out at the exact moment the door handle disintegrated beneath my fingers. I hit the ground as another bullet tore the air above my head. Ten yards away, a freestanding rack held a fire hose. Stay here and be shot or try for the rack's protection. I got up and ran. As I reached the stand, I felt a sharp jolt as a bullet pierced my shoe.

I looked down at my feet. The bullet had shredded the rear half of my shoe's sole, but no blood.

I wasted a moment in reflection. Having broken into a nuclear power station for no valid reason apart from following a girl, I was under fire from someone who seemed keener to kill me than arrest me. That meant the shooter was probably not part of the power station security force. The shots were muted. A legitimate security team would not use suppressors.

Sometimes it's better not to reflect.

Whoever was shooting had skill. It wouldn't take long for them to change their position and come at me from another direction. My sanctuary was temporary. Time to retreat. I sprinted back to the door that I had passed through less than two minutes earlier. As I shoved it open with my shoulder, wood splintered beside my head when two bullets shattered the doorframe in quick succession. Someone was trying to double-tap me. Professional.

In the protection of the corridor I took a second to catch my breath. Then I had the most ill-timed thought. When Bruce Willis's character has just been attacked by terrorists in *Die Hard 2,* his response was, "How can the same shit happen to the same guy twice?"

Another bullet through the corridor wall above my head shook me out of my stupor and sent me barreling down the corridor toward the exit.

I flung the door open, bolted for the fence, and saw the light in Elena's car go on in the distance. I needed to make a decision. If I headed for the fence and my sniper came out the door after me, I would be exposed with nowhere to run. Yet I couldn't stay where I was.

My marine combat instructor had always said, "If your back is against the wall, do the unexpected." The unexpected was all I had left. I turned around and ran back up the corridor toward the shattered doorway leading to the floodlit yard. As I charged toward the door a figure dressed in black came in through it. In his right hand he held a large black Glock, deadly accurate up to fifty yards in the hands of a professional. He was two yards away.

The difference between us was I was expecting him, and he had no idea I would be there. We both fell to the ground on impact, but I was first to get up. Before the man could turn his gun toward to me, I unleashed a powerful kick with my right foot. It smashed into the side of his face. I heard bone crack. He shook his head but kept getting up. I didn't expect that. Resting on one knee, he raised his pistol. I kicked again, slamming my foot into his hand and sending the gun hurtling down the corridor. An instant later the man was on his feet again and charging at me. This guy was a juggernaut. He grabbed me around the waist, taking us both back down to the floor. He was strong. If this became a long fight, I would lose.

As my assailant rose and drew back his arm, fist clenched for what he thought was going to be a knockout blow, I waited. Just as he was about to connect, I twisted my head to the right. He didn't have time to pull his punch, so his fist, with all his weight behind it, crumpled against the concrete floor.

I had a chance, a window, but it afforded an ugly view. As his fist hit the floor, I wrapped both my arms tightly around the man's neck, his body tensing in surprise. I pulled his head in tight and, using my own body weight, smashed the crown of his head hard against the floor. A second later, it was over.

I sat there panting until my breathing slowed to an acceptable level. While I knew this guy would be out for a while, I didn't know whether he had any friends that were about to come through the door to take up the fight. The balaclava over his head and the silencer on his gun meant the unconscious man on the floor in front of me was definitely not a member of the power station security team. Now I needed a plan. I liked plans.

The smart thing would be to retreat outside and through the fence while there was a chance I could make it without a bullet finding my back. On the flip side, most of the trouble I'd caused myself in life stemmed from my being more curious than I was smart. I needed to know what was going down. Armed intruders infiltrating a nuclear power station under the cover of darkness could mean nothing good, yet if I approached them, the power station guards would arrest me before I could even try to persuade them something was amiss. I looked out the door leading back outside toward the fence. Elena's car had vanished. She'd done it again. Put me in the middle of a firefight and disappeared. "How does the same …"

Against my better judgment, I shrugged, turned around, and crept in the other direction toward the inner workings of the complex.

Eight doors and four corridors later I found myself standing in the most confusing workspace I had ever seen. There were hundreds of pipes, large and small, three levels including a main floor, two gantry-style levels, and an abundance of complex machines, many with flashing consoles. Up on the highest level I could see two large blue cylindrical objects. I didn't need to be a nuclear scientist to figure out I must be in the plant's turbine room.

Fortunately, the room also provided numerous places for me to hide as I tried to work out what to do next. I slid behind some enormous silver pipes and crouched down. Voices murmured from above me. I assumed they belonged to plant workers, but at this point nothing was certain.

It was strange that I'd been able to get this far undiscovered. Dumb luck. Or the man I'd taken out had already laid a path to get here through either violence or bribery.

It seemed logical that Elena was allied with my unconscious friend back in the corridor, and that there could be others in their team—many others—who I hadn't yet encountered. Remaining undetected would be paramount. The next and most obvious question was what were the intruders doing here? Assumedly something nefarious, but what?

Further penetrating the complex, I figured these people were aiming to cause some damage; at a nuclear power station, damage could endanger hundreds of thousands of people. Stopping that was a responsibility I really didn't need in my life.

The most perplexing question about Elena's conduct—her sudden departure from the complex—wasn't to be answered now. Given the situation's urgency and my position's precariousness, that could wait.

If lives were at stake, I had no right to protect my own

freedom: I would contact security, try to tell them what I suspected, and accept my arrest. But if corruption were involved, members of the security team could be compromised. Would I be handing myself over to the enemy?

I decided to give myself ten minutes to see if I could get a grip on the situation. If I couldn't, I would just hand myself in, pass on the information, and risk whatever consequences.

Footsteps on the metal stairway above me brought me back to the moment. My hiding place would not be secure for very long. Edging my way along to my left, I tried to conceal myself behind the pipes and metalwork while inching toward a door that was visible near the corner of the chamber. Fortunately, the rhythm of the footsteps receded as I edged further along. Abruptly, a man in dark-blue coveralls appeared. I ducked and held my breath. He seemed oblivious to my presence and approached a control panel on the other side of the room. I exhaled and continued creeping toward the door.

At this point I was attempting to think like the intruders. If I broke into a nuclear power station wanting to do as much damage as possible, what would my target be? What would hurt the most? Even in my scientific naivety, I easily worked out the answer, and it sent a chill down my already cold spine.

Chapter 6

I opened the door gently, trying not to make a sound. I had no idea what was on the other side.

A few seconds later I found myself in a narrow space between two sections of the complex. I knew what I was looking for, and I figured it wouldn't be too far away from the plant's turbine room.

A short walk and a couple of precious minutes more and I was staring at a red wall painted with white stripes. Next to a door was a large blue sign:

NUCLEAR SAFETY
THIS DOOR FORMS PART OF A
HAZARD-SEGREGATION BOUNDARY AND MUST
REMAIN CLOSED AND LATCHED

The door was open.

Moving into the room, I found myself in a space that dwarfed even the turbine area. Again, machinery and piping filled my view. As I moved, I pressed myself along the outer wall.

No matter what I'd read about the safety of nuclear energy, I was now acutely aware that I was standing in the middle of a state-of-the-art gas-cooled nuclear reactor.

I was also almost certain that someone intended to destroy

this reactor, tonight.

Only six minutes until I was to surrender my freedom.

I thought through the mechanics of the situation. A well-placed explosive or two in this environment would at the very least stop the cooling process. My military training had taught me to understand that the uranium dioxide fuel used in the reactor would then cause untold damage if it was unleashed. Not too long ago a tsunami had caused a similar incident in Japan.

The question now was where the explosives would be placed for maximum impact.

I heard voices. Two men talking, workers.

"When you're done, can you get someone over to Reactor Two to check it as well?"

"Sure thing, Boss," came the reply.

Reactor Number Two. I hadn't even thought about that. How many were there in total? What if the explosives had been set in another reactor?

Five minutes left. Goodbye freedom.

I saw one of the men descend the stairs above me and leave though the doorway I had just used to enter. The other man was directly above me. As his boots stomped the steel grating above me, I felt like a caged animal. I couldn't move without fear of discovery. Surely he would see me.

Another precious minute later, the second man descended the stairs and left the reactor area. I had four minutes. I felt certain the intruders would only need to plant explosives in one reactor, but if I was in the wrong reactor, it was all over.

I looked around the room; the technology was beyond me. I couldn't begin to hazard a guess at the deadliest spot to place the charge. Then I heard a sound. Movement on the edge of my vison. Something black. Apparently, I wasn't the only one waiting for the plant workers to leave.

I crept around the bottom of the stairwell, keeping the structure between me and where I had noticed the movement. My senses were charged, but I had to move silently. Ahead of me a large man stood clad in a familiar dark outfit, complete with black balaclava.

I saw this as a blessing. I could have looked for hours for the explosives, but if I did this right, this guy would lead me right to them. I watched.

He moved carefully and efficiently. He must have only entered the reactor shortly before me because he carried his bag as though it was heavy. His work was yet to be done. Pulling a package out of the bag, he placed it against a pipe, then took out a smaller object wrapped in tape. As a marine I had been trained in how to place C4 plastic explosive and attach a detonator. I recognized the process.

I now had to decide whether to confront him now or wait, let him plant the explosives, and leave. It was better to wait. His associate had been a professional. If we fought and I lost, which was entirely possible, the intruders' plan would continue unhindered. Many could die.

Definitely better to wait.

But my plan failed immediately. The figure in black glanced up from his work just as I ducked back to my hiding spot behind the stairs. He saw me. This man was also a professional and didn't falter for a second. As he dropped the bag, he took from it a Desert Eagle Magnum. Damn these people and their guns.

His plan was obviously better than mine. It was simpler too. He was just going to shoot me.

All I could do was lunge for the cover of the nearest bit of solid-looking machinery. I reached a large yellow metal container when the first bullet hit. The gun was suppressed, but suppressors are overrated. The shot still echoed through the cavernous room and then cracked like a whip when it ricocheted on the metal casing inches from my head.

This was not a good place for bullets to be flying around.

I decided to keep moving. He decided to keep shooting. I dodged and weaved my way from one piece of equipment to the next in a bid to close the distance between us. I wasn't making much ground and was crouching behind a section of white square metal piping when suddenly the shooting stopped.

I had a brief opportunity. If he was reloading his gun, I would have a few seconds to reach him. If I was wrong—I'd be dead wrong.

It turned out I was right.

As I left my flimsy cover, the man in black stooped and reached into his bag—for ammunition. I had a chance.

I moved quickly. The man's eyes widened when he realized I was on him and it was too late to use his weapon. He ditched the pistol and grabbed at my clothes as he feverishly clawed his way upright. I felt myself being pulled off balance, so I followed the motion. Together we hit the floor hard. I was desperate to make my first punch count. As I connected awkwardly with the side of his jaw, my opponent grunted. Yet it wasn't enough to stop him landing an open-palmed blow to the side of my head, its power dazing me.

My brief stupor allowed my opponent a window. Before I could react, he'd staggered to his feet and, with desperate ferocity, unleashed a series of forceful kicks to my head and body. I was still down and struggling as each blow further numbed my consciousness. I was all but out when, unexpectedly, he stopped.

His reason for stopping became clear as he reached into his belt and unsheathed a knife large enough to decapitate a man. As he pulled it back to strike down at me, I dug deep, searching for the strength and presence of mind to respond. Using my last ounce of will, I kicked up at his groin with both feet. It worked.

My attacker maintained his forward motion with the knife, but he hesitated for a second. That was all it took. I slid right and reached above me to grab the wrist of his knife arm. Using the body weight he had already invested in his thrust, I pulled him to the floor. He kicked frantically but made no substantive contact. Still holding his wrist down, I struggled to raise myself up onto one elbow. The masked face below me faded in and out of focus as I wrestled with my own consciousness. Instinct and training took over: I headbutted his face. It wasn't enough. I could still feel his attempts to escape my grip and bring the knife back into play. I headbutted him again, hard. He went slack.

In close-quarters combat, victory very often goes to the combatant with the quickest recovery time. For less than two seconds, we both lay winded on the power station floor. I knew we were both desperate to be the first man up.

Despite my need to close my eyes and fade away, I was the first to my feet.

Without hesitating, I stomped on the back of his head with all the force I could muster. Then I did it again. There was an anguished groan, and the man in black was out for the count.

Relief engulfed me as I bent over his prone body and tried

to catch my breath. If the intruder had had more friends in the area, they would have come out when they heard the shots. For that matter, so would any plant workers. No one came. I was alone in the reactor.

My path forward was now clear. Take the detonator out of the C4, look for any other explosives the intruder may have managed to plant before I arrived, grab his bag, and make a swift exit.

I had been right about most of the bag's contents: several taped bundles of C4 and a pile of detonators, plus spare ammunition for my assailant's Desert Eagle. No surprise there. What worried me was the last item in the bag. It was some sort of enclosed explosive device, a little like a very sophisticated pipe bomb. It was welded closed at each end, so I couldn't get inside it to disarm it even if I knew how, which I didn't. I assumed this must have been their backup device if the C4 failed.

In the center of the device was an LED readout. It looked a bit like a radio microphone, something with which I was very familiar. But the readout here was very different to a microphone's. It took me several seconds to realize what the figures on the readout meant. Then it hit me like a truck that I'd just thrown away several valuable seconds. The figures were a time stamp.

From what I was seeing, I had exactly three minutes and twenty-two seconds to get the explosive device away from the reactor and the power station. I'd slowed them down, but that wasn't enough.

No plan required. I gripped the device tightly, picked up the bag, turned, and ran. I ran for my life, and for the lives of the untold thousands who would die if I was too slow.

I didn't think, I didn't stop, I didn't yell out, I didn't do anything, except run.

The only way out I knew was the way I had entered the complex, so that was the route I took. Back through the turbine room, back along the maze of corridors, through the floodlit courtyard, back into the outbuildings, and out the other side. No one tried to stop me, no one tried to arrest me, no one tried to question me. No one saw me at all.

When I reached the fence, I still hadn't thought about what I planned to do with the device or the bag. I looked at the readout on the device: forty-seven seconds to detonation. Then the answer was staring me in the face. I ran down to the foreshore and sprinted across the beach. The sand felt sluggish, but I just pushed harder. I glanced at the timer: twenty-three seconds.

I wasn't going to make it.

I sprinted straight into the water and kept running until I could go no further. Standing there in the ice-cold water with foam lapping all around me, I heaved the device and then the bag as far as I could into the sea. I seemed to find some sort of adrenaline-based super-strength, because I had never thrown anything of that weight that far before in my life.

As I stood there, the sea erupted as though an active volcano lay submerged fifteen yards out. I wasn't sure whether it was just the explosive device or the C4 as well. I stood there drenched in a spray of freezing brine, fighting to keep my balance as the underwater blast pushed against me like a tsunami.

Behind me, a siren blasted and security lights all around the complex turned night into day. At last someone on the power station's nightshift had noticed that not all was well.

It was time to go.

I stayed in the water and half waded, half swam parallel to the shoreline until I was level with my car. All attention seemed to be on the power station complex, not the area around it. Every part of me hurt, and every part of me was exhausted as I ran from the sea, struggled across the sand, and crossed the foreshore to my car. Flinging the driver's door open, I climbed in and took off like the proverbial bat out of hell.

Of course, although I didn't realize it, I wasn't leaving hell at all. I was stumbling toward its gates, demanding sanctuary.

Chapter 7

The wide waters of the Thames meandered into the distance. On the river's left, the London Eye stood as a beacon for contemporary tourism and engineering. A long line of people queued for the experience. On the right bank stood the houses of parliament and Big Ben, representing all that was traditional in British life. The river itself was a frenzy of activity. Large barges plowed through the chop toward the southern docks, and numerous roof-decked ferries carried excited tourists along the river, even on this cold but clear winter's day.

The view was as breathtaking as it was expensive. From the window of my suite at the Savoy Hotel, I could be forgiven for feeling like I owned the world. I didn't. I wasn't even paying for this room. Although the tour couldn't really afford accommodation of this kind, Antonio Ascardi had insisted that we stay here as his guest. The Savoy was where his friends stayed, so his artists should stay here as well. It was a very generous gesture.

I had driven hard through the night to get here after the events at the Cinaed power station. Where possible I had avoided main roads and motorways, figuring the less CCTV that caught an image of my car the better. It meant that the drive had taken longer. I pulled into the Savoy at dawn, exhausted.

After a sleep and a shower, I felt only marginally better. My body ached like my muscles and joints were being torn apart on a medieval rack. The events of the previous evening looped in my head. There was just so much that wasn't right. I couldn't seem to make any sense of it, nor could I make sense of the fact that I had somehow landed in the middle of some terrorist plot. Nicholas Sharp, wrong place, wrong time ... again.

The one thing that kept hammering my mind was Elena's appearance. Was it a coincidence running into her again? I thought not. Why had she left the power station almost as quickly as she had arrived? I had no idea. And the big question: what was the nature of Elena's relationship with Antonio Ascardi? I had no clue.

It was just after 1 p.m., and I was tired, and my head pulsed with pain.

As I contemplated a small scotch to clear my mind and dull the ache, a knock at the door rang in time with the throb in my head. I moved away from my spot by the window. Before I got halfway across the room, Greatrex had let himself in. I'd left him a keycard at reception.

"You certainly are living the life," he said.

"And this is only one room; you should see the rest. How's your accommodation?" I asked.

"Fine, but it's not like this for us humble crew members."

I knew he had a single room on a lower floor. This was the Savoy, one of London's finest hotels, so he wouldn't be too hard done by. Greatrex moved over to the window and took in the view.

"I heard you got in quite late last night. What held you up?" He asked.

"Before I answer that, you better sit down." I moved over to the drinks trolley. "Scotch?"

Greatrex looked at his watch, a questioning frown on his face. "Really?"

"Trust me," I responded. "When you hear what I have to tell you, you'll be begging for another."

I poured us both a drink, gave him his, and eased myself into an elegant Chesterfield chair, the crumpling sound of its maroon leather relaxing me. Greatrex sat opposite me on the couch.

"Shoot," said my friend.

"Bad choice of words," I said. Then I told him everything.

Thirty minutes later we sat in silence.

"Shit," said Greatrex.

"That just about sums it up. I've got nothing." Nicolas Sharp, font of all wisdom.

"You know what I like about touring with you, Nicholas?"

I wasn't sure that he was expecting an answer, but I gave it a shot. "My inquisitive nature?"

"Not so much. Probably it's your ability to take something perfectly normal, like a drive through the Scottish countryside, and turn it into a life and death battle for survival."

"As I said, my inquisitive nature."

Greatrex let out an amused sigh.

"All right, let's unpack this one more time," he said as I poured our second scotches. "It seems to me that this all revolves around one thing: this Elena's knack of appearing in your life at the most inopportune moments."

"I've been thinking about that all night. I just don't get it," I said.

"It's almost like she's some sort of emotional tease—provocateur, if you like. She provokes you into a situation, you react, and then she does the vanishing bit."

"I know. It happened in L.A. and it happened again last night, but why? What does she have to gain?"

"Maybe it's not her but rather somebody else who's getting something out of all this," said my friend.

"Possibly, but I can't see any relationship between what happened in L.A. over a year ago and what happened last night."

"Nor can I."

"The other key thing here is Elena's relationship with Antonio Ascardi. What's that all about?" It was like an eternal question, never to be answered.

"You know my feelings about Ascardi," said Greatrex.

"Yes," I responded, "but I just can't see Antonio Ascardi having some deep sinister involvement in blowing up a nuclear power station. It just doesn't ring true for a man in his position."

"You're a convoluted man, Nicholas Sharp. You easily see the best in others, but never in yourself."

We both let that little pearl of wisdom hang in the air.

"Maybe I just don't want Elena do be on the wrong side of all of this."

Greatrex raised an eyebrow to that but said nothing. "Has there been anything on the news about the power station break-in?"

"I haven't looked since you got here," I said, reaching over for the television remote to turn it on. I flicked through a few stations until I got to a 24-hour news network. We didn't have to wait very long.

A young reporter, obviously out in the field, came into view with the front gate of the Cinaed Nuclear Power Station as his backdrop. "We have just been issued a statement saying, and I quote, 'The Cinaed power station was broken into last night. There appears to be no significant damage, and the station's operations were unaffected.'" The reporter then looked directly down the camera's lens. "There are reports an antinuclear group was responsible for the break-in, and that it was staged as a peaceful protest against the use of nuclear power rather than to cause any disruption to the station." He then signed off.

"Well, there you go," said Greatrex.

"There you go," I repeated mindlessly. "It certainly is a strange sort of peaceful protest that involves attacking and shooting at an unarmed man and planting military-grade explosives in a nuclear reactor."

"Even stranger that the situation has been covered up," observed the big fella.

"Asian shadow theater," was my response. "Silhouettes maneuvering behind screens."

"I will have to talk to Elena," I continued. "There is no other way around it. Everything hangs on that. We need answers that only she can give. It's most likely Antonio Ascardi has absolutely nothing to do with this. There is even a strong possibility he is being set up."

Greatrex looked at me as though I was a child struggling with a difficult concept. "To ask her anything, you will need to find her."

I paused for a second. "No, I won't," I responded. "I won't have to look for her at all because she's going to find me.

That's how she operates."

I got up from my chair and walked over to the window. The sky was clouding over, but the beauty of the river view was not lost. Nor was the frantic heartbeat of a city full of life; Londoners and tourists alike braced themselves against the winter chill as they scurried to attend to their affairs. I took another sip of my drink. I could feel that Elena—mysterious soul, the elusive provocateur—was out there somewhere. I knew she was not done with me yet. I also knew that she would find me whether I wanted her to or not.

Despite Greatrex's sarcasm, there was no doubt I was consumed by my Achilles' heel, curiosity. Even though I knew this girl meant trouble, I was sure there was a bigger issue to explore.

The problem was that, despite my outward protests, I knew I would probably welcome not only Elena but also perhaps the trouble she brought with her.

Chapter 8

It was just after 3 p.m. as we stood outside the Royal Opera House in London's Covent Garden. To say the building was impressive was an injustice. I was in awe as I eyeballed the majestic Roman columns spiraling upwards toward the beveled eaves and the grand balcony suspended above the entrance like a regal guardian. This was a place where kings and queens had championed their chosen artists for centuries. History was unveiling itself before me.

As Patrick Jay and I pushed through the opera house's front doors, the foyer struck me as equally impressive. Plush red carpets and gold-embossed railings suggested luxurious formality. The wide staircase under a majestic archway promised an experience that those performing would have to honor. As we paused to digest the atmosphere, a short, balding man in an expensive-looking charcoal designer suit appeared out of nowhere.

"Mr. Sharp, Mr. Olden, it is a pleasure to welcome you here. I am Norbert Fontana, Mr. Ascardi's personal assistant here in London. Mr. Ascardi has asked me to make your visit to this wonderful venue as memorable as possible."

We shook hands, and Norbert Fontana raised an arm to lead us toward a closed door on the far side of the foyer.

"This way please, gentlemen. Ms. Byrne is in the greenroom backstage. Mr. Ascardi will join us later, after he has fulfilled some business commitments."

We followed.

"This sure is a long way from an Uluru desert sunset," said Patrick Jay.

"About as far away as you can get," I agreed, surveying the grandness before me.

It had been over forty-eight hours since my return from Scotland, and nothing more had eventuated. No contact from Elena and nothing more in the news regarding the events at Cinaed. As perplexing as the situation was, I was starting to doubt that anything further was going to happen.

It was time for a change of focus. Our London performance was tonight, and we were here to do a job. There was a sound check to be done and a show to prepare for.

Fontana led us down a series of corridors, left, then right then who knows where. We followed him through the labyrinth until finally we entered a large sitting room furnished with generous couches, comfortable armchairs, and a bar. The surrounding industry-green walls were tempered by a series of ornate paintings tracing the building's cultural heritage and punctuated by large framed mirrors. You couldn't go astray allowing for a performer's vanity. It almost felt like we hadn't left the Savoy.

The beautiful Aislinn Byrne was perched on a sofa across the room; she was looking very much like the elegant leading lady that she was.

"Hi, Aislinn," said Patrick Jay. "What about this place?"

"It's glorious," she responded. "I can't wait to stand on that stage and feel the presence of all those greats who have performed here before us."

I sat down next to Aislinn; Patrick Jay lounged on a chair.

"Well, you may have to wait a little longer than you expected," echoed the voice of Jack Greatrex as he appeared in the doorway. "I'm afraid there are a few technical issues with the sound system. Nothing major, but it will probably take an hour or so to sort them out. It looks like some unauthorized idiot has messed around with the wiring." Greatrex disappeared down the corridor as quickly as he had arrived.

Rather than look crestfallen, both Aislinn and Patrick Jay appeared as though they were ready to settle in with caviar and Cristal. No diva tantrums here.

I got up from the sofa, feeling restless. I'd been edgy for a couple of days now. A distraction was called for.

Obviously sensing my unease, Norbert Fontana, who until now had been standing quietly in a corner of the room, made a suggestion. "Mr. Sharp, would you like to take this unexpected opportunity for a personal tour of the building? Mr. Ascardi is very well connected here. I'm sure we could arrange access anywhere you wanted to go. Oh ... and of course anyone else who would like to join us."

I didn't think he expected a positive response from Patrick Jay or Aislinn, and nor did he get one.

"I'm fine here," said Aislinn.

"Likewise," echoed Patrick Jay.

Fontana looked directly at me.

"Mr. Sharp?"

"Why not," I answered. "Let's go."

As it turned out, Norbert Fontana was a terrific tour guide. There wasn't much he didn't know about this grand old building, and what he didn't know was provided by an older gentleman called Cedrick, who had joined us. Cedrick had apparently worked at the Royal Opera House for thirty-seven years. He knew the building and its history forward and backward. He also had keys to access all areas.

Walking through the massive backstage rehearsal chambers was like gliding through a parallel universe. Sets, props, and costumes seemed to beg you to listen to their story. The space was large enough to host its own performance. Fontana spoke of the venue's recent history. "Not too long ago there was a major rebuild and remodeling of the entire building."

"It took years and cost millions," added Cedrick, "but the result is a world-class modern facility cloaked in the guise of an historic landmark."

As we headed toward the main stage, where Greatrex worked on my keyboard rig, Cedrick stopped and pointed his hand upward.

"This is the fly tower," he said.

I craned my neck to get a look.

Cedrick continued. "It spans fifteen stories to facilitate the largest of sets and backdrops."

The black void above me was seductive. A tall metallic canyon soared into the darkness. Racks of lighting towers, scaffolding, and gantries formed on all sides. It was something like the heart of the Death Star.

Norbert Fontana seemed to sense my fascination. "How are you with heights, Mr. Sharp?"

Memories of hot roofs and exposed hilltops in Iraq flashed through my mind, only now I didn't have an M40 sniper rifle in my hand.

"Mr. Sharp?"

"Not bad," I responded, snapping out of my daydream. "I've done a little work in elevated situations."

Fontana smiled.

"We don't normally do this," said Cedrick, "but Mr. Fontana has made arrangements that allow me to take you up to the rooftop of the fly tower. It has one of the best views in London."

I looked at them both. "Again, why not?" I answered. "As long as we have time."

"Oh, we'll have time," responded Fontana with certainty.

"Lead the way," I instructed.

Twenty minutes later, after ascending the fly tower by a series of stairs and a lift, we found ourselves on a gantry overlooking the metallic canyon we had previously been surveying from the ground. From fifteen stories up, I had a heavenly perspective on the Bard's words about all the world's men and women being players on a stage.

"Quite something, isn't it, Mr. Sharp?" asked Fontana.

I couldn't argue with him.

"Come this way," instructed Cedrick as he led us along a high gantry toward a locked door.

A moment later, he had pulled some keys out of his pocket, unlocked the door, and was leading us up the remaining few stairs. He opened the final door, and light flooded into the darkened space in which we stood. "The rooftop," he announced.

We passed through the door and out onto the roof of the building. To our left was some plant machinery covered in some sort of tin housing; the rest of the rooftop was clear. There was a parapet all the way around to ensure the safety of the few people who ventured up this high.

As we walked around, from every angle we could see the famous buildings and iconic monuments that were London's signature. To the south was the Thames, leading down to the Tower Bridge; to the west were St James Park and Buckingham Palace. Virtually adjacent to the building where we stood was the Covent Garden Market.

"Take your time, Mr. Sharp," said Norbert Fontana. "Enjoy the experience. Not many people are granted this opportunity."

He was right: this was a rare privilege, and despite a blustering winter wind cutting though my exposed skin, I was glad to be there.

All good things must end. Thirty minutes later, we were back down on the stage level and I was thanking Norbert Fontana and Cedrick for their time.

Greatrex walked hurriedly around the corner. "Good timing, Nick; we're ready to do the sound check." Tour over—time to get to work.

The applause of the crowd washed us in a sea of acclamation. We had just finished our final piece, and Patrick Jay and I were standing either side of Aislinn, soaking in the atmosphere. Looking out from the stage, it seemed like the room was wallpapered with people, all the way up to the ornate circular ceiling. People in the balconies were clapping, those in the stalls were cheering. It seemed like we had won quite a few hearts. Patrick, Aislinn, and I looked at each other. Our smiles were not forced; we were feeling good. We had just played the Royal Opera House in London. Not bad for this former marine from Venice Beach, California.

Off to the side of the stage, I noticed Antonio Ascardi

grinning and applauding vigorously; next to him Norbert Fontana was doing the same. I could even see old Cedrick just in the shadows, smiling and clapping. Music for all people.

We took another bow and left the stage. The audience kept applauding, but we had already performed an encore. As the saying goes, "Leave them wanting more."

Ascardi was the first to greet us; after all, he was footing the bill. "Bravo, bravo. You three are magic," he enthused as he kissed Aislinn on the cheek. "Just listen to that crowd." The audience were still carrying on. It was hard for us not to be affected by their reaction.

"Well done," said Fontana, as he shook our hands.

I looked around for Jack Greatrex. In a world of gushing fans, Greatrex was the one I could always count on for an honest appraisal of a performance. I saw him standing on the other side of the stage, holding his hands out in the classic "two thumbs up" pose. We must have been all right then.

Antonio Ascardi announced, "After you shower and greet some well-wishers, I am taking you out to dinner. One of my favorite restaurants, Rules, is just around the corner, and they are reserving a private room for us." It was more of a command than an invitation.

I sat across the table from Tony Ascardi, quietly observing him as he spoke animatedly to Aislinn Byrne on one side and Patrick Jay on the other. He was again holding court, and again we were his audience. From his excessive manner, you would think that it was he who had just performed onstage at the Royal Opera House. It didn't matter; everyone had enjoyed the sumptuous meal, and contagious laughter rippled around the table. My own appreciation centered on the expensive scotch in my hand.

"Paris next. They will adore you, it will be 'amour,'" Ascardi said, over-gesticulating as he spoke. Everyone laughed some more.

I was still finding Ascardi hard to read. At times like this he was the gregarious extrovert. Other times I'd seen him zone in on the minutest details, repeatedly checking figures over and over, ensuring the logic of the results provided were to his standard. Earlier I noticed him giving the ticketing manager for the concert a not-too-subtle grilling. Like the wine incident, it was done quietly, not for show. I supposed his was an empire built on detail. Despite his proclamation of love for our music, I wondered why the entrepreneur was so involved in the tour. In fact, I questioned why he was involved in the music industry at all. Surely the income we were generating paled in comparison to his primary business activities. Maybe, as Greatrex and I had discussed, we just didn't understand the philanthropic nature of the new generation of tech tycoons. As I looked at Antonio Ascardi across the table— animatedly telling stories, enthralling his subjects in amusement and awe—I concluded that I didn't really know the man at all.

So I ordered another scotch.

Fifteen minutes later I had downed the Glenfiddich and made my apologies, announcing, "I'm going to swing back via the opera house and pick up Jack." Greatrex had stayed back to supervise the pack-up. I was on my feet and out the door before anyone had the chance to object.

It was a short walk back to the opera house. I entered though the stage door. Almost immediately I heard Greatrex call out, "Five minutes, Nicholas, then you owe me a drink at the American Bar back at the Savoy."

"It's a deal," I responded, looking around for a way to amuse myself for a few minutes while I waited.

To my surprise, Cedrick appeared out of the shadows.

"Good evening, Mr. Sharp."

I turned to him. "Hello, Cedrick. Thanks again for your time today. That was one heck of an experience up on the fly tower."

"It was an absolute pleasure, Mr. Sharp, as was hearing you play tonight," he responded.

"Thank you, I appreciate that."

"It's a peculiar thing though," he said.

I looked at him a little awkwardly, I thought he was talking about our music. "I know our sound isn't to everyone's taste," I said.

"No, it's not that. Your performance was wonderful. What seemed peculiar to me was the tour."

"I know you don't take many people up there, Cedrick, but was it that unusual today?"

"No. Again, I'm sorry; I have not made myself clear," he said. "It wasn't the visit to the rooftop that was so peculiar, it was the fact that Mr. Fontana had arranged it yesterday, before you even arrived."

"You're sure of this?" I asked.

"Yes, sir."

As if on cue, Jack Greatrex strolled up. "Ready to go, Nicholas?"

I stared at him vacantly.

"Nicholas?"

"Yes," I said, distractedly. We said goodnight to Cedrick, and I led Greatrex out the stage door.

Out in the alleyway, my friend turned to me. "What's wrong?" He could read me like the proverbial book.

"Let's find that bar," I said. "We need to talk."

Chapter 9

The morning sun penetrated my brain like ray guns from outer space. I knew I should have closed the curtains. My head ached from too many drinks. The only redeeming factor was that the scotch had been of a high quality; otherwise the pain would have been worse.

Greatrex and I had sat up until the small hours, drinking and chasing ideas around the room. We had started at the American Bar downstairs and ended up in my suite.

It was clear to us that I had been manipulated by Norbert Fontana to tour the opera house, including the fly tower and the roof. For the life of us, neither of us had the faintest idea why. What could Fontana possibly have to gain by delaying the sound check and showing me the sights of the venue? Fontana worked for Antonio Ascardi. Ascardi knew Elena. I had been manipulated by Fontana and Elena. Was I being manipulated by Ascardi as well? Pass the scotch.

About 4 a.m. we had given up, or perhaps our brains had given up on us. Greatrex returned to his room, and I clambered into bed.

Now my head hurt. I should have closed the curtains.

Just as I was drifting back off to a merciful sleep, my laptop chirped. I'd forgotten to turn that off as well. I climbed out of bed and walked a little unsteadily over to where the computer sat on the coffee table. There was a message. No surprise there: that's what the chirp meant.

"We need to talk urgently. Dukes Hotel Bar in Mayfair. Tonight, 8 p.m. E."

That was it, the whole message—simple but world changing. It didn't require Hercule Poirot to figure out who "E" was.

I sat on the sofa, lost in thought. Then I got lost some more.

Finally, I decided on three definite courses of action. First, I was going to meet Elena, no matter the consequence. Second, I would tell Greatrex about the email later today.

The final course of action was a little more straightforward, and could be done immediately. I closed the curtains and went back to bed. Merciful sleep, please overpower my aching mind.

I like to walk. I particularly like to walk in London, where the people and the buildings are a maze of variety, ideology, and perspectives. It was dark by the time I walked across Piccadilly Circus, one of the most hectic and colorful intersections anywhere in the world, and on toward Mayfair. It was there that I would find Dukes Hotel and Bar, and Elena. The cold night air had brought me to my senses after a lazy, contemplative afternoon. I was aware that the meeting with this girl could go in a number of directions, not all of them good. The bottom line, however, was that I wanted answers, and meeting with Elena was the only way I was going to get them.

Greatrex had wanted to come with me, but I had said no. If Elena was going to reveal anything at all about what was going on in her cryptic world, I felt she would reveal it only if I went alone. Jack was not happy, but he understood the logic.

As I entered St James's Place, I was comforted by the upmarket neighborhood. I told myself that nothing bad could happen here. Then again, I supposed Charles Manson's victims had thought the same thing. Dukes Hotel was at the end of the short laneway. As I walked up the steps, I was greeted by a doorman in uniform. "Good evening, sir. May I help you?" He was all British class, but his build indicated he could take me down just as quickly as he could take my coat.

"The bar please," I requested.

I was shown into a small but obviously exclusive bar. There were plush chairs surrounding small tables. The windows were thickly draped, and pictures with heavy traditional wooden frames adorned the walls. Waiters in white coats and black ties hovered over the few guests. I half expected to see Bond in a secret meeting with M in a corner.

I scanned the room for Elena, but she hadn't arrived. A waiter showed me to a table near the bar, where I had a good view across the room. I said I would order when my friend arrived. He gave me a cocktail menu and the *Evening Standard* to look over in the meantime.

I must have sat there for around ten minutes. I was on time but not early and had begun to wonder if the girl was going to be a no-show.

Then she walked in.

To say the room stopped as she strolled through the doorway may be an exaggeration. I'm sure someone in that room was doing something apart from looking at Elena, but I didn't notice if they were. Along with everyone else, I was beguiled by the cascading dark hair, the inviting face, the slender frame supporting an exquisite black dress, and those deepest of green eyes.

As she sat down in the chair opposite me, I felt the envy of every other man in that room. I also felt a little bit afraid. What was I getting myself into here?

"Hello, Nicholas. It's been a while."

I realized I was holding my breath. Great first impression.

"Hello, Elena. It *has* been a while."

"It's good to see you," she said.

Her voice was captivating, the familiar traces of her Georgian accent only just evident. I sat there, hypnotized by the deep Atlantic-green whirlpools that were her eyes. I realized I was losing ground here. That had not been my plan.

"As I recall, the previous times we have run into each other, it hasn't gone so well for me, Elena. The battle with the thugs at the Marina Del Rey in California and then the more recent attempt to blow up a nuclear power station in Scotland. I think you owe me an explanation."

I was gaining ground, but I had to look away. Each time I looked into those eyes, I felt my will abandoning me.

"Yes, Nicholas, I do owe you an explanation. I can see why you are angry."

Angry? I felt like a puppy lying on his back.

She continued. "It is very complicated, and the lines have been blurred."

"Lines—what lines?" I asked.

"The lines between right and wrong, between black and white."

She was right: now I was confused.

"Before we talk any further, may I suggest a drink. After all, this is one of the most famous undiscovered bars in the world," she said.

I nodded my head in agreement and signaled for the waiter.

Elena continued. "They say this bar was the local London drinking hole of many artists, authors, and musicians, including Ian Fleming. Legend has it that this is where Fleming decided James Bond would be a martini drinker."

I was enchanted by her. It also seemed I wasn't far off about Bond meeting M in a corner after all.

The waiter came over. "Madam, Sir, what may I serve you?"

Elena took the choice out of my hands, "Two martinis please—the Vesper."

Of course, I thought. Was there ever any doubt?

We waited as the waiter brought a trolley to our table and made quite a show of mixing the drinks in front of us. He explained every move like a patient teacher sharing his knowledge with a couple of attentive students.

After he left, we each took a sip.

The martini's taste vied with the sight of Elena's eyes for the most captivating experience I'd had in the last hour or so.

Attempting to refocus, I brought myself and the conversation back to the point of being here. "Elena, I need some sort of explanation, and I need it now." Nicholas Sharp, man of steel.

She sighed. "First, Nicholas, you need to understand that I am not an evil person."

I took a sip of my drink and said nothing.

"I have done bad things for bad people," she continued, "but I have done them for good reasons."

"What exactly do you do?" I asked.

"You could almost say I work in recruitment, kind of freelance."

I looked at her blankly. This conversation was becoming more ambiguous with every word.

"I do not really expect you to understand," she said. "In my position I have had limited choices, and sometimes that has meant choosing the least harmful of an array of awful options."

"All I'm hearing here is your justification for what you have done, Elena. I'm none the wiser about what happened in California or in Scotland. I need facts." I thought I sounded quite tough.

"I know you think I have used you, and I probably have. The situation required it, and dreadful circumstances have turned out well because of it."

I'd had enough. I took a large sip of my martini and said, "Cut the crap now, or I walk."

Suddenly, she looked sullen and vulnerable. The girl in front of me then took a long gulp of the very strong drink in front of her and declared, "All right, I will tell you what I can now, and later, at a more appropriate time, I will explain the rest."

It was a start.

"I can tell you nothing about California; you would get too angry. But I can tell you about Scotland. You see, I needed you to be there. I needed you to stop them destroying that power station. A nuclear detonation would have cost too many people their lives."

"Go on," I said, dumbfounded.

"I could do nothing to stop those men, but you are resourceful and clever, Nicholas Sharp. When someone is in trouble, you help them. I've seen it."

"How did you know about the plan to blow up the power

station?" I asked.

"I cannot tell you that. In fact, if some people knew I was talking to you tonight, my life would be forfeited."

I wasn't sure if Elena was being entirely honest, but all my senses were telling me she was in sincere fear for her life. I looked down: our drinks were empty. Apparently, honesty makes you thirsty. I ordered two more.

We spent the next few minutes in a considered silence as I weighed the impact of her words.

After the drinks arrived, Elena continued. "I know you need more from me tonight. I will give you what I can."

I just looked at her. The martinis were making me a little more contemplative and a little less judgmental, or maybe just a little more drunk.

"Why didn't you go to the authorities with your information?" I asked.

"If I had done it anonymously, no one would have believed me. If I had gone to them in person, I would have been arrested."

That sounded a little like how I had felt at the power station. I recalled thinking it was better to sort things out myself than bring in the authorities and be arrested. I gave her an inch of wriggle room.

"So, you accidentally came across me on the highway, knowing I would follow you into the power station?" I questioned.

"It was no accident, Nicholas. I left Edinburgh a minute before you. I was parked around the corner from your hotel, waiting. That was my plan."

"Now we're getting a little honesty," I said.

I was maneuvering into position for the big question. Then

I fired. "What, if anything, does Antonio Ascardi have to do with all of this? I know that you know him. I saw you at his castle, that evening in the courtyard. I want the truth here, Elena." My voice sounded harsh and confrontational. I was okay with that.

There was a silence between us. Silence usually means someone is thinking up an answer, often a mistruth. We looked at each other and drank some more.

"Nicholas, you won't believe me, but I cannot answer you."

She was right. I didn't believe her.

"I do not know Tony that well. He is, well, a friend of a friend. We have a few mutual friends actually. He had asked me to come to Scotland to meet him."

I thought for a moment. It was hard to identify the truths among the deceptions. I was, however, certain she was in some sort of significant trouble.

"Did he tell you why he wanted to see you?" I asked.

Elena looked away, across the small room. Then she looked at her drink as though it was fascinating, and then she looked at me. I could tell she was worried about answering the question.

"Yes," she said. "He wanted to see me in Scotland because he'd discovered that I knew you."

There it was—the bombshell.

I sat there for a few minutes, soaking it all in. The truths, the lies, the martinis. I think in essence, I believed that Elena was not a terrible person, although I had a hundred reasons to convince myself otherwise. I looked across the table at her. Her eyes were drawing me in again. I could see defiance and fear in the swirling green Atlantic mist of her soul. I didn't know which was stronger, the defiance or the fear.

Elena just sat there, alternating between staring sadly around the room and then turning back to me. Each time she looked at me, I felt a little of my resolve disappear. I was becoming a moth to her flame.

Finally, as if making up her mind, she threw her head back and broke the silence. "Really, I do not care anymore what you or anyone else thinks, Nicholas. I have made my bed, as they say. I will lie in it."

Ah, defiance.

Then Elena looked at me. I saw the depth of emotion in her eyes.

"Nicholas, I don't want to be alone tonight."

Ah, fear, but I didn't know if it was hers or mine.

The memory I will always hold from that night was the generous and open way in which Elena gave of herself after we went upstairs to her room. She was passionate and aggressive but also timid and coy, but then again so was I.

I knew that in the morning I would consider myself a fool for my weakness. I also knew I would never regret it.

Chapter 10

"So, now you're emotionally involved." Greatrex made the statement sound like a judge handing down a sentence.

"Not so much involved as emotionally kidnapped," I responded.

Even I didn't believe me.

We were onboard the Eurostar, having left St Pancras Station in London an hour or so earlier. At two hundred miles per hour, it wouldn't take us long to get to Paris. Jack sat opposite me, a table separating us, in a first-class carriage. Other members of our tour group were scattered around the carriage. Antonio Ascardi preferred us to travel in a manner that left a smaller carbon footprint. Train was better than plane.

"Well, what did you find out about the elusive Elena? At least, what did you find out that will help us work this thing out?"

I told him about the conversation in the bar.

"There's still a lot of gaps in her story," he said when I had finished.

"I found out at least one important thing. While there's no doubt that Elena is not a totally innocent party in all this, I do believe her intentions are essentially good."

"Is that an unbiased assessment?" the big fella asked.

"As unbiased as I'm capable of right now," I said sheepishly.

"When will you be speaking to her again?" Greatrex probed.

"Well, there's the thing," I said. "When I woke up this morning, she was gone, checked out, no forwarding contact."

Greatrex didn't say a word; he didn't have to.

"All right. I suppose in all your undercover activity"—he laughed—"sorry, in your investigation of the girl's activities you may have missed this in the news." He passed me his cell phone, open at a news website. "This was posted late last night." The headline read:

MYSTERY DEEPENS IN NUCLEAR POWER STATION BREAK-IN

The copy went on to say:

A radical environmental protest group known as the Natural Earth Army has not only claimed credit for the recent break-in at the Cinaed Nuclear Power Station in the east of Scotland but has claimed the media did not report all the facts. The group says that several cakes of C4 explosive were planted in one of the station's nuclear reactors and that they had intended to destroy the power plant. The Natural Earth Army are quoted as saying, "No matter the human cost, we must save the planet from the excesses of mankind." The group did not elaborate on why their plan did not "succeed."

Inquiries by this news agency and other mainstream outlets have yielded no further information about the group or their objectives. It is, however, clear that the group was very active on social media. Apart from the NEA's initial statement, all their current social media sites have been taken down and their digital footprint effectively wiped. A representative of the Scottish police stated, "It is as though the Natural Earth Army never existed."

Since the NEA posted their statement, a significant number of people have now gathered at the site of the Cinaed power station to protest the facility's apparent vulnerability to attack.

I stared at the article for a good five minutes, thinking about the events in Scotland a few nights earlier. The Natural Earth Army had certainly got their facts straighter than the initial media coverage. But no mention was made of the two intruders I had left behind or of my own role in the affair.

"Perplexing," I said. "It takes a great deal of technical know-how to come close to wiping someone's digital presence."

"There's one more thing," added the big fella.

"Of course there is," I responded, waiting patiently for Greatrex to continue.

"That news site that posted the article. It was the first source to uncover the link to the supposed Natural Earth Army."

"So?" I said, feeling a little less patient.

"So, that site is owned by the Ascardi Media Group," replied the big fella. I was sure I saw a slight smirk on his face.

"Crap."

"Perplexing," said Greatrex.

"Totally," I eventually responded. "I wonder if it was possible that Elena worked in some way for the Natural Earth Army?"

"But that wouldn't explain why she wanted you to stop them," said Jack.

"An enigma wrapped in a situation that makes no damn

sense at all," I said.

We sat in silence looking out the window at the fast-changing view.

It didn't help.

"I don't understand why this NEA group would make a claim like that and then disappear. Wouldn't they have been better off keeping quiet and then planning another attack?" I asked.

"Maybe there's more to this than we can see. There are too many players and too many pieces for any picture to be clear," said Greatrex, the chess master.

"So, we can do nothing but wait," I said. "I don't like waiting when I feel something ominous is lurking around the next bend."

As I thought about it, I realized that again we were at an impasse. There was nothing we could do. We still didn't know for sure if Antonio Ascardi was involved in any of this. We didn't know if nor when Elena would reappear. We didn't know how the hell the self-proclaimed "Natural Earth Army" fitted in. Each day added more questions and subtracted more answers.

It was time to change our focus and concentrate on the tour and making music. That's what we were here for. As far as everything else went, we would have to bide our time.

"We wait," I repeated. "We have no choice."

Factories flicked past us. Peering out the window, I saw the language of their signs and billboards had changed: we were now "waiting" in France.

As we climbed down from our carriage at the Gare du Nord train station in Paris, we were met by our drivers and a few security personnel Antonio Ascardi had arranged. We were not well enough known to require massive protection, but Ascardi had certainly provided VIP treatment for the group. Ascardi himself was not with us; we were told he would be arriving in Paris later that evening.

Like any major transport hub, the Paris Gare du Nord was hectic. The French set about their business in a no-nonsense manner, their foot traffic frantic but purposeful. We worked hard to keep up as Patrick Jay, Aislinn, and I remained glued to our escorts hustling through the crowd. Aislinn pointed to a piano sitting in the middle of the station concourse. "What is that for?" I asked one of our guides.

"It is not that unusual in Europe. Anyone can play it. We like to promote culture among the people," was his response.

Patrick Jay looked at me questioningly. I was tempted to sit down and play, but the thoroughfare was just too crowded. "Music for the people," I thought out loud.

Before long we were flying through the streets of Paris in two dark-gray luxury SUVs on the way to our hotel.

Once again Ascardi had provided us with obsessive luxury. The Four Seasons Hotel George V was situated only a few steps away from the Champs-Élysées. I thought our host couldn't beat the Savoy in London, but this place would've made the Sultan of Brunei jealous.

"I could get used to this lifestyle," announced Patrick Jay.

"Yeah, millionaires for a month and then back to our humdrum lives," I responded. Nicholas Sharp, embracing the downside.

"It's just lovely." Aislinn, as ever, singing a positive note.

A short while later we had been shown to our suites. From

my balcony the roofs of the Paris skyline pointed upward like rows of doll's houses in pastel shades. It seemed like every struggling artist in the world has spent some period of their creative time honing their craft in one of these attic apartments high above the streets, as they allowed the view through the expansive dormer windows to inspirit their work. I would've appreciated the ambience more if I weren't too tired, too perplexed, and now a little too worried about Elena and what lay in wait on the rest of the tour. I needed sleep, and I was damn well going to get some.

An hour later I lay awake on the huge bed staring at the ornate ceiling. Elena, the Natural Earth Army, nuclear reactors and a hundred other strange and intrusive terms had hectored me into wakefulness. Some people count sheep to get to sleep; I was counting complications, and I was getting angry with the whole damn mess. I got up, poured myself a scotch, swallowed it in two gulps and then had another. I lay back down on the bed and thought about the previous night. Despite my best efforts, I felt a smile creep onto my face, and I was asleep in five minutes.

I must have slept right through the night because the morning sun flooded my room as I awoke to a loud knock on the door. I knew who it would be.

"Greatrex, do you have to bash so loudly?" I said as I opened the door. "You'll wake up half the freakin' hotel."

"Come on, Rip Van Winkle, it's a big day in tour-land," announced my friend. "We set up and sound check today. Tomorrow is the big show."

He was right. The next night was one of the biggest shows of the tour. We were performing at the Palais Garnier, one of the greatest opera houses in Europe. Most of the European music press would be there. After a decent sleep, I was beginning to feel a rising excitement at the thought of playing such an iconic venue. Just as it had been in London, a performance in such a celebrated environment filled me with almost youthful anticipation, only slightly muted by a dash of realistic trepidation.

"Give me half an hour and we'll grab some breakfast," I said. Greatrex left. I looked out the window at the sun shining down on the wonders of Paris. The problems that had kept me awake started to recede. What could go wrong in an environment like this?" Nicholas Sharp, eternal optimist.

As things turned out, "Nicholas Sharp, naive fool" would have been more appropriate.

Chapter 11

We weren't walking into a building as we ascended the steps to the Palais Garnier from the famed Avenue de l'Opéra. We were walking into history. To a musician there is no moment that matches your realization that you are no longer observing the rich tapestry of cultural evolution but are now part of it.

Aislinn, Patrick Jay, and I looked at each other as we entered the cathedral of gilded majesty that was the building's foyer. Before us, the venue's Grand Staircase beckoned like a stairway to the heavens.

"Oh shit," said Patrick.

"I couldn't have put it better myself," I responded. A child in an amusement park.

"This is beyond any expectation I could have ever had," pronounced Aislinn.

"Oh shit," said Patrick again.

"What are we doing here? How can we do this?" asked Aislinn.

"Well, someone thought we were up for this," I said.

"Antonio," replied Aislinn.

"Always loved the man," responded Patrick. There was a certain irony in his tone.

We had arrived early to get a feel for the place. We should

have arrived much earlier.

Before we knew it, the now familiar figure of Norbert Fontana came barreling up. Obviously, Fontana covered Paris as well as London for Antonio Ascardi.

"Aislinn, Patrick Jay, Nicholas, I am so glad to see you. Can I show you to your dressing rooms?"

We looked at each other. I felt that I spoke for all of us when I said, "No thanks, Norbert, I think we'd just like to wander around for a while." Everyone nodded in agreement.

"Oh well, you have plenty of time. Just call me if you need me."

And so it began, Dorothy, the Scarecrow, and the Lion walking along the yellow-brick road. The Tin Man couldn't make it. This place had enough heart for us all.

We must have wandered around for over an hour. I had never seen a place so grand, so inspiring, and so intimidating. The regal architecture bathed in ornate gold leaf, the countless statues and figures decorating walls of rooms so large you could land a plane in them. We hadn't even got to the main auditorium yet.

Eventually, time and reality caught up with us. "Ah, my talented runaways." It was the voice of Antonio Ascardi. "So good to see you all."

We hadn't seen Ascardi since we'd arrived in Paris. He'd been busy with more "business commitments." The man looked tired—a bit of lost sleep maybe. I wondered what could be bothering him.

After we had greeted each other, Ascardi announced, "I know it's time for you to go to work now. But tonight, I have booked the finest restaurant in Paris. We will have a fabulous dinner in your honor."

With that, he led us off to the backstage area. I couldn't help but feel like a naughty student being pushed around by the headmaster. It made me uncomfortable. Also, I was beginning to question if the headmaster was hiding some sordid little secrets. That made me more uncomfortable.

"It is with great honor that I introduce to you tonight three very special people. I have brought them to this magnificent city to share the magic of the enchanting music that they make together." Antonio Ascardi's voice resounded around the cavernous private room in which we all sat. The table was large and elegantly decorated. Heavy blue velvet curtains framed the room's ceiling-height windows, overlooking the alluring lights of the Parisian streets. The sheer scale of the room itself was nothing less than you would expect from an exclusive French restaurant with three Michelin stars. Opulence laced with extravagance. We were certainly playing out of our league.

Ascardi continued. "It has been my privilege to bring these great artists together, first to record and then to bring them to you live on stage." I was starting to think he was going too far—it was getting a little embarrassing—then it occurred to me that Tony Ascardi probably didn't understand the term "too far."

I looked at Jack Greatrex sitting across the table from me. He rolled his eyes and sipped some more soup. Next to me, Patrick Jay wriggled in his chair, looking decidedly ill at ease. Only Aislinn looked as though she was born to be there.

At the end of the table, Ascardi was on his feet. He was dressed in a black dinner suit with his hair swept back. He looked like he was thriving in his role as visionary entrepreneur and host. There were positive murmurs from guests around the table, then some polite applause. I wondered if the appreciation was more for Antonio Ascardi's benefit than our own. Everyone in the room knew he wielded great power and influence. He was winding up. "Ladies and gentlemen, I give you the delightful Aislinn Byrne, accompanied by two of our label's most accomplished musicians: Mr. Patrick Jay Olden from Australia and Mr. Nicholas Sharp from California in the USA."

More applause and Ascardi sat down. Thank God.

We had arrived about an hour earlier after being ferried across town in our black chauffeur-driven SUVs. Strolling through the restaurant doors on the first floor of a classic seventeenth-century building near the banks of the river Seine, I was met with a picture way beyond what we expected. Judging by the venue, our host was really laying it on thick, almost too thick. Maybe I was just being ungracious. Was that a chip that I could feel on my shoulder?

The thing I hadn't expected was the guest list. There were politicians, movie stars, celebrities, and members of Paris's social elite. All for us? I didn't think so. Patrick Jay and I had mingled uncomfortably before dinner. The ever-gracious Aislinn, of course, was right at home in this elite company. She had won everybody's hearts.

Patrick Jay sat to my left, and an elegant middle-aged gentleman who had introduced himself to me as Gabriel Arquette, France's minister of culture, was on my right. While they were each distracted in other conversations, I took the moment to retreat into silent observation. A professional habit for a creative ... and for a sniper.

Ascardi chatted comfortably with those around him. No

matter how rich or influential the company he kept, he was never out of his depth. He was a tall man, classically good-looking, charming, and mega-successful, a combination that made him a powerful social aphrodisiac. Judging from the way some of the women around the table were looking at the entrepreneur, maybe the aphrodisiac wasn't just social. Was Greatrex right when he said there was something troubling under that outward warmth? We'd already seen that there were layers to this man. I wondered how many people had managed to peel off those layers and see the real Antonio Ascardi.

I was sure that I had caught moments when he looked a little too sorrowful for his surroundings, his face a little blotched, his mouth drawn tight as though he was carrying some private burden. But then the look would vanish, and the warmth returned. If I was right, he wouldn't be the first soul on the planet to wrestle with his demons. As if I could talk. Looking at him here, charming the A-listers and entertaining those around the table, I thought guiltily that any doubts I'd had about him seemed unfounded.

"Do you know Tony well?" The voice of the minister on my right shattered my daydreams.

I turned to him and answered, "No, not really. We haven't been working together that long. We're just getting to know each other." Nicholas Sharp, diplomat.

"He's a fine man and so talented," continued the minister. "Apart from his own gargantuan success in the field of social media, he has been a generous benefactor to the arts as well as many other causes across Europe. His contributions have been appreciated, and he is well respected."

"You sound like you know him well," I observed.

"Yes, we go back a long way. Years ago, I spent some time living in Italy. I got to know Tony Ascardi just as his business was beginning to grow. I was aspiring to get into politics, and he was a great support to me. It's wonderful to see him back to his normal self."

I was reluctant to interrupt his flow, but I asked, "Normal self?"

"Yes, he went through a very bad period a while ago, when his younger sister died."

"I'm sorry. I didn't know he had a sister."

"Yes, her name was Vittoria. He named his record label after her. He believes music stands for so much that is good in the world. That's why he gave the label her name, and why he spends so much time and money supporting it. Of course, that is probably why you and your colleagues are here, Mr. Sharp."

The minister became distracted by his phone ringing. "Pardon."

I took another moment to let my mind navigate these new facets of Antonio Ascardi's world. Clearly, I'd read too much subversion into this whole damn thing. The possibility of Ascardi's involvement was becoming more and more remote. It was time to back off.

I was staring vacantly in the minister's direction when I noticed a deep look of concern envelop his face as he listened on his phone. "You are sure?" he asked. Then a sadder look of resignation.

Another phone rang at the table, then another. Three minutes later it seemed like half the people in the room were talking animatedly on their cell phones, including Antonio Ascardi. Greatrex and I looked across the table at each other;

we both shrugged in ignorance.

A minute later Ascardi was back on his feet. "I do apologize to you all. For those who have not yet heard, I have just been informed that the British Chancellor of the Exchequer, Sir Phillip Morton, whom I'm sure many of you know personally, has been assassinated."

Murmurs of shock reverberated as more people reached for their phones. Assistants started dribbling into the room seeking instructions from, or passing on information to, their masters.

"Poor Phillip," said the minister next to me.

The room was abuzz.

"Where did it happen?"

"When did it happen?"

"Have they caught the assassin?"

No one seemed to know the answers.

Antonio Ascardi turned to the tuxedoed gentleman on his right, who alternated between listening attentively on his phone and barking instructions to two lackeys who had appeared out of nowhere. "Jacques?"

Jacques put up a hand to block any interruption. The minister next to me leaned in and said, "That is Jacques Milland. He is our Ministre de l'Intérieur. If anyone knows what is going on, he will."

Milland finished his call and stood up. "I am very sorry, but I will have to say goodnight." He looked in Aislinn's direction and nodded to Patrick Jay and me. "I particularly apologize to our guests of honor." He then gave a short bow to Ascardi, who looked like he was expecting more.

"Can you tell us anything before you leave, Jacques?"

Milland looked at Ascardi then turned to the table of

guests. He shrugged and said, "I am thinking you will all find out by the morning anyway. As you have just heard, the British Chancellor of the Exchequer, Sir Phillip Morton, has been assassinated. The information that I have just become privy to has not been released yet. I'm sure, however, in this era of social media"—the minister glanced sideways as Ascardi—"and the constant news cycle, it soon will be available to all. The fact is, Sir Phillip was actually murdered in the late afternoon yesterday, in an apartment in Covent Garden, London. The investigation is already twenty-four hours old."

"Why the delay in reporting it, Jacques?" asked Ascardi. Everyone nodded; it was a reasonable question.

Milland seemed to hesitate for a moment. "It would appear that the chancellor was not only away from his own home when he was shot"—the room was quiet—"but also that he was not alone." More murmurs engulfed the table. With that announcement, the Ministre de l'Intérieur turned and left. Next to me, Gabriel Arquette smiled sadly and said, "Yet they say that it's we, the French, who are the amorous ones."

Jack Greatrex and I sat alone in the back of our SUV as we were driven back to our hotel. The party had broken up quickly after the announcement of the British chancellor's death. There were too many important people in that room who would have to react to the news.

We both had our phones out and were scouring the news sites for details. Ascardi's sites had no more information than the rest.

"It says here that British investigators put a news blackout on the assassination for twenty-four hours while they tried to establish the identity of the person in the apartment with the chancellor," said Greatrex.

"I'm assuming it was a woman, although in this day and age in politics that's a pretty big assumption," I responded. "I'm also assuming that the so-far-unnamed person survived, or they would have been identified."

"Makes sense," said Greatrex. He tapped on another website. "It says here that authorities are looking for a yet-to-be-identified witness."

"Survived and fled," I added. "Well, as traumatic as these events are, they have little bearing on us and the tour, except for interrupting an exclusive but way too boring dinner party."

"Too damn right," said Greatrex. "Although one thing is certain. Every British and European government agency is going to be looking for that missing woman."

What neither of us could have possibly realized at the time was that within twenty-four hours I would be desperately searching for that same woman. I would be looking for her not only to ensure her survival but also to guarantee my own.

Chapter 12

They were in front of us, they were above us, and they surrounded us.

As we walked out onto the stage at the Palais Garnier, the audience sat like expectant shadows, silhouetted by the dimming house lights wherever we looked. It was the nature of the classic horseshoe design of the opera house. The audience on the floor rolled out to the back of the room, but then there were four levels of people in boxes around the walls all the way up to the roof. And what a roof it was. The ceiling was well lit and painted in bright, luminous colors, a tribute to the great composers of opera. The layers of balconies were supported by huge ornate gold columns that rose out of the floor. On three of the upper levels, individual boxes provided luxurious comfort for the aristocracy. It was a pallet of muted gold and red velvet.

As I walked toward the piano, I inhaled deeply. Nothing could prepare a performer for this moment. The room was an ocean of anticipation—that of the audience but also that of the ghosts of legends past. Across the stage I noticed that Aislinn's and Patrick Jay's faces seemed to reflect my own trepidation. No matter how many shows we had done, this was big.

I sat at the piano, adjusted my stool, and stretched my hands. Aislinn stood straight and erect at the microphone; she was in the zone. The start of the show belonged to Patrick Jay. As the applause died down, he shifted on his seat to make himself comfortable. The end of his didgeridoo rested on the stage floor in front of him, its traditional brown and yellow ochre markings luminescent under the warm stage lights.

The audience grew silent. Patrick Jay drew a long, extended breath and began to play.

You could hear the audience gasp at the power of the sound. Most would never have heard a didgeridoo live before, certainly not in an atmosphere like this. The ancient, haunting sound seemed to permeate every corner and crevice in the room. As his circular breathing deepened, Patrick seemed to draw on millennia of ancestry to allow the audience to immerse themselves in the low, fathomless drone. The cry of a thousand souls.

I sat there staring ahead, allowing a couple of minutes to pass by. The didj was casting its mystical spell, defying intrusion. When the timing was right, I raised my fingers to the keyboard. Beforehand, we had only agreed on the key of the music; everything else would be in the moment. Now it was my moment. I played a few gentle chords, just enough to introduce the piano without distracting the audience from their Patrick Jay–induced trance. Gradually, I let the didgeridoo envelop the piano and encourage it to explore. At first, I lightly worked my way up the keyboard, then, before long, gently cascading waves of arpeggios eased their way back down.

I knew it was me playing, but I didn't seem to have any

control over what was happening. The music wasn't coming from me, it was coming through me. I slowly allowed the sound of the piano to grow in complexity, weaving in and out of the didgeridoo's rich tone. Gently but consistently, the almost unidentifiable chords seemed to build. The intensity grew as the sound moved toward a searing climax.

Then I backed off … it was time.

If Aislinn didn't have the voice of an angel, the angels certainly sang through her. Her first tender, almost frail note left her lips, quivering in the air, high above the digeridoo and a world away from the piano. Then came a second note, higher, stronger. Before long, her melodic seduction soared and danced through the room. Only a stone heart could have remained unaffected.

Three minutes later, our sounds were entwined, flying, swooping, writhing across the room. Questioning, answering. It was totally out of our hands now, as piano, didgeridoo and voice complemented, challenged, and serenaded each other into another realm.

We had begun.

The next fifty minutes seemed like five. Then the audience were on their feet, clapping loudly, cheering, and this was only the intermission. We had twenty minutes to rest, take a drink, and reenergize. Playing into the darkness as we did, with every note and phrase an improvisation, takes it out of you. Patrick Jay, Aislinn, and I gave each other a smile and then disappeared to our dressing rooms to freshen up. Words were unnecessary.

The second half of the show began differently. Aislinn stood alone at the center of the stage. Patrick Jay and I stood in the wings, waiting for our delayed entrance.

The audience grew silent in anticipation. Then there it was again, the angel's voice. God's enchantress. She began low and quiet. I stood there taking in every note and nuance. Her voice began to rise. My heart rose with it. She was captivating. The room was hers.

Suddenly, I heard some commotion behind me, then I felt a tugging on my sleeve. The moment was broken. I turned, annoyed. Greatrex was standing there with Antonio Ascardi. They both looked worried.

"We have a problem," said Greatrex.

"Look at this, Nicholas," said Ascardi, producing his cell phone. A text message was displayed on the screen. I read it carefully.

There is a bomb. It will not destroy the entire building, but if it explodes many lives will be lost, important lives.

Monsieur Antonio Ascardi, you must immediately deposit the equivalent of 5 million American dollars in cryptocurrency in the following account. The account is untraceable, as is this phone number.

If the money is not deposited by the end of tonight's show, the bomb will be detonated. If you stop the show and try to evacuate the building, the bomb will be detonated.

We do this as a statement of solidarity against the corrupt politicians and business leaders who are guiding Europe on a path of economic and cultural self-destruction.

The note was signed:

The Ghosts of the Revolution

The account details were below the signature.

I looked at Greatrex and then Ascardi.

"Holy shit," was all I could say.

In the background, Aislinn's voice climbed in pitch and intensity. The audience sat besotted.

"I've notified security," said Ascardi. "There is little they can do without causing panic that would lead to the bomb being detonated. They are looking for anyone behaving in a suspicious manner."

"Who may or may not be inside or outside the building," added Greatrex.

"And they are covertly inspecting the building for anything unusual," finished Ascardi.

Reading the concern on our faces, Patrick Jay had wandered over. I showed him the message. He grimaced but said nothing as he passed the phone back to Ascardi.

Aislinn's rich tone reverberated through the air, penetrating the atmosphere with unbridled emotion.

"Nicholas, Patrick," said Ascardi. "You must ensure that the show continues until we have apprehended these people, found the bomb, or deposited the money."

I sighed. No pressure there. The expression on Patrick's face indicated he was thinking the same thing.

"How long will it take you to deposit the money?" I asked.

"At least an hour, maybe more. Five million dollars is a lot of money to gather together at no notice. I've got Norbert talking to my accountants as we speak."

Her voice was rising higher, growing more intense with every note.

My thoughts were muddled; I needed to clear my mind. I was due on stage in about three minutes. The prearranged cue would be Aislinn hitting a peak and then pausing with a small nod of her head.

I desperately needed time to think.

Her voice had reached its upper range. Each note she sang was piercing and powerful, flooding the vast space with pathos.

"Why would anyone do this to us?" Antonio Ascardi was visibly upset. I couldn't blame him.

"That's a question for another time," I responded shortly. "For now, we just have to find that bomb."

I looked at Greatrex. He just shook his head in frustration.

Where would I plant a bomb to cause some, but not total, destruction in a building like this? I had no definitive answer.

I looked at my watch; it was now about two minutes until I had to walk back on that stage acting like nothing was wrong.

Her dynamic was building, climbing to the heavens. The climax was close.

Think, damn it, think.

Ascardi looked around expectantly, as though the bomb would just appear through willpower alone. It didn't.

"Show me the message again," I said urgently. I read through it, then read it again.

Aislinn's voice was so high and so intense that it seemed to cut through the air like shards of glass.

Maybe I had an idea, or maybe I was losing the plot.

Her voice soared through the air, infiltrating every soul in the room.

Focus, fool, it's right in front of you, somewhere ...

Then ... it wasn't in the message. It was the signature.

The Ghosts of the Revolution

Greatrex looked at me, trying to read my thoughts.

"Who's in box five?" I demanded of Ascardi. "Do you know?" I knew I sounded desperate. I was desperate.

"Why yes, of course I know that—box five is my box. I am hosting Jacques Milland, the Ministre de l'Intérieur."

"Anyone else?" I pleaded.

"Yes," said Ascardi. "Your new acquaintance, Nicholas: Gabriel Arquette, the minister of culture, and a couple of very old friends from my early years in Italy."

One minute until I was on stage.

It was as though Aislinn's spirit had enshrouded the room, singing the song of truth.

I looked over at Greatrex; I was agitated, he was perplexed. "That's it, box five. The bomb is in box five!" I yelled as I turned and began to run. The big fella was one step behind me.

Her voice was so high now it was about to peak. The entire room was on edge, focused on the purity, the purpose, the sound ... until the explosion.

I felt the shockwave before I heard the blast. In an instant the room was filled with smoke and the sound of panicked screams. I was almost at the rear curtain at the back of the stage when it exploded. I turned to look. In the place where box five had been perched to the right of the stage, there was nothing but a tangled mess of wreckage. No one could have survived. Below, flaming upholstery still rained on an innocent audience. There were bodies, some deathly still, others writhing in pain.

I then looked at the center stage. Aislinn was lying sprawled across the stage floor. Without thinking, I ran to her.

She was barely conscious and badly dazed. Her dress was torn and her face scratched, but I could see no obvious injury, thank God.

"Aislinn, are you all right?" I asked as I cradled her head in my arms. Her eyes opened and she nodded.

"Nicholas, what was that? What just happened?"

I gave her the briefest explanation I could and then asked, "Are you okay to walk?"

"I think so," she said. I helped her up. Greatrex had joined us. He took her other arm and we guided her off the stage.

It was shattering. In the space of a split second, a moment of beauty had become an eternity of anguish.

Within minutes there were first responders everywhere. Greatrex, Patrick Jay and I helped evacuate the uninjured audience members on the ground floor. Security personnel led the way. We moved as fast as we could. I didn't think there was another bomb, but there was always a chance. To her credit, Aislinn recovered quickly. She ignored her own discomfort, found a first-aid kit side of stage, and moved directly into the audience area, helping the ambulance personnel treat the injured. Our songbird was much tougher than anyone thought.

As everything that could be done was being done, I paused and took a moment to look around the room. I saw destruction, I saw pain, I saw suffering. It was the human—or perhaps more accurately, inhuman—face of terrorism.

What evil bastard would do this?

Chapter 13

It was around four in the morning when we staggered back through the lobby of the hotel and up to our rooms. We had been extensively questioned by the French authorities for several hours. As we stood by the lifts, we didn't say much to each other. We were talked out, exhausted.

Up in my suite I poured myself the required scotch, but it hardly touched the sides. I lay on my bed, certain sleep would elude me. Again, I stared at the ornate ceiling. I felt I would get to know it very well over the next few hours. I was too tired to think, and too filled with adrenaline to sleep. I got up again.

Poor me … another one.

The next day at noon, Greatrex and I had arranged to meet downstairs in the hotel's "La Bar" for a coffee. I felt like I needed more than one. As Jack entered the room a few minutes after me, he looked beaten.

"I've ordered coffee," I said.

"How much?"

"A limitless amount," I responded. That seemed to satisfy him.

"We need to talk," he said.

"We do. Conversation might even help me think. I seem to be having trouble with that at the moment."

"You did all right last night," he said. "In fact, tell me, how the hell did you work out where the bomb was?"

"It doesn't really matter now. The point is, I didn't work it out in time, and people died because of that."

"Don't go all guilt ridden on me," said my friend. He took a large gulp of the newly arrived coffee and gave me the sort of look that only one good friend can give another. The one that means, 'Don't give me any of your shit'. "Not your fault, Bucko; you didn't plant the explosive device among a crowd of innocents."

I knew he was right. For better or worse, my need to protect was a natural trait that had only been strengthened further by my time as a marine sniper. Watching from rooftops, M40 rifle in hand, scouring the streets for the potential threat of insurgents as US troops performed their duties, day after day, month after month ...

"Anyway," continued Greatrex, "I don't really think there was an opportunity to save those lives. The more I think about it, the more I think the bomb was intended to go off anyway."

As I thought about it, what the big fella said made sense. We hadn't broken any of the "rules" laid out for us. We hadn't stopped the concert nor evacuated the building.

"Then why?" I asked. "Why go to all the trouble of sending Ascardi the message asking for the money?"

"Let's come back to that," directed Greatrex. "So, back to my question. How did you know the bomb was in box five?"

"Well, this will sound a bit stupid," I said, "but it was a mixture of things. The first was the note. It said not only that lives would be lost, but it specified 'important lives.'"

Greatrex nodded, but his face still looked like a human question mark.

"So, I figured that the 'important people' at that venue, in fact at most opera houses, would be in a private box," I said.

"That makes sense, but why box five?"

"Well, this is where it gets a bit weird. Most musicians are aware of the famous story of the Phantom of the Opera." I explained.

"Lloyd Webber wrote a musical about it. Just a minor success," said my friend sarcastically.

"Well, that's the thing," I continued. "I know it sounds like a bit of a disconnect, but the original Phantom story took place in Paris, at the Palais Garnier in fact."

I had Greatrex's attention.

"In the original story, box five was set aside as the place from which the Phantom could view his opera. In fact, he blackmailed the opera company that a catastrophe would befall them if they did not follow his instructions and leave that box free for his use. But it was when I looked at the text message the second time that something twigged. It wasn't in the message but rather in the signature."

Silence from across the table.

"It was signed by the 'Ghosts of the Revolution,'" I said. "We all assumed that to be some sort of reference to the French revolution, considering we were in Paris."

Greatrex nodded.

"Well, the 'revolution' wasn't the key word, it was 'ghosts.' In the Phantom of the Opera story, the Phantom is referred to as the 'Opera Ghost.'"

"That's a bit of a long bow to draw," was Greatrex's response.

"Well yeah, I was thinking that as well," I admitted. "That's why I hesitated. But the thing was, when I asked Ascardi if he knew who was in that box and he told us it was the minister of the interior and the minister of culture, it all connected ... 'important lives.'"

Greatrex was silent for a moment. "Sherlock freakin' Holmes" was his only response.

There was silence. The coffee seemed to be working as another thought bounced into my mind.

"There is one more very important aspect to consider," I continued. "It seems to me the issue is not only who was in the box but also who wasn't in the box."

"You mean ..."

"Yes, I mean, Antonio Ascardi."

As a thoughtful silence overtook our conversation, the familiar faces of Aislinn Byrne and Patrick Jay Olden appeared at the door of the bar.

"Here they are," announced Aislinn, turning to Patrick Jay.

"Mind if we join you?" asked Patrick as they wandered over to our table.

Before either Greatrex or I could say anything, they both sat down. Deal done.

"Coffee?" I asked. Two nods, and I waved the waiter over and ordered fresh coffee for all of us.

Looking at our two colleagues, and friends, it was fairly obvious that the events of the preceding evening had drained them. Patrick Jay looked worn out. Aislinn looked a little brighter, but there was a sadness in her eyes that I hoped was only temporary.

"How are you two doing?" asked Greatrex.

Patrick was the first to reply. "The news this morning says fifteen dead and twice that many injured. It's bad, but I've seen bad before. You know, I've seen injustices dealt to my own people on our own land," he continued, "but nothing could prepare anyone for what happened last night. For the rest of my life, the Palais Garnier will always be a black hole of despair."

"For a knockabout didgeridoo player, you're pretty goods with words," I said.

"I couldn't have put it better myself," chimed in our songstress. "The tragedy of last night will forever be etched in my mind. I don't think the memory will ever fade," she added.

Greatrex and I looked at each other.

"It does fade," I said, "but it never leaves. It's how you deal with it from here on that will define who you are and how you let it change you."

Both Patrick Jay and Aislinn looked a little puzzled. Greatrex answered for both of us.

"In another world, a different time, and doing a different job, both Nicholas and I have had to work through more than our fair share of trauma," he said.

Neither Aislinn nor Patrick Jay asked for more information. We appreciated that.

"Has anyone seen Ascardi today?" I asked.

"Yes, we just left him," said Aislinn. "We bumped into him in the foyer. He looked very shaken and upset."

Again, Greatrex and I exchanged a look.

"He has already cancelled the next show in Munich. As you know, it was scheduled two days from now," added Patrick Jay. "He thought we needed time, and that the authorities here would want to talk to us some more."

"The one thing he did request," said Aislinn, "was that we resume the tour when we are ready. He was hopeful we would perform in Venice, at the Gran Teatro La Fenice ... if we felt up to it."

I had a feeling this tour was not done with us, whether we wanted to end it or not. It felt like a roller-coaster ride you couldn't leave halfway through.

"How do you two feel about that?" I asked.

"I'm okay with it," said Patrick Jay.

"I think the music will help us heal," offered Aislinn, "so I'm in. Besides, we can't let these bastards win," she added.

I looked at Greatrex, who smiled and shrugged his shoulders.

"Okay," I said. "We go on. We begin again in a week's time in Venice."

"I am worried about Tony," added Aislinn. "He doesn't seem his normal self. This has affected him badly. I think we need to keep an eye on him."

I was worried about Ascardi as well, but for a different reason. We would certainly be keeping an eye on him.

Our coffee meeting broke up. Aislinn and Patrick Jay returned to their respective suites while Greatrex went off to find Ascardi's people to talk tour details.

I was halfway across the expansive hotel foyer when I noticed a small, very official group of people striding through the front entrance. They moved too purposefully to be just well-heeled tourists on holiday. The leader of the group was a stout man with thinning brown hair. He seemed to look around the room as if searching for something or someone.

He looked in my direction, then beckoned the others to follow him.

"Monsieur Sharp? Monsieur Nicholas Sharp?"

"Yes, that's me."

"Bonjour, I am Capitaine Pascal Barre from the Direction Régionale de Police Judiciaire de Paris, the Sous-direction anti-terroriste, to be specific." He then held out his hand.

I shook it. "Pleasure to meet you, Capitaine. That is quite a title you have there." I find it's best to stay on the good side of law enforcement officers.

"Oui—yes, pardon—but I think it is best people know who they are speaking with."

I nodded.

The Capitaine continued. "I would like to introduce Monsieur Jasper De Vries from the European Counter Terrorism Centre of Europol."

A tall, thin man with blond hair, arctic-blue eyes and a smile of ice stepped forward. No hand—he just nodded.

I assumed this would be more questions about the previous night. Sometimes it seemed like every law enforcement officer wanted to hear your version of events for themselves. I wondered if they ever spoke to each other.

Capitaine Barre continued. "We have phoned ahead and arranged for the hotel manager's office to be made available for us all to sit and talk. I hope that is agreeable for you."

The manager's office: this was new. "Of course," I said. "Lead the way."

The Capitaine did lead the way, but I sensed Jasper De Vries from the Counter Terrorism Centre of Europol breathing down my neck as we walked. When we arrived at the manager's office, the flunkies who followed the group were told to wait in the anteroom. Barre, De Vries, and I went in. I was shown to a chair between the two of them. The whole thing felt awfully prearranged.

Forty-five minutes later I was tired, irritable, and bored. That's a bad combination for me. I had told them the story of the night before, twice. The first time through they stopped me when I explained how I'd worked out which box had the bomb in it. A non-committal "unbelievable" was the only response I got from Capitaine Barre—nothing from De Vries.

I thought we were done and about to wind up when Jasper De Vries asked his first question, his accent more Northern European than French. "Tell us about your background in the US Marines, Monsieur Sharp."

The question floored me. "I can't see how that has anything to do with the tragic events of last night," I said, feeling irritated. "But if it helps you, I was a decorated Marine Sniper Scout for several years, and I served my country on three tours of duty in the Middle East."

I looked them both in the eyes, in a way that I hoped looked defiant. Nicholas Sharp, making a stand.

"Please tell us about your reasons for leaving the military," requested De Vries, his voice as cold as a winter wind.

"That is personal," I said. "I don't see why you need to know that." I was becoming agitated. Not a smart thing to do when being questioned by a couple of law enforcement officers. I should have known better.

Barre and De Vries glanced at each other. Barre nodded. I felt like I was being played.

"Well then, Monsieur Sharp," continued De Vries, "perhaps you could explain these." He reached into his case and removed a tablet. He unlocked it, looked at it briefly, and passed it over to me. "Well?"

There was a picture on the screen. It was of me. It took me a few seconds to figure out the context. I appeared to be looking out across a view of London. Then I realized it: the photo must have been taken while I was on the roof of the fly tower of the Royal Opera House in London.

"Swipe through, there are more," said De Vries. He sounded dryly self-satisfied.

There were more shots, different angles. I couldn't recall either Norbert Fontana nor old Cedrick having a camera or getting out any sort of device when we were up there.

"I don't see the point of these holiday snaps," I said, sounding as angry and frustrated as I felt. "I would like to help you gentlemen. You see, a very bad person did a very bad thing last night, and you should be investigating it, not wasting time here showing me irrelevant pictures and asking me irrelevant questions. So, if you don't mind ..." I got up to leave.

"Please sit down, Monsieur Sharp. Let us explain the relevance," said Barre. His tone of voice had gone from "good cop" to interrogator.

Jasper De Vries sat up in his chair. "Monsieur Sharp, let's be clear. What we have asked you and shown you is most relevant. I assume you are aware that the British Chancellor of the Exchequer was assassinated the day before yesterday.

"Yes, of course." I didn't like where this seemed to be going.

"Well," continued De Vries, you may be aware that the chancellor was shot in an apartment in London—Covent Garden, to be exact. The British police have calculated the trajectory of the bullet that killed him. As it turns out, the bullet was fired from an M40 rifle on the rooftop of the fly tower of the Royal Opera House, coincidentally, from exactly the same spot where you, a former military sniper of some note, were photographed casing the lie of the land a few days before." De Vries paused, just looking at me, staring me down. "It would appear that your activities at the time of the murder are unaccounted for. No one in Paris saw you for at least fifteen hours. Plenty of time to get to London and back," added Barre.

I thought of the long sleep in my suite in Paris. Of course there were no witnesses. Suddenly, the room felt cold.

"So again, you may forgive us if we have found a connection—a relevance, if you like—between the questions we ask, the assassination of the Chancellor of the Exchequer in London, and the murder of fifteen innocent people last night in Paris. And that connection Monsieur Sharp ... is you."

Both men searched my face for a reaction.

I didn't know what to think. The only smart thing I could possibly do was not to speak at all. So, I asked, "Where did you get those pictures? Who took them?"

"That is not your concern, Monsieur Sharp. What you do need to do is explain to us the circumstances of your presence on that rooftop," said De Vries.

I explained. I told him about the delayed sound check and the impromptu tour.

Capitaine Pascal Barre exploded at me. "Do you take us for fools, Sharp? That bad person to whom you refer killed fifteen innocent people last night, including my boss, Jacques Milland, the Ministre de l'Intérieur. Jacques was my friend, my good friend. In fact, I have just spent the morning comforting his devastated wife and children. So forgive me if I don't believe a word of your pathetic story. I believe that you are that very same 'bad person,' and it is taking every bit of my professionalism and experience not to inflict my own interpretation of justice on you right now."

I turned away from Barre's furious red face. I could understand his pain, and his reasoning. I knew there was no way I could persuade him otherwise. Not right now anyway.

I looked across at Jasper De Vries of Europol. "The fact that we are having this conversation here and not at the office of the Direction de Police Judiciaire de Paris at the famous thirty-six Quai des Orfèvres tells me that you do not have enough evidence yet to arrest me, Monsieur De Vries." Nicholas Sharp, cool under pressure.

De Vries' knuckles turned white as he gripped the arms of his chair, but he said nothing.

"I am going to go now. You are both wrong. You are wrong about me, and you are wrong to stop looking for whoever's behind all of this." I paused for a second as it occurred to me that there was now a likelihood that it really was one person behind all of these events. "I will show you that you are wrong. I'm just not sure how yet."

"Do not leave Europe, Monsieur Sharp. Be certain that we'll be watching you closely." Jasper De Vries seemed very sure of himself. "Because of this musical tour, you have a profile and you have influential friends; accordingly, we cannot arrest you until our case is bulletproof. Believe one thing, Monsieur Sharp, our case will become bulletproof. Your best future lies in a lifetime in jail. You should know there are many on our two forces who believe that to be too good for you." I could feel De Vries' veiled threat through his frozen stare.

Capitaine Pascal Barre was silent. He appeared to be battling to rein his fury in.

I got up to leave. Trying to convey a calmness I didn't feel, I traversed the room. It was a relief when I could steady myself on the doorframe. I turned and looked at the two lawmen. They were looking for answers, and they were searching for justice. In their position, I would have done the same. They had made it clear that, in their minds at least, I was now on the wrong side of the law and the sole focus of their investigation.

I turned my back on them and walked out of the room.

Nicholas Sharp, moving target.

Chapter 14

I made it across the foyer, up the elevator and into my room. Anger and confusion raged within me. As if I hadn't been disturbed enough by the explosion at the Palais Garnier. To now be accused of being responsible for that carnage—and the political assassination in London was like being struck by a lightning bolt with a vengeful streak. Of course, it was all made so much worse by the fact that Barre and De Vries seemed to have some very concrete and damaging evidence against me.

I needed to think, and I needed to think alone. I knew that soon enough I would call on Jack Greatrex to come up and help me work through this, but right now I needed the counsel of my own thoughts.

I sat on one of the large lounge chairs and stared out the windows toward the Paris skyline. Twenty-four hours ago, the city had been a beckoning dream; now it was a waking nightmare. I didn't even pour myself a drink. I needed every bit of mental clarity I could muster.

Emotion be gone. It was time to focus on the big picture.

First question. What the hell was happening here?

I had left the military because I couldn't, or wouldn't, stay in a job that required me to kill on order. In that world, a successful mission had always ended in somebody's death. I was over that, and had moved on. It was a hard decision, and I was fully aware that there were ghosts that still needed to be laid to rest. When I turned to music as my tonic, the future was unclear. As it turned out, I had grown accustomed to civilian life, and thanks to a few breaks that had come my way I had found some success. Now I was confronted by my past clawing at me, again.

Neither Capitaine Barre nor Jasper De Vries saw me as a musician. How had they described me? "A former military sniper of some note." It seemed the person I had tried to leave behind was still here. No matter what I decided for myself, others would always see the part of me they wanted to see. Obviously, I had no say in it.

I was angry, I was tired of people pulling my chain, and I was furious with myself for being caught in the middle of this mess. On the other hand, it was my own curiosity that had inflamed events. Stupid over-inquisitive man.

Back to being angry at myself.

I moved away from the window and lay down on the bed, staring at the now very familiar ceiling. I had no idea how much time was drifting by.

Finally, I decided something I should have decided long ago. If I was the product of two contradictory worlds, then so be it. I am what I am.

I hope the world knew what it had asked for.

Nicholas Sharp, victim no more.

I needed a plan. Two people could help me, both of whom I trusted implicitly. One was several thousand miles away. The other was staying a few floors below.

I called Greatrex. "Can you get up here now? Things have gone from bad to WTF."

Phone down, he was on his way.

I waited. It's difficult for men like me to admit fear. But I realized there was some of that, as well as the anger. Everything was pointing to my guilt. If I wasn't me, I'd probably think that I was guilty as well.

Five minutes later, while I was still waiting for Greatrex to arrive, my cell phone rang. I didn't recognize the number, but I recognized the voice.

"Nicholas."

"Elena," I responded blankly.

"Nicholas, I must speak to you, I must see you. I'm in serious trouble."

"Elena, I'm afraid your timing is way past bad. I'm in a fair bit of trouble myself." I couldn't see how catching up with a girl who seemed to specialize in causing me grief could help anything. Then she explained.

"Nicholas, I know you are still angry with me, and you have every right to be." She paused. I could hear her take a deep breath. "But my predicament is part of your problem."

I couldn't understand how Elena could even be aware of the issues I was facing, so I said nothing. She seemed to take my silence as a cue to continue.

"I have knowledge of the circumstances of Sir Phillip Morton's death. I also have some ideas regarding what happened at the Palais Garnier. You and I need to talk, for both of our sakes."

Then silence.

"Okay, start talking, Elena," I said.

"No, not on the phone; it is too exposed. We must meet."

I felt all my antennae sounding off in alarm. Foolishly, I also felt the stirrings of anticipation. "Are you in Paris?" I asked.

"No, I have had to drop off the grid, so to speak. There are people who I think—no, I am certain—wish to harm me," came the reply.

I may be many things, but I don't regard myself as an idiot.

"Wherever you are, Elena, I can't come. I have too much to sort through here," I said.

"Nicholas"—her voice rose in pitch, quavering— "if the other night meant anything to you, you must come. I don't think you understand; helping me is helping you." Her last statement was almost shouted: "You need what I know."

I sat frozen with the phone to my ear. Probably the most stupid thing I could do now is go and help this girl.

It was my turn to take a deep breath. "I make no promises, Elena, but tell me where you are."

There was a palpable sigh of relief from the other end of the phone. "I am in Füssen," she said.

"Where the hell is that?" I demanded, already cursing myself for showing weakness.

"In Bavaria, Germany. You will find me," she said. "It is the land of Sleeping Beauty."

I didn't understand, and I certainly didn't need any vague fairy-tale references.

"Just tell me where you are, Elena," I repeated. She gave me an address to meet her.

"Don't count on me, Elena," I continued. "Please don't count on me."

"You will come, Nicholas. I know it." And with that, she

hung up.

Sitting there, I began to wonder about the "Sleeping Beauty" reference. A beautiful girl who just couldn't wake up. Was Elena trying to tell me something? Was I meant to read anything into what she said? I didn't know, but I did know I didn't need this extra layer to a very complicated situation.

At least I thought I knew.

So much for La Ville-Lumière—the City of Light.

A couple of minutes later came the knock on the door that I had been waiting for. I opened it, and Greatrex walked straight in and sat down on the chair opposite me.

"How long has it been since our get-together in the bar downstairs?" I asked him.

He looked at his watch. "Around ninety minutes," he replied.

"Well, the world has changed a lot in the last ninety minutes," I said, "and not for the better."

I explained to him the meeting with Capitaine Pascal Barre and the glacial Jasper De Vries. Greatrex shook his head, sighed, and began to speak. "You are in deep …"

"I know, but there's more," I interrupted, telling him about the call from Elena.

Jack Greatrex just looked at me without saying a word. It was only a minute or so, but it felt like an hour.

"Of course you're not going to meet her." His inflection indicated statement rather than question.

I decided to treat it as a question. "At this point, no, I won't be going."

"At this point," mimicked my friend skeptically.

We spent the next hour posing questions and searching for

answers. It was like riding on a merry-go-round. Everything led back to where we had started.

Were the break-in at the nuclear power station, the assassination of the Chancellor of the Exchequer, and the bombing at the Palais Garnier all related? Outwardly, it seemed not. The groups online that had taken credit for the bombing and the break-in appeared to have no connection to each other.

Whoever was behind the British assassination had not yet come forward. The only common link appeared to be me, as Barre and De Vries had so maliciously pointed out. They hadn't even mentioned, or I presumed had knowledge of, my involvement in the power station incident.

If Antonio Ascardi was a common link, the question was what would he have to gain from any of these events? Yes, it was convenient that he had been called out of box five at the Palais Garnier just before it was blown up, but were we reading too much into that? Ascardi had seemed very upset on the night, and Aislinn indicated he was extremely perturbed the next day. He had cancelled the Munich show, which was only going to cost him money. Though he knew Elena, there was no proof he was involved in any of this.

Of course, this led to the huge question of Elena. If I put aside my first meeting with her in California, what had she really done? She said she had met Ascardi only once. Was that the truth? She led me to a situation where I stopped a dangerous incident at the power station. Just two good Samaritans? Yes, she had disappeared, but so had I. Elena didn't appear to have anything to do with the Palais Garnier attack or the death of the British Chancellor of the Exchequer, yet she had mentioned both those events in her phone call to me. The obvious question was whether we could believe anything she said anyway. Her track record on trust was not strong.

All of this led back to the pictures of me on the roof of the fly tower at the Royal Opera House in London. Who had taken them? I was certain it was neither Norbert Fontana nor old Cedrick, yet somebody had gone to a lot of trouble to photograph me up there. Surely it was no coincidence that I'd been led to the exact place that later concealed the assassin of a significant British political figure. If I had been set up, who was behind it? Fontana? Or did the circle lead us back to Ascardi? If so, how would Antonio Ascardi benefit from Sir Phillip Morton's death?

"My head hurts," announced Greatrex. "We've laid it all out, but nothing adds up."

"When nothing adds up, it's been my experience that our lack of answers stems from a lack of useful data. We need to know more," I said.

"You have to be careful," advised Greatrex. "In fact, you have to be beyond careful. The authorities have good reason to suspect you and firm facts to back up their suppositions. Nicholas, you can't afford one misstep."

"And I can't afford to just sit here and wait to be arrested, or for an 'accident' to befall me." I was thinking of Jasper De Vries' perhaps not-so-veiled threat.

"There is one person we can turn to," said Greatrex.

"Yes, I know. I think we need to call him," I responded.

I reached for my cell phone and dialed a number I'd committed to memory. It was an international call, to Maryland, Virginia.

Twenty seconds later, a familiar voice answered.

CHAPTER 14

"Hello, General, it's me."

Chapter 15

Former Lieutenant-General Colin Devlin-Waters, retired, had been Jack's and my commanding officer for much of our time in Iraq. He was a good man with a clearly defined moral code. He had supported us in the warzone and come to our aid in near-disastrous circumstances that spanned Iraq and the Isle of Wight in England. The incident could have had a calamitous effect across the globe. The General had helped us intervene. He was also exceptionally well connected. If anyone could help us dig underneath the surface here, it was him.

I told our former leader everything we knew, including my role in all the events of the last few days. I told him of our suspicions in multiple areas and about our lack of proof in those same areas. He listened carefully, interrupting with a few pertinent questions.

When I finished, he said, "Nicholas, can you put me on speakerphone please?" I did so. The General's clear and authoritative voice echoed through the room. "Jack, Nicholas, you are to do precisely nothing. I will need a little time to gather information and do some research. In the meantime, the safest course is for you to stay in Paris and leave only when it is time to go to Venice for your next performance. Do not—I repeat, do not—run around playing detective. Chances are you will only dig yourselves deeper with the authorities. I have people available; that is why you called me. Now let me and them get to work. Is that clear?"

A general becomes a general partly because people listen when he gives orders. We were listening. "Yes, sir," we both responded in unison. You would've thought we were still in uniform.

"Good. We will talk soon." And with that, the great man was gone.

I allowed myself to feel a small amount of relief that someone with the General's authority was now on my side, but was that enough?

Greatrex looked at me with a satisfied smugness. "I told you so," he said. "The smart thing to do is wait."

I could tell that he was waiting for affirmation. I thought for a minute about the wisdom of the General, the cleverest man I knew. I looked across the room at my friend, a man whose guidance and loyalty I appreciated every day. Then I thought about my newfound resolve—no more victim.

I got up and went into the bedroom. A minute and a half later, Jack walked in behind me. I had my suitcase laid out on the bed and had begun placing my clothes inside it.

Greatrex didn't ask what I was doing; he already knew. He did ask, "Are you sure?"

"In no way whatsoever," I responded, "but I have to."

He shook his head in a kind of acceptance. "Call," he instructed. "Twenty-four hours without communication and I'll be there."

"I know it and appreciate it, but I have to go alone. One question," I said, looking at him.

"Shoot."

"Where the hell is Füssen, and how in God's name do I get there?"

We shared a reckless laugh.

I made it out the front door of the hotel and halfway down the steps before I heard, "Nicholas, are you going somewhere?"

It was Antonio Ascardi.

I hesitated for a second but recovered quickly. "Hello, Tony. Yes, I'm taking a few days off. Last night shook me up quite a bit. Don't worry; I'll be in Venice in plenty of time for the show."

"The lone wolf rides again," he said, irony in his tone. "Do you think that's wise? Won't the authorities think that you are disappearing—man on the run type of thing?"

Ascardi's eyes gave away much more than his words. I was sure he had a greater knowledge of the situation than he was saying. My eyes must have been giving away my own secrets because he continued with, "A couple of policemen came to see me, asking about you. It appears you may be under some sort of suspicion."

There it was, out in the open. "What did you tell them?" I asked.

"Why don't you let me give you a lift to the airport or train station, wherever it is you are going? We can talk more in the car." He pointed in the direction of a large black limousine with a uniformed chauffeur waiting beside an open door. I was so surprised to see Ascardi I hadn't even noticed it.

"I don't want to take you out of your way," I said.

"It's not a problem. I think we should talk. Maybe I can help you."

I thought for a moment. I did tell Greatrex I was on an information-gathering mission. Maybe a talk with Ascardi could help that.

"Thanks," I said.

As we headed toward Gare de l'Est, the crowded Paris streets flew by. The car was so soundproofed that the people outside appeared as though on a muted TV screen.

"Drink?" asked Ascardi nodding at the bar.

"No thanks."

"So, Nicholas, tell me, where are you off to?" he asked.

"I don't know really," I lied. "I think I just need a few days away."

"Just hitting the road, eh? Sounds terribly romantic."

A small alarm rang in my head. What did he mean by "romantic"? Did he know who I was meeting? No chance.

"I'm just really chasing some thinking time," I said. "You're right though—as absurd as it is, the authorities do seem to think I may have something to do with last night's bombing."

"Then again, I ask, is it wise to leave? Would you not be giving the impression of guilt?"

There was probably wisdom in what Ascardi was suggesting, but I knew I still had to go.

"As you say, just being a lone wolf," I replied.

Ascardi turned and looked me directly in the eye. "I know it is absurd that you could be responsible for this tragedy," he said, "and I told the authorities exactly that. Please let me help you, Nicholas. You know I am not without influence."

Again, I hesitated. Was this a genuine offer of aid from a good and well-connected man, or was this more like a snake asking a hungry man outside for a bite?

"Thanks for the offer," I responded. Then I changed the

subject. "How are you feeling, Tony? Aislinn said you were pretty upset by the whole situation."

"Yes, it has distressed me greatly. All those innocent people who died. Losing several friends and almost losing my own life. The whole affair is frightening." For a moment, the entrepreneur appeared to linger in thought before adding wistfully, "I wonder if it really needed to happen."

I thought the final comment strange but continued to probe. "Do you have any idea who would want to do this? Anyone who would bear such enmity for you or what you stand for?"

"I am a very successful businessman, Nicholas. One man's success can lead to another's pain, no matter how accidental. But to be the subject of such an intense hatred. No, I can assure you that I was not the primary target of this terrorism." I looked directly into Ascardi's eyes; he was very convincing.

"What about the principles you stand for?" I pushed the point.

For a brief moment, Ascardi just stared at me. Again I was having trouble reading him. Then he slowly turned his gaze to the world outside, seemingly distracted by the street life passing by. A long minute elapsed. We would soon be at the station.

Finally, the entrepreneur turned back, his expression softening. "Nicholas, you and I do not know each other very well. Perhaps you have purposefully kept a little distance between us. Let me say something to you. It is no secret that I have been fortunate, but my life has also been a very passionate one. I've been lucky that my passion has brought me opportunity. You need to understand that I love all the things that life could be. You know I passionately promote alternative solutions to the world's problems, and you know I promote that as a society we ease the pace, look after the planet, and enjoy what we have. I believe that those racing toward a faster existence using technology as some sort of religion are like lemmings running off a cliff."

"But you have built your empire through increasing the world's use of technology," I pointed out.

"Yes, you're completely correct. That is exactly what I have done." Ascardi momentarily looked as though some sort of internal debate was taking place in his mind. I was taken by surprise when the expression on his face grew intense and troubled. His brow furrowed, and the lines around his eyes read like a roadmap to a place he didn't want to go. He continued. "I built what I built to make the world better, to open honest communication and dialogue between people without the continual interference of governments and corporations. That is why we neither edit nor take responsibility for what appears on our social media platforms. The content reflects who we are as a society, not who I am as a businessman."

As Ascardi spoke, his voice changed. I could feel a depth of frustrated anger as his tone deepened and the intensity of his inflection verged on malevolent. There was no trace of compassion at all. "Nicholas, the problem with social media is not of my making, despite what many suggest. The problem is that what we see on social media is who we really are." He then waved his hand dismissively at the people on the crowded sidewalks outside the car. "My friend, over time I have learned just how vile people can be when hidden behind a mask of anonymity. What you see on my media platforms is a frightening window into the very essence of human existence."

It was just a few seconds and then he clicked back, as though nothing had happened. Ascardi then offered me his winning smile. "I ask you, Nicholas, who would possibly want to hurt a man who stood for such liberty?"

As he finished speaking, the car pulled up at the station. I thanked my host for the ride, opened the door, and climbed out. I could offer him no more.

As I walked away, I felt perplexed, unsure of what had just happened. Had I just been listening to a sincere and thoughtful man questioning how anyone could hate someone for their altruism? Or ... had I just seen a glimpse into the hidden canyon of a predator's soul?

Chapter 16

About four hours into the drive to Füssen, Germany, and with another four to go, my tired eyes began to challenge my wisdom of driving through the night. I'd left the station right after Ascardi had dropped me off and hired the most nondescript car I could find for the trip, an aging white Volvo SUV that was too old to be electronically tracked. The girl at the hire car company had seemed surprised when I asked for a paper map book rather than using my cell phone for directions. I worked out a route that headed east across France, over the German border and into Bavaria. The forecast was for rain and snow. The rain didn't bother me, but the snow could be problematic. Füssen had just been covered in four feet of snow, with more to come. The long road ahead wound into darkness, its bright reflectors zipping by like fireflies. Drive on ...

It was well after midnight when my headlights illuminated a signpost heralding my destination. The SUV also lit up the endless snowbanks that made a gully of the road. It was still traversable, but the last hour of driving had taken a lot of concentration. I had also kept a vigilant eye open in my mirror for any headlights following me for too long. Apart from one car that sat on my tail for a good two hours, I saw nothing.

Entering Füssen, my tiredness had escalated into an outright battle to stay conscious. I ached for sleep. Knowing nothing about the area except that there was an old and a new part of town, I headed to the older section, as Elena had directed.

I slowed right down on the slippery roads outside what I assumed to be the small train station and bus terminal. The next corner revealed a vision that suggested my fatigue was messing with my eyesight. Floodlights exposed centuries-old Bavarian buildings painted in pastel greens, yellows and blues, each of their sharply pointed rooftops perched under a blanket of thick snow. The narrow streets had been plowed, but the snow that had been pushed away created a three-foot-high dirty white wall along the side of each street. The Christmas card vignette was completed by bright lights decorating eaves and windows, reflecting off a glowing wash on the icy ground. I wondered if the town would have presented the same enchanting picture one hundred years ago. It was a comforting thought.

I pulled over to check the map's directions. Then, slowly heading down a series of glaciers posing as laneways, I finally came to the Hintere Gasse. It was a narrow backstreet that seemed more dimly lit than the rest of the town. Old limestone buildings two stories high lined its snow-covered footpaths. I pulled the car over in one of the few available spots, grabbed my overnight bag, and trekked down the street until I found the number Elena had given me.

It was freezing cold, but I hoped I would be warm soon, one way or another. When I arrived outside the old whitewashed building that displayed the address I'd been given, I knocked loudly on the weathered timber door. I hadn't told Elena I was definitely coming, in case reason overtook foolhardiness and I changed my mind. Despite the hour, she must have been awake, because a moment later the door in front of me opened and there she was, again.

I had just spent eight hours telling myself to be distant and professional with this girl. I'd spent the final two hours convinced that she'd tell me everything she knew, and I'd soon be on my way. For the few minutes it took to walk down the street, I had felt my resolve start to weaken. When Elena opened the door and stared at me with those mesmerizing green eyes, my resolve abandoned me. When she threw her arms around me and kissed me fully with her soft lips, I couldn't even remember what resolve was.

When I awoke the next morning, the aroma of simmering fried eggs filled my nostrils. I could hear Elena rattling around on the apartment's small stove. Hunger outweighed my need for more sleep as I got up, threw on some clothes, and joined her.

I hadn't taken much notice of the apartment when I'd arrived late the night before. Other things had been on my mind. Looking around, I felt the history of the place wrap me like a reassuringly warm blanket. As I padded across the bedroom's blemished polished floorboards toward the steps leading up to the lounge, I paused for a second. The worn, oversized doors framed her beauty. Elena's hair spilled down around her face as she worked at the small stove. A log fire crackled in a fireplace in the corner. It was a picture, but not the one I'd come for. Despite that, I felt sure that googling "romantic hideaway Bavarian alps" would surely bring up pictures of this place.

"You certainly picked a spectacular spot to run off to," I said as I put my arms around her as she cooked. Then I wondered how the hell was I suddenly feeling so domesticated. I withdrew my arms.

"Yes," she said, ignoring my movement. "I used to come here as a girl, with my family. It was always my favorite place to be." Again, I was enjoying the touch of Georgia in her accent.

"The town certainly looked quite something as I pulled in last night," I said.

"Yes, it is breathtaking, but there is more to this place. Neuschwanstein Castle is not far from here."

"Nootsch—... Newtsh—"

She laughed. "Neuschwanstein is the castle of dreams; it has been used as the location for many Hollywood films. It is the Disney castle, Sleeping Beauty's castle. To a young girl from Georgia, coming here was a way to touch a dream."

Elena turned to me and buried her head on my shoulder. "I just wanted to come here, one last ..." She didn't finish the sentence. A tear rolled slowly down her cheek.

She seemed so fragile. Nicholas Sharp being drawn into the vortex.

"We need to talk," I said, trying to reassert some self-control.

"Yes, we do, Nicholas—we must. I know that is why you are here. But first we eat and then walk while the sun is out. Then we talk."

As much as I desperately wanted information, I accepted her rules. The thought of some small amount of sanctuary from what I'd just been through was too tempting. Our morning turned out to be easy and slow. We ate, we lay down for a while, and I even let sleep, which had been denied me in the previous twenty-four hours, claim back some time. It was like we had walked away from the world; maybe that was the fairy tale.

Around midday we put on some warm clothes and went downstairs. The cold air hit us like slivers of ice penetrating our skin. Thankfully, the sky was a clear blue, allowing the occasional ray of warmish sunlight to spring to our defense. As we walked down the narrow streets, it became obvious that the township of Füssen was just as beautiful by day as it had appeared the night before. Thick quilts of snow covered almost every available surface. The old buildings, the quaint shops, and the restaurants were peeking at us through a veil of white. I could see why the girl walking beside me had chosen this place to escape the life that troubled her.

The snow-covered statue in the main square looked like a soldier wading through an ice field. I knew how he felt. Although the beauty of this small village may have been timeless, the pressures and doubts I felt niggling at me were very much of this moment.

At one point I heard a growling rumble above me. Elena laughed. "Come here," she said, taking my hand and stepping under the eave of the shop we were strolling past. Another growl, and a crag of ice thudded on the snow where we had stood.

"That would have hurt," I said.

She laughed again. "Yes, when there is a lot of snow on the roof, the schneefang holds it there. As the snow melts, or there is too much for the grating to retain, the snow and ice break off and tumble down. Don't worry; it won't kill you. Besides, most times you hear that rumble just before it happens. The locals know to step out of the way."

We walked down a gently sloping street that opened up to

reveal the surprise of a wide, fast-flowing river. Suddenly, the Christmas card had turned into a scene from a kid's storybook. Pine forests surrounded the smattering of steepled roofs with gleaming red and blue trims belonging to the homes that lined the riverbanks. Like two ordinary lovers, we strolled toward the water, leaned against a rail, and gazed out at the view before us.

"The Lech River," said Elena softly.

"We need to talk—now," I responded, perhaps a little harshly. Nicholas Sharp, man of steel, becoming impatient.

"Yes" was all I got back.

In the military I had been trained that silence is key to interrogation. Current affairs journalists did the same thing when interviewing reluctant politicians. I continued to look out across the view but remained silent.

"Nicholas, you may think less of me before this day is over, but I will answer your questions," she said.

Silence. The key to interrogation. Besides, I didn't know which questions to ask.

Three minutes later: "All right," she sighed. "I will tell you what I can."

We both remained looking straight ahead over the river, avoiding eye contact. It seemed easier that way.

"First," she began, "I told you on the phone that I may have some knowledge about the murder of Sir Phillip Morton, the British Chancellor of the Exchequer. Well, that is true. Before I tell you any more, you need to understand that I had no idea the authorities would blame you for the shooting."

I nodded silently.

Elena carried on without waiting for me to speak. "You may have read that the police are looking for another person who was with Sir Phillip when he was shot—a woman, in fact."

I was starting to anticipate where this conversation was going, and I didn't like it.

"Nicholas, the woman that the authorities seek is … me."

I had no idea what to say.

Elena turned to look at me, just for a second, and then turned back toward the river. "I know you are shocked; I can see it in your face. You probably should be shocked, but there are some things you need to know before you judge me."

I'd uttered no judgment, but I'd sure as hell passed one.

"First, I want you to understand that I had no prior knowledge that Phillip was going to be shot. No idea at all."

I said nothing.

"Secondly, I desperately want you to understand and believe that I was not involved with Sir Phillip Morton in any romantic or physical way."

I was starting to wonder if this story was turning into a fairy tale; was anything Elena said true? Still I made no comment.

"You do not believe me, Nicholas; I can feel it."

For the first time, I turned to Elena and spoke. "Then help me here, Elena. You were in a Covent Garden apartment with a high-profile British politician when he was shot, but you were just there to say hello?"

"No, I was asked to be there."

There was no stopping me now; my mind was racing. This was about my survival as much as Elena's credibility. "Did you think whoever put you there needed you and Sir Phillip there at a specific time so that the assassination could occur? They also needed the shooting to take place in that apartment because they had photos of me on a nearby rooftop." Abruptly, my knuckles tensed into a ball. I knew the depth of my antipathy must be showing.

"But Nicholas ..."

"No, Elena," I interrupted. You set me up for a murder charge, whether you meant to or not. *Why* were you there with the chancellor? And *who* arranged it?"

This time the silence was Elena's. For two long minutes we watched the water flow. I knew she was wrestling with herself, and I knew I was running out of patience.

"I knew Phillip socially. We moved in some of the same circles. He was a good man; he never suggested anything improper or inappropriate to me."

I waited. "Good ol' Sir Phil. So what?"

Elena continued. "I have been thinking about this for the last few days, and I don't understand it even as I'm telling it to you, Nicholas. Sir Phillip Morton himself asked me to meet him at that apartment. He said he had some information to give me. No one sent me there, and no one asked me to go there apart from the very man who was murdered."

I was grasping for a lucid thought that would decipher all I was being told. Why would such a man invite this beautiful woman to his own murder? What information could he have for Elena? It was nonsensical.

"What information did Sir Phillip pass on to you?" I asked impatiently.

"Nothing," she replied. "He was shot before he could tell me anything."

Convenient for someone.

We didn't talk for another few minutes. The sound of the gentle mountain waters flowing past seemed to moderate my anger. Something needed to. One minute I'm lying in bed, infatuated with this mysterious angel next to me, the next she appears to be the angel of death, wielding a scythe in bony hands.

"All right," I said, "let's suppose what you say is true. What did you do after the chancellor was shot? Why did you run?"

"I tried everything I could to help Phillip, but he was gone." She paused, as though reflecting. "I quickly realized I would be held accountable. I also knew his name would be publicly sullied. The media love a story like that, particularly the British media."

What Elena said rang a bell of truth.

"I must have some sort of connection to the killer. The killer knew we would be there; he knew I was there."

Elena was trying to be strong, but the shaking gave her away. You can't fake the shaking.

"So you ran," I offered.

"Yes, I ran and ran. I was covered in Phillip's blood. I have no idea how I got out of there without being stopped. I wondered later if the assassin had allowed me to escape."

"Explaining why the authorities didn't get to you in time is straightforward. The killer would've used a suppressor on his rifle. It wouldn't have been silent, but it could easily have been mistaken for a car backfiring. So no one would have been looking for a murderer immediately," I said.

I paused for a minute before continuing. I was trying to gauge her reaction to my words.

"Explaining why the killer let you go is more difficult. I don't have an answer to that," I concluded.

Elena started shaking again. My own thoughts were a bit of a mess. Did I believe everything I had just been told, or had the story been carefully crafted just for my ears? Looking at Elena, I realized I wasn't going to get any more out of her in the state she was in. Besides, there was a small part of infatuated Nicholas who wanted to look after her, protect her.

"We have more to talk about, but not right now," I said, guiding her gently away from the railing. "Let's go back to the hotel."

It wasn't until later that I realized that in my semi-besotted state I'd failed to ask one vital question.

Who was Morton's information intended for?

Chapter 17

The rest of the day passed without a lot of conversation between Elena and me. There were too many things to sort through, probably in both our minds. One minute I felt infatuated, a moment later suspicious and resentful. Too much going on here.

As the afternoon progressed into evening, Elena calmed down. We agreed that we would eat and then talk. I needed to know what she knew about the Palais Garnier bombing.

"I will cook, then we will talk, Nicholas," was all I got out of her on the subject.

What worried me the most was that wherever there was some sort of trouble, Elena seemed to either be there or have some insider knowledge. This girl was everywhere. It also worried me—more than worried me—that every hour I spent with her dragged me deeper into her enigma. I was treading water and losing breath.

The daylight had surrendered to darkness, and Elena was preparing dinner when she announced she'd forgotten to get salt. "We will need it."

"I'll go," I said. Didn't we just sound like the perfect domesticated couple.

"No," she answered, "I know where the shop is, and I know

what I need. It's only a five-minute walk." She grabbed her white puffer jacket from the hook by the door, climbed into some waterproof boots, and was gone before I could object further.

The fire crackled away as I sat beside it. Amid my brooding, guilt made an appearance. I shouldn't have let her go on her own. Then I glanced up at the shelf on the kitchen wall. There it was, in clear view. Salt.

Shit!

I ran into the bedroom. All her clothes were there; if she'd done a runner, she hadn't packed a bag. Elena had been scared, really scared, when we talked earlier in the afternoon. She was convinced people were after her, and I had let her go out on her own.

I grabbed my own coat and boots and headed out the door.

Outside the temperature had dropped drastically. Thick snow was building up on the street, making it difficult to navigate. Elena wouldn't have stayed out in this weather any longer than she had to. I had no idea which direction she would have gone in, so I just started to walk. I convinced myself this would be a big misunderstanding that we would be laughing about back in our room later in the evening. Then I turned a corner and saw the flashing blue lights of the cops.

I felt a chill that had nothing to do with the weather. I jogged down the narrow street as quickly as I could. A small crowd gathered round a crew of medics attending to someone on the ground. As I got closer, my fears exploded. The medical workers moved with no urgency—nothing they could do. Then I saw what I didn't want to see.

The body lying on the white snow was clothed in a white puffer jacket. Blood made a grizzly red slushy of the snow.

I ran the last few feet, only to be stopped by the arm of a member of the polizei.

"Halt," he said. I couldn't hear him. I couldn't hear anything.

I ducked and stepped in closer. My chest tightened. Elena lay on the ground a few feet away from me, deathly still, her long hair cascading across the ice. Her face was turned away, half buried in the snow, but there was no doubt. It was her.

I turned and threw up.

The officer who had tried to stop me appeared by my side. "Kennst du sie?" he asked. I knew it was a question from his inflection, but I didn't understand.

"Sorry. I don't ..." I began.

"Do you know her?" he repeated in English.

"Yes," I said. "Yes, I do." I wasn't thinking, and it was a foolish response. The blue lights of the emergency vehicles cast ominous alternating shadows over her body, like some macabre discotheque.

"I'm sorry," said the officer.

I forced myself to focus. "What happened?" I asked.

"What is your name please, sir?"

I stared at the officer as though I hadn't heard him. "What happened to her?" I could feel my voice rising.

The police obviously decided on a different approach. "I'm afraid, Herr ... sorry, I didn't get your name."

I said nothing.

"I'm afraid she has been shot," said the officer. He began to pull out a small notebook when another police car pulled up. More flashing blue lights. A tall, slim, suited man with pocked skin and a weary expression climbed out. From the reaction of the other officers I assumed him to be the detective in charge.

"Muller, bitte hier druben," he commanded.

The officer standing next to me seemed to hesitate. He turned to me and said, "Please remain here." He then strode over to his superior.

I stood there motionless, wrestling with the shocking image in front of me. I forced my mental cogs to start turning. Giving the police my details and becoming a suspect in another murder would not help me find Elena's killer. This was likely a professional hit. Local law enforcement could well struggle to handle this.

I needed to disappear, but it was going to be difficult. The policeman I had spoken to was keeping a watchful eye on me as he was talking to his boss. I edged behind the man next to me in the crowd. The policemen's eyes followed me. Worse still, from their body language it looked like the cops' conversation was winding up.

The man who was now in front of me seemed nervous, stepping from foot to foot. He kept turning his head every which way, asking questions of those around him. His behavior spoke of a highly-strung disposition. A murder in this small village would put the whole town on edge. That gave me an idea; it wasn't mind-bogglingly brilliant, but it was all I had.

I tapped the man in front of me on the shoulder. He jerked his arm away in surprise. I then leaned forward and quietly spoke to my jumpy friend, "Excuse me, my German is not good."

"That is all right," he said, calming a little when he realized I posed no threat. "I speak a little English."

"Did I just hear correctly that the police were talking about some sort of airborne virus that was used in this attack, I mean before the girl was shot. And look over there, is that policeman getting masks out of his car?"

Instantly, the man's nerves got the better of him as he yelled out, "Es liegt ein Virus in der Luft!"

I had no idea what he said, but the crowd reaction was instantaneous. People were suddenly yelling out questions to the police. Others were running back up the street. A couple were just screaming. It was the moment of chaos I needed.

Feeling faintly surprised that my little ruse had worked, I took the onlookers' reaction as my cue. Edging quickly toward the perimeter of the crowd, I eased my way out of the glaring brightness of the surreal lightshow. Once in the shadows I moved hastily up the street, my feet searching for traction in the thick snow.

Forcing myself to think as logically as I could, I realized I'd never been to this town. The room was in Elena's name. The only thing that identified me was the hire car. It wouldn't take the authorities long to find out where Elena was staying. They would also figure out pretty quickly that she wasn't here on her own. Grief would have to wait. I would have to compartmentalize. I'd done it before.

The streets were mostly deserted. Everyone who was outdoors had gathered at the scene of the crime. Elena's murder was a dramatic occurrence for the village. I knew in time it would torment me as well. I just couldn't allow that to kick in yet.

I rounded the last corner. I was close; our small gästehaus was within sight. No sign of the polizei—I was going to make it.

Then I heard, "Nicholas Sharp, do not move. I have a

weapon pointed at your back,"

I froze.

"Now turn around please." That was a phrase you didn't want to hear when someone pulled a gun on you. If he wanted you to turn around, that meant he didn't care whether you saw him or not. That meant—

"Who are you? What do you want? Why did you call me Nicholas Sharp?" I was trying everything. Just throwing mud.

"Please," said my assailant, "do not insult me. I am a professional, as you once were. There should be mutual respect."

I couldn't pinpoint the accent, but it was European, possibly from the south.

"Now, Mr. Sharp, please do exactly as I say. I will not pretend that if you do, you won't get hurt. You are about to get hurt very badly. If you scream or call out it will only make the result more instantaneous."

I matched the man's stare. He was the walking definition of nondescript. Dark clothes that wouldn't stand out, not too tall, not too short. He had an inoffensive face, but even in the streetlight I could see that his eyes were gray and lifeless, like a shark's. He was, as he said, a professional.

"Now, Mr. Sharp, let's not drag this out. Please continue to walk down this street, go straight past your gästehaus and then turn left down the next laneway."

I had no doubt that he intended this to be my final few minutes on the planet. The man in front of me had probably already committed one murder this evening; a second wouldn't bother him.

"Who sent you?" I asked, inquisitive to the end. To be honest, at this point I didn't really care. I was just stalling for time.

"Turn and walk, or it all ends now."

I turned and walked. Our procession of two passed the doorway to Elena's apartment as he shepherded me down the icy footpath. I thought about feigning a slip to give me a chance to spin around and incapacitate my executioner-to-be. Glancing behind, I saw he was close enough to watch me but far enough back that I couldn't strike him. Any attempt to incapacitate him would be futile and end lives.

We were almost at the laneway. Letting him take me down there was a bad idea. Then I heard it. I stopped and turned around. My assailant seemed unfazed.

"If I am going to die tonight, at least tell me who has ordered my death," I said. Although I was going for defiance, I really just didn't want him to move.

I received no response bar a wave forward of the gun. Then came the sound again, the growl. Again, it went unnoticed by the man pointing the pistol at me. Under the streetlight I now recognized it as a 9mm Glock 17. It had a capacity of seventeen rounds. I knew that because I had one at home in L.A. I also knew that this man wouldn't need anywhere near that number of bullets to do the job. That being said, he could shoot me all he wanted, and I still wasn't going to move from that spot. Now I was feeling defiant.

With a shrug of the shoulders he raised the gun and pointed it at my chest just as a mound of ice and snow plummeted from the rooftop above us. As the assassin's finger tightened on the trigger, I threw myself to the right, under the shelter of a large eave. The snow and ice tumbled down, collecting my would-be assailant and knocking him off his feet. The man let out a surprised cry as his head thudded down on the hard ice.

In a second I was standing above him, but he reacted with surprising speed, raising his gun toward me. I desperately kicked out with the heel of my shoe, sending the weapon spinning across the street. The assassin showed the same quick reaction, clawing at my ankle, finding his grip, and twisting hard. Sharp pain shot through my leg as I lost my balance, smashing to the ground. I landed awkwardly, bending my wrist as I fell. Despite the additional pain, I knew that staying down would be fatal. My assailant was already on his feet. I had no doubt he'd come with more than just a gun. Then there it was: he produced a long hunting knife from under his coat. Clambering backward, I ripped my own coat off and wrapped it around my hand and wrist, just missing his first jab with the blade as I retreated. As he came at me in a full-on attack, he slipped on the ice, just for a second. I was standing now, so I changed plan, unwrapping my coat and throwing it into his eyes. As he swiped it away, I sprang forward, my left leg hooking behind his right knee. He lost his purchase and hit the ice like a falling rock. I had one chance. I put all my weight behind the biggest punch I could muster, my right hand aiming directly at his heart—that would have to slow him down. At the same time, I reached for the knife with my left hand. I knew it was a dangerous move, I could easily grab the blade rather than the handle, but my choices were limited to non-existent. As I grabbed the knife a second punch to the heart did its job. My attacker loosened his grip on the knife and I ripped it from his hand.

I then had a millisecond to make a decision. I knew the man struggling below to be Elena's killer. I could give no room nor show any weakness. I plunged the knife directly into his eye. It had been a life-changing decision ... I had decided to end his life.

Chapter 18

I stepped over the dead man's body and ran back to our gästehaus. Unlocking the front door, I took the stairs two at a time and entered the apartment. Was it only less than two hours ago Elena and I had been happily ensconced there? I knew that any minute now the polizei would splinter the door and it would be over. I only hoped they hadn't discovered my car yet. Two minutes later I was leaping down the stairs, bag in hand, and out the front entrance.

I jogged as quickly as I could down the street, trying not to draw too much unwanted attention. I found my car, scraped what snow I could off the windscreen, climbed in, and started the engine. As I pulled out from the curb, the flashing blue light of a police car appeared in my rearview mirror. I floored the gas pedal; the wheels spun on the ice but the car refused to budge. I tried again with less power. Still no forward movement. I released my foot and tried yet again. It seemed to take forever for the wheels to find some traction as I eventually eased slowly up the street. I made it to the corner just as the police car pulled up outside the gästehaus. That had been way too close.

I had to extract myself from the immediate area now and figure out where I was going later. As I turned the first corner, I saw more flashing blue lights fifty yards ahead. It was a polizei roadblock. There would be no talking my way through that. I spun the wheel and the car lurched violently to the left, my rear wheels sliding out on the icy road. As I headed down a small alleyway that wasn't much wider than my vehicle, I prayed that none of the police at the roadblock had seen my clumsy attempt at avoidance. I was driving too fast, following the laneway as it veered gradually round to the right. Suddenly, a large building dominated the headlight's beams. I slammed on my brakes, skidding on the ice. It was a dead end; there was nowhere left to go. Hemmed in and completely out of alternatives, I slapped the wheel in frustration.

A flickering streetlamp on my right caught my attention. It was lighting a narrow walkway. The path was clearly not designed for cars. I backed up slightly, then inched forward, turning the wheel to the right. If the last road was a tight squeeze, this was almost impossible. I held my breath as the car crept along the path. The sound of solid limestone scraping against the metal door handles told me I had less than nothing to spare. Midway along I was forced to a stop as the car's wheels began to spin wildly in the snow, fighting against the friction of a particularly narrow spot between two buildings. As if on cue, the reflection of flashing blue lights appeared in my mirror, growing brighter as they bounced off the walls behind me. A police car was driving down the laneway I'd just vacated. A minute later, the car had reached the dead end, its lights pointing straight ahead into the same building at the end of the street. The pulse of the flashing blue seemed to be everywhere. Well, almost everywhere. Fortunately, my walkway remained in shadow, out of their reach. Flicking my lights off, I stopped the engine, hoping that there was enough darkness on the footpath to conceal my car from all but a thorough search. I waited, well aware that if they ventured down my walkway I couldn't even open a door to run.

A few seconds later relief flooded through me as the flashing blue lights started to recede. I presumed the police had reversed back up the laneway. After some cajoling of the gas pedal I was eventually released from my limestone vice and drove forward down the walkway.

Relieved at my newfound freedom, I drove a couple of miles down the road before pulling over onto a cul-de-sac sheltered by a thick strand of pines. My first priority was to get clear of Füssen and then try to get out of Germany. The more distance—bureaucratic and physical—I could put between myself and the German police force, the better. I was only a couple of miles away from the Austrian border. If I could cross it without having to produce any identification, I might have a chance.

Twenty minutes later I was in Austria. At least I thought so. I wasn't really sure because there had been no border guards and no apparent border. Thank God for small mercies. I pulled over at the next town. The sign I passed said it was called Reutte. I stopped the car and checked my map again. Yes, I was definitely in Austria, a little further out of the hands of the German authorities.

It was time to develop a plan. The last twenty-four hours seemed to involve a lot of reacting and little or no forethought. Where to now? I knew I needed to make my way to Venice. But I was tired, way beyond tired. I'd been exhausted when I'd arrived in Füssen. I couldn't drive all the way through the

Austrian Alps and onto Venice in my current state. I looked outside the car. Snow pelted down, building an impenetrable cold white wall standing between me and freedom. If it kept falling at this rate the roads through the alps would quickly become impassable, yet I couldn't stay where I was.

I looked at the map again. The town of Innsbruck was around two hours away, probably four in this weather, presuming the roads remained open. It would be too late for a rail link from Innsbruck to Venice tonight, but I could most likely get one tomorrow. That was it, then: ahead of me I had an all-night drive on a dangerous alpine road through heavy snow with nearly zero visibility. Nicholas Sharp, unto the breach.

An hour later I was seriously questioning my judgment. The car's headlights seemed to light up only the pounding snow. I was traveling slowly, testing every facet of the Volvo's reliability. The drive grew more treacherous with each mile. Thick snow now layered the roads. There had been no snow-clearing machinery, nor any other vehicle, for at least thirty minutes. I didn't need a weather forecast to tell me things were getting worse, but I couldn't turn back now; it was only forwards.

Every now and again, dim lights shone from distant towns way down in the alpine valleys. Seeing them didn't encourage me. They only reminded me of the consequences if I missed a turn. The tires were finding it harder and harder to grip the frozen slurry. I drove on.

I wanted to stop and think, but I couldn't afford to. I may not have been able to get going again. So much had happened in the last few hours, but the driving needed all my concentration. Several times, back in the military, I had been single-minded in my focus as I concentrated on performing an extraction. Reflection comes later. I had to be in that mindset to extract myself from this situation now. But I felt myself slipping ...

I kept seeing Elena lying in the snow, soaked in her own blood. My stomach heaved every time.

Concentrate on the road.

Then I thought about our last night together. No, focus, damn it.

Back to the road.

Then came the questions. I wondered what Elena hadn't told me. While I was in mid-thought the car shook and lunged violently to the left. I corrected, but in the challenging conditions I overdid it, and the car counter-lunged to the right, where I'd just seen distant lights in the valley below. The Volvo wouldn't stop; despite correcting and braking, I had no control. It slid toward a void of blackness. I was going to go over the edge. Close your eyes and accept it, Sharp.

Almost too late, the car found some grip and straightened up. I braked. The vehicle stopped as the engine stalled. It left only the sound of the wind outside and my throbbing heartbeat within.

Focus on the road, you damn fool, or you won't be around to ask any questions. Compartmentalize or perish.

Five and a half hours after my journey began, the road started to widen and flatten out. I was past the worst of it and could put on a little speed. Sometimes you don't feel the depth of the stress that has engulfed you until it stops. I felt my breathing and my muscles begin to relax as the road ahead became more manageable.

An hour later, and again I was arriving in an unknown European town in the small hours of the morning. This time there would be no warm greeting. I desperately needed sleep, even just a few hours. If I slept in the car in these temperatures, I would freeze. All I could think to do was find a bland corporate chain hotel and hope I could check in for a few hours without having to produce any identification. Twenty minutes after that I was standing in the foyer of the very comfortable Marriot-Innsbruck hotel. The check-in clerk was professional but not overly attentive. When I explained that I'd accidentally left my passport in my car and didn't want to go out in this weather to get it, she understood. Just bring it in in the morning, she instructed.

Ten minutes after that I was lying on a large double bed. I knew I wouldn't be awake for long. The last thought I had as I drifted off to sleep was how odd this all seemed. Today I was a fugitive, yet in forty-eight hours I was meant to be stepping on a stage in Venice in front of a thousand people. Go figure.

Chapter 19

The morning light hit me like a slap on the face as I awoke to a world without Elena. I had slept soundly; my body wouldn't let me do otherwise. Up until now there hadn't been any real chance to think, or to grieve. Now my waking thoughts were bouncing around my head like colliding atomic particles. The depth of my feeling toward the girl had been surprising. I knew she was a dangerous place to be, yet I had gone to her. Her death left a void in my world. That was surprising too. I would never have been able to completely trust her. Now she was gone, and I had killed her murderer. But I was certain that I hadn't even begun to deal with the person who ordered her death. That would come.

I got out of bed and opened the curtains fully. The weather had cleared. It was gray and overcast, but the snow had stopped. Innsbruck was a much bigger city than it had seemed last night. From eight floors up, I could see the snowcapped mountains surrounding the city, standing as sentries for the busy streets below. Directly in front of my window less than a mile away was an enormous ski-jumping stadium. It loomed out of the mountain like an artificial dragon. This was the land of winter sports.

I made myself a coffee. It was good for hotel-room coffee.

CHAPTER 19

Despite my grief, it was time to move forward and chase the big picture. I had gone to Füssen in search of more information. I had gained some, but not in the manner I would have chosen. It was pointless to dwell on it now, but I should have asked Elena if she knew who was behind the explosion at the Palais Garnier. That conversation had been relegated to the evening together that never came.

Then I felt as though I had betrayed her by just having that thought. Either way, it was too late for recriminations.

I glanced at my watch. The train to Venice would leave at 1:22 p.m., just over two hours away. My first act would be to contact Greatrex. He would be worried, not to mention annoyed, that I had been out of communication so long.

I got out my laptop and skyped him. It took all of five seconds before his face appeared on my screen. The big fella's drawn skin and the blackness around his eyes told the story of a sleepless night; he was a screenshot of worry and frustration.

"Well, back from the land of the lost." Attitude.

"Sorry, it was out of my hands."

"I had started throwing my things in my bag and was about to come looking for you." My friend sounded a touch irritable.

"There are things you need to know," I explained. I think he picked up on my own angst and frustration because his tone softened slightly.

"I've just been talking to the General," he said. "I think the three of us need to have a chat. Where are you?"

"Austria."

Greatrex paused for a moment. "Wasn't expecting that."

"I haven't expected much that's happened in the last twenty-four hours," I replied.

"Why don't I see if I can get the General back online? Then

we can all talk together."

"Done deal." I sipped my coffee and waited.

A few minutes later the image of General Devlin-Waters' face appeared on my screen next to Greatrex's. He looked pissed.

"Good morning, General," I said.

Fifteen minutes later I had filled in Greatrex and the General on the most salient points of the events in Füssen and my struggle to get to Austria.

There was a moment of silence before I heard the General's voice say, "And which part of 'do not run around playing detective' did you not understand?" Now he sounded pissed.

"Yes, sir, you were right, and I know I'm in a bigger bind than I was when you said that but... on the other hand we have some more vital information regarding Elena's involvement in all of this." Nicholas Sharp for the defense.

Greatrex allowed a smirk to appear on his face. He was obviously amused at my being reprimanded.

"And the young lady has now lost her life," added the General.

Smirk gone - silence from both of us.

"Well," said the General. "I have some more information as well. You may as well get comfortable; this could take a while."

I took another large sip of my now cold coffee.

"My people and I have done some serious digging around in the life of Antonio Ascardi," he began. "It seems there are two schools of thought about the man. There are those - and I must say that they are in the clear majority - who believe he has done great work and deserves all the success that has come his way. They say he is a man of conviction who truly believes in what his media group and other interests stand for. They say he is what he appears to be."

"And the other point of view?" questioned Greatrex.

"Well, that's where things get a little more complicated," responded the General. "Even his detractors say he is a man of principle, but they do question some of his ethics."

"In what way?" I asked.

"Let's go back a bit. No one really knows where Ascardi got his start, but everyone we spoke to said he was bankrolled at some point early in his career. His money and initial success almost seem to come from nowhere." The General hesitated as if deciding what to say next. "It's possible, with Ascardi's Italian heritage, that connections to the mafia could be an easily argued point. We have, however, found no definitive proof of that."

I interrupted. "I know of one man who knew Ascardi right from the beginning. He was there with him through the journey to success."

"Who's that?" asked Greatrex.

"Well, it won't do us any good," I replied. "It was Gabriel Arquette, minister of culture in the French government, and now he's dead, killed in the explosion at the Palais Garnier."

Again, there was silence over the line. The General broke it. "Let me continue. It would appear that the common view of those who question Antonio Ascardi's morals is that things changed for him after the death of his younger sister, Vittoria. His critics say he was badly affected by her passing. The word is his passions turned into obsessions. He began to ignore his closest advisers, discarding their views as ignorant and inconsequential. He seemed unable to temper his judgment with his usual reasoning. They say his modus operandi changed from consultative to compulsive."

"How did his sister die?" I asked.

"She was murdered," answered the General. "Culprit unknown."

Greatrex began to talk. "Let's think for a minute about Elena's involvement in the murder of Phillip Morton. How does Ascardi fit into that?

"I haven't got an answer to that," I said. "It's highly possible he had nothing to do with it."

"Nicholas, did you ask Elena who introduced her to the chancellor and who the information that he wanted to share was intended for?" asked the General.

That was it—the question I should have asked when Elena and I were by the river.

"No," I said sheepishly. "She just said they moved in the same social circles."

"Hmph," mumbled the General. "There are other sides to this. There are also some interesting aspects to Ascardi's business dealings," he continued.

Greatrex and I both waited for more.

"Antonio Ascardi's business, the Ascardi Media Group, has two head offices, one in London, the other in Milan."

The General had our attention.

"He also has three homes: the Scottish castle you have already visited, a very expensive London townhouse in Belgravia, and a palatial home just off the Grand Canal in Venice."

"Lucky man," said Greatrex.

"A couple of points here," continued our former commanding officer. "Ascardi has been spending more and more time in Italy. Yesterday he moved his main man, Norbert Fontana, to work out of the media group's Milan office."

"Nothing unusual in that," I observed.

"The unusual thing is that Ascardi has not been seen a lot in the Milan office lately. The people there have been told he is spending more time at his Venice home."

"I'm guessing someone that rich can spend as much time at home as they like," noted Greatrex. "He would have people like Fontana to run the business for him."

"Now, here's the strangest thing," observed the General. "Our man on the ground in Venice is saying Ascardi has been spending increasing amounts of time away from his house there."

I thought for a moment. "He's been absent from the tour on several occasions. We've been told he's off dealing with business matters. It didn't seem unusual at the time for such a successful entrepreneur to be spending his time that way, but in hindsight ..."

"If Ascardi is not at one of his offices, nor spending much time where he had led people to believe he is ..." began Greatrex.

"Then where the hell is he spending his time?" I finished the question for him.

"That's the question that needs answering," said the General. "But there is one more bit of information that you two need to know."

We waited.

"Our group has a person very well placed in the Ascardi Media Group in Milan. She has observed an unusual practice in that office. At first she didn't think it important, but taking current events into consideration, it may be. The Ascardi Group deals with two shipping companies in Milan. Despite most of their work being in the digital domain, they move products all around the world; Ascardi Media would be good customers."

"Makes sense," I said.

"They also use a much smaller business to ship goods from Milan to Venice. Two things struck our person as unusual about this. The first is that this smaller company specializes in the shipping of ultra-high-spec equipment, the kind needing to be handled with extreme care."

"Why would Ascardi be shipping high-spec equipment to Venice?" asked Greatrex.

"We don't know," replied the General. Our person can't get a look at any of the manifests or the destinations."

"You'd assume it would be his house," I thought out loud.

"You would, but it would pay to be sure." The General always erred on the side of caution.

"Can your person find out any more?"

"As I've said to you gentlemen before, the group I am part of observes and provides information. We can support governmental decisions, but our people are not operatives and they are not rogues. They are just people with a conscience."

Greatrex and I looked at each other on the screen, just like a couple of rogues.

"This shipping firm is called Tech-Safe. Its ownership is concealed behind a number of trusts and shell companies across the world. Eventually, we tracked our way to the source. Two of the names listed on the board of the controlling company were of particular interest. The first was Norbert Fontana. The second was one …" the General paused, like he didn't want to say what he was about to say.

"Go on," I said.

"Elena Beria."

"Shit," said Greatrex.

I said nothing.

After we hung up, Jack Greatrex and I just stared at each other on our screens. "That's a game changer," he said. "What are you going to do?"

"I'm meant to be traveling on an afternoon train to Venice," I said. As I spoke, I was already thumbing through the map book I'd had with me in the car. "I really don't have to be there for a couple more days, so I think I'm going to change my plans."

"Milan?" he asked.

"Milan," I said. "I need to get a look at those manifests and find out where in Venice that equipment is being sent to. I don't know why it's important, but I feel that it is." I glanced at the map on my lap. "I can get off the Venice train in Verona and catch another train to Milan from there."

Greatrex gave me the look. "Let me get this right," he said. "You're probably being pursued by the German police for murder, you're definitely under investigation by British and French authorities, not to mention Europol for murder and terrorism. There's also every chance the person who is really behind those deaths is after you as well, only not to arrest you but to kill you. All of this, and you decide that you, Nicholas Sharp, the man with the tech brain of a pineapple is going to go to Milan and break into an international shipping company that specializes in high-end technology."

"It doesn't sound so good when you say it out loud," I replied.

"I'll call you later tonight when I arrive in Milan," he said.

"I can't let you—"

The line went dead. I knew I couldn't stop him either.

Chapter 20

A ten-minute walk down the Maximillianstrafe followed by a brief wait at the Innsbruck Hbf Station, and I was on my way. I caught the train to Italy because I was way too exhausted to drive. I also wanted more time to think. Events were speeding up, and my pursuers were closing in. I felt like a lone soldier lost on a battlefield; any wrong step could trigger a mine.

Settling into my first-class seat, I stared out the window. The sky was clearing, and there were scattered patches of blue. The weather seemed to lighten my pensive mood. The journey would take us through the Brenner Pass, reputedly one of the most scenic rail journeys in Europe, particularly in winter. As the journey progressed, I decided the reputation was well earned. Thick layers of white snow covered the countryside as the train cut its way through the hills. Deep valley floors smattered with small villages and undulating farms came and went. The bright white sentinels that were the Austrian Alps towered all around, protecting the peaceful naivety of the chocolate-box view from the outside world. As we continued to climb through this fairyland, my immediate stress began to dissipate. Bring on the inner child.

I even allowed myself the luxury of ordering a glass of pinot grigio to ease my burden. A female attendant who was doing her very best to look and act like Amy Winehouse delivered it in a particularly nonchalant manner.

I had purchased my ticket all the way through to Venice, though I planned to get off at Verona. On the off chance that anyone was following me, I wanted to keep them guessing.

The afternoon rolled on. I taunted myself with the thought of another pinot. When I finally decided to have one, the bar attendant was nowhere to be seen. Maybe Amy was off doing a gig.

I even dozed a little. When I woke up and checked my watch, there were still a good couple of hours to go. Despite the comfort, my legs felt stiff and cramped. One of the great things about European trains is that you can walk their length while they are still moving. This wasn't always easy with the train swaying from side to side, but at least I got some exercise. I got up and walked.

I first noticed him in the door's reflection at the end of the first carriage. The figure was climbing out of his seat at the far end of the carriage and slowly making his way toward me. It shouldn't really have been an issue, except that for some reason the figure looked vaguely familiar. I took the opportunity of opening the door to turn sideways and glance back at him. As I did so, he turned to look out a window. He seemed relaxed, not like a man on a mission. Again, he looked familiar, but I couldn't place it.

I walked as quickly as a moving train would let me to the end of the next carriage and glanced around once more. The man behind me had just entered the carriage I was about to leave. He still looked unhurried and relaxed.

I continued my walk to the end of the next carriage and passed through that door. This time I didn't glance around;

I'd have revealed my suspicion that he wasn't simply looking for a steward.

The following carriage opened to a long corridor on the left and sparsely occupied compartments on the right. Halfway down the carriage the compartments made way for a long, unfurnished section with a wooden deck for freight. Here, the Amy Winehouse attendant sat next to her trolley on a makeshift seat, listening to music on her headphones as she gazed out the window. So much for first-class service.

This was an opportunity. I quickly slipped open the door, moved inside, and closed it behind me, too quickly for my pursuer to see. Amy looked up, surprised a paying passenger had invaded her refuge.

"Oh, hi, can I get you something?" she asked awkwardly. Her English was good but the Italian accent apparent.

I tried to look as though I was deciding what to order. As I did so I stepped back against the wall, concealing myself as much as possible from the corridor. I counted seven seconds until I saw the man who had been behind me walk past. He appeared not to notice either Amy or me but was now moving with more purpose. For the first time I got a good look at him. He had short blond hair, wore a gray suit, and moved as though he was fit. Familiar, but I still couldn't place him.

As I watched the figure disappear into the next carriage, I noticed Amy frowning and edging herself away from me along the seat. Perhaps I'd taken too long to order. "I'll have a long white coffee, thanks," I said. Now was not the time for pinot.

"I'll bring it straight up to you," she said. "I know where you are sitting." Before I could feel too flattered, I realized there weren't many people in first class. She'd probably know where we were all sitting.

"Great, thanks," I responded. I opened the compartment door to leave. I think she was a little happy to be rid of me.

I went back to my seat. There was no point in changing location. If the man was looking for me, he could find me anywhere on the train. Besides, despite my concerns about being pursued, I wanted my coffee. Something in my gut told me I wasn't being paranoid, although after the events of the last few days I had every right to be. This situation, however, did leave me with a problem and the usual number of annoying questions. Who was this person? What did he want? And more to the point, who had sent him? A lot of people seemed to be interested in my activities at the moment. Then there was the biggest question of all: how can I lose him so I can get off the train at Verona undetected?

For the first time in two days I turned on my cellphone. It would be common knowledge that I was heading for Venice. In fact, that was a perception I wanted to encourage. I put a call through to Greatrex. No answer. He was probably in transit, but if he picked up soon enough, he could help. I left him a detailed message.

Now I had to figure out if I was in imminent danger. Screw it—I was almost past caring.

A couple of minutes later, Amy Winehouse showed up with my coffee. She looked a little chastened, like she'd been caught playing truant. I paid, thanked her, took the coffee, and sipped it. It was cold and bland, but I still drank it. I was just beginning to think that I'd imagined the whole "being pursued on a train" thing when I heard those ominous words: "Hello, Mr. Sharp."

I looked up. The tall blond man causing my paranoia was

standing in the aisle looking down on me.

"Do you mind if I join you?" he asked. The heavy Northern European accent and the intensity of his tone added menace to his outwardly innocent words.

I said nothing but waved a casual hand toward the seat on the other side of the table in front of me. For a moment I regretted my choice of seat. Maybe I'd seen too many movies where the thug pointed a gun under the table at the righteous man sitting opposite him. Maybe.

"You know my name," I said. Nicholas Sharp, astute observer.

"Yes, Mr. Sharp. You've obviously realized I'm here to keep an eye on you. In such a restricted environment, I expected that you may catch on. Anyway, I thought, why keep up the pretense? I am Thomas De Vries. I believe you know my brother, Jasper."

That explained the familiarity. The man sitting in front of me had the same Northern European features as his brother—the blond hair, the cold blue eyes, the square jaw. Basically, he was Jasper De Vries of Europol, model 2.0.

"Are you in the same line of work as your brother?" I asked.

"Yes, I'm afraid so," he responded. "We both work for Europol."

I glanced under the table. No gun.

"Well, on the positive side, being from Europol means that you're not here to kill me," I said. Although I did recall the threat from the lips of Capitaine Barre from the Direction Régionale de Police.

"No, I am not here to kill you, Mr. Sharp," Thomas De Vries assured me.

"I'm thinking that you're not here to arrest me either," I said.

"If you were, you would have arrived with a few extra friends and arrested me at the station in Innsbruck before we got on the train."

He just nodded.

"Then what are you really doing here, Mr. Thomas De Vries of Europol?" I tried not to let my relief show.

"As I said, I am here to simply observe you, Mr. Sharp, and to ensure that you don't attempt to leave Europe or …"

"Or?" I mimicked.

"Or get yourself into any more trouble." With that, De Vries 2.0 sat back on his seat, looking annoyingly smug.

"What do you mean by trouble?" I knew exactly what trouble meant, but I was trying to see how much he knew.

"Every time you disappear off the grid, reports of nefarious activities follow in your wake."

He was giving nothing away.

"My brother, Jasper, has asked me to ensure that you arrive safely in Venice for your next show … and whatever else awaits you," he added.

I was beginning to wonder if European law enforcement officers were all trained in the art of the "veiled threat." I seemed to be getting my share of them.

It was time to end the conversation. "Well, thank you for at least putting an end to the charade of tailing me," I said. "You know very well that I'm heading to Venice for our next show, so why don't you pop on back to your seat and we can catch up in the city of gondolas." I thought I sounded suitably detached and unimpressed.

"As you wish." With that, Thomas De Vries, brother of Jasper De Vries, promptly stood up and strode down the aisle to his original seat. No new friends today.

I sat there evaluating the change in circumstance. I was now very glad I'd bought a ticket to Venice. I knew that would have been the first thing the Europol man would have checked out. As I heard myself talking to De Vries, it also occurred to me that I was becoming a convincing liar. Oh well—you learn the skills you need in life.

My problem was that it was going to be very hard to shake this man. He was obviously smart and professional. Europol does not employ fools. It was vital that he not get off the train with me at Verona. I didn't care if he later worked out where I'd alighted; I just couldn't have him follow me. But every tactic I thought of seemed ludicrous. He'd see through them all. Then I had an idea: with no alternatives, why not embrace the ludicrous? Be obvious, use the obvious as a distraction. So, I began to implement ludicrous idea number 33A from the amateur spy playbook.

Having made my palms sweaty by holding them against the train's heating vent, I clutched my stomach and began to groan. Then I wiped the sweat over my forehead and cheeks. I got out of my seat and turned toward De Vries. "I'm off to the bathroom," I announced. Using a little amateur method acting, I contracted my stomach muscles and inhaled heavily in slow breaths, almost convincing myself that I was sick. I could nearly feel the fictitious bile in my throat. "I must have eaten something bad back at the station."

De Vries looked skeptical, as any professional should.

I slouched to the men's room at the end of the carriage. De Vries followed me for a way. After a little fake vomiting and superbly underperformed groaning, just enough to be heard through the door, I reappeared ten minutes later. He was still waiting. I nodded at him as I pushed past and returned to my seat. Act One over.

Act Two. According to the train's schedule we would soon be coming into Rovereto. When I estimated we were five minutes out, I warmed my hands again, wiped the sweat back on my face, and made my way back to the bathroom. I turned to De Vries and shrugged as I went. Again he followed, but not quite so closely. I waited in the bathroom while the train stopped and took off again a few minutes later. When I came out, De Vries loomed outside the bathroom door. This was not a man who trusted easily.

Again, he followed me back to my seat.

The second part of Act Two was to follow the same process ten minutes later. I really poured the sweat on for that one. This time De Vries didn't even get up. All I received was a curt nod as I returned to my seat.

I waited a while longer, wriggling in my seat, clutching my stomach in distress, and perfecting the understated groan. My performance functioned as the perfect distraction as I transferred anything I really needed out of my bag under the seat and into my pockets, using the one hand I kept hidden from my observer's view. The map showed we were fifteen minutes out from Verona.

It was time for the final act. I got up and repeated the previous process. De Vries followed me down the aisle, but at a distance; he didn't seem as focused this time. Fifteen minutes is a long time to stand in the corridor outside the men's bathroom on a train, especially when people were beginning to stand at the exit getting ready to leave. I hoped that if De Vries was there, he'd grow bored and return to his seat. After all, he knew I was ill. I sat on the toilet until the train lurched to one side, which always seemed to happen when a high-speed train braked. I gambled on De Vries being back in his seat and distracted by the sudden jolt. In one movement I opened the bathroom door and slipped into the now crowded corridor by the carriage exit. I closed the bathroom door behind me. There was no cry of alarm.

A long minute later the train pulled up to the platform at Verona Porta Nuova. I was first to climb off, but I waited on the platform until other disembarking passengers had surrounded me. I then strolled purposefully off amid the crowd, making our way down the platform toward the exit.

I wasn't clear yet. It was dark on the street outside the station. A crisp breeze acted like a numbing agent on my unprotected skin. I didn't want to remain exposed here too long, and not just because of the weather. A few seconds later I saw the flashing lights of a small gray Fiat one hundred yards up the street. I walked briskly up the footpath, checked the driver's seat, opened the passenger side door, and climbed in.

"Let's go," I said.

"Already moving," replied Jack Greatrex, his eyes intensely focused on the road as he accelerated away from the curb. The big fella was bulging out of the small car's driving seat. He had obviously heard my phone message. "How did you get away?" he asked as we sped into the evening traffic.

"I think we need to thank Pavlov and his dogs." I told him what I'd done.

"Who would've thought that conditioned stimulus would have worked on a Europol agent?" Greatrex laughed as he said it.

"I know," I responded. "It's ludicrous."

Chapter 21

We cleared Verona and headed off past the waters of Lago Di Garda toward Milan. It was a relatively easy drive on a multi-lane highway. As we drove, I filled Greatrex in on the train trip and answered a few of his questions about the events in Füssen.

"No wonder you look like shit."

He had flown to Verona from Paris and picked up the hire car.

"What would you have done if I hadn't been able to leave the train unnoticed?" I asked.

"Gone to Milan without you." It was good to feel needed.

"I'd like to check out the Ascardi Media Group building first, just to get a feel for it before we try and access the Safe-Tech building," I said.

"Agreed. I've been doing some research on Safe-Tech's security." Greatrex was a very capable tech-head. He always seemed to be able to find information that was hidden in the darkest recesses of the internet. And there wasn't much he didn't know about security systems and how to disable them. Despite my protestations, I was glad he was with me. "From what I can gather they seem to have a state-of-the-art system there. That's surprising considering it's only a small company.

On the other hand, they do deal in technology."

"Security seems to be a vital component of their trade," I said.

"Yeah, I'll need to eyeball it when we get there, but we can expect them to have security cameras, motion detectors, glass-break detectors, along with door and window switches."

"Great," I said. "How the hell are we going to get through all of that?" I looked across to my friend. Although he had his usual look of intense concentration when driving, a smirk appeared on his face. "You have a plan, don't you?" I asked.

"Sure do." I waited for him to say more. There was nothing.

"You're going to make me ask?"

"Yep." Jack Greatrex, having his moment.

"All right, I'm asking."

"Well, seeing as you're asking," he replied, "it's pretty simple. Antonio Ascardi is going to turn the alarm off."

Now, why didn't I think of that?

We drove in silence for a few minutes until I could no longer contain myself. "Okay, I'll buy in. Please explain."

Again, the smirk. "Well, the model of alarm system they have at Safe-Tech can be deactivated two different ways. You can use a straightforward numbers code with thumbprint recognition, or it can be turned on and off with voice recognition."

I still had no idea where he was going with this.

"Well, obviously we don't know the number code, and we can't reproduce anyone's thumbprint."

"I'm sure Tom Cruise did that on *Mission Impossible*," I said.

Greatrex rolled his eyes without taking them off the road ahead. "Well, this isn't Hollywood, but we do have some 'industry skills' we can use."

I waited.

Greatrex continued. "The number and thumbprint system is the conventional way to switch these systems on and off. In fact, that's what the manufacturer recommends."

I nodded to myself.

"In this model of alarm, the voice recognition system has a limited memory. It will usually only respond efficiently to one or two voices. The manufacturer recommends that these voices are those of the security chief and perhaps someone high up the food chain, like the CEO."

As I sat there thinking, the throaty growl of a high-revving engine echoed through our cabin. A red Alfa Romeo sports car shot past us, spraying water on our windscreen. No little gray Fiat could match it. There were times I really missed the old V12 Jaguar XJS I drove back in Cali. It would have made the Alfa look like a traffic light. A distraction is a distraction.

"It seems to me," continued Greatrex, "that if Fontana owns part of Safe-Tech, Ascardi would be somewhere in the background."

"It figures," I responded.

"Then it also figures that the system would recognize Fontana's voice."

I waited some more; Greatrex was quietly enjoying himself.

"I think the other voice would most likely be the CEO's, in this case the undeclared Antonio Ascardi." Greatrex stopped talking and glanced in my direction. The smirk on his face spoke of unrestrained pride.

"I don't know if you realize this," I said, with a little sarcasm in my voice, "but even if you're right, I can't see Antonio Ascardi popping over to let us break into his covert shipping company so we can find out where in Venice he's shipping his secret tech equipment." Take that, big man.

"Ye of little faith," he responded. "Ascardi won't even know he's doing it."

"We're going to kidnap him and knock him out after slipping him some memory-wiping drug?"

"No, Mr. Bond. We're going to kidnap his voice."

I thought Greatrex may have been be losing his grip.

He went on. "Ascardi has made hundreds of speeches and done countless media interviews through the years. They're all recorded. I listened to several while you were away adventuring in Germany."

"But a recorded voice wouldn't fool a high-quality voice recognition system," I said.

"Not normally, no. You know I have Pro Tools HD audio on my laptop in case we ever want to do some recording or writing while we're on the road?"

"Yes," I said.

"Well, on the plane on the way over I may have taken some of Ascardi's interviews and speeches and messed with them a bit. You know my headphone monitoring is studio quality. A little bit of background noise reduction here, a filter there, and maybe some additional equalizing as well, and there you have it. Antonio Ascardi, in the flesh ... the voice. Whatever."

I stared vacantly at the road ahead, consistently amazed at the big fella's resourcefulness. Then I saw a problem. "Won't there be something specific Ascardi has to say into the system?"

"That's the hard bit; we need to make a calculated guess about that."

"A calculated guess," I repeated vacantly. Then I glanced over at Greatrex. His classic "I know something you don't know" twitch of the mouth reappeared. "You reckon you've figured it out, don't you?"

The smirk. "Yep."

If I turn on your laptop and play Ascardi's voice, he's going to say just one word, isn't he?"

"Yep."

For a minute we just listened to the sound of the car belting down the highway. Then at the same time we both said "Vittoria," the name of Antonio Ascardi's dead sister.

We were twenty minutes out of Milan when I said to Greatrex, "What if we're wrong?"

"Then we'll both be arrested for breaking and entering," he replied.

"Hell, they can just add it to my list of charges." I vainly attempted to smile as I said it. The trouble with sitting in the passenger seat is you had time on your hands to think. I didn't want to think, plus I'd never been a good passenger; I like to be in control. I closed my eyes, my mind drifting to Elena lying on the bloodied snow in Füssen, the red of her blood merging with the torn red velvet that littered the Palais Garnier, cushioning rows of corpses amid the rising smoke. Fade to black.

I was in control of nothing.

Chapter 22

An hour later we were driving through outer metropolitan Milan.

"Head north," I said. "The Ascardi Media Group office is at Porta Nuova." Map book on my lap, I guided Greatrex through the streets of Milan.

Soon we were sitting in a carpark in front of a majestically curved modern glass building. The twenty-story structure towered above the neighboring buildings like a custodian of modern architecture. There was artistry and grace in its elegant minimization of straight lines, just as there was a clear message of opulence in its grandeur. The hour was late, and no one was at work now, save for security staff.

"It's quite a building," I said. "Very chic."

"Would you expect anything different?" I asked.

"Not from the doyen of social media. My research tells me that the Ascardi Group own the entire building," said Greatrex. "The man has style, influence, and money."

"Makes you think twice about taking him on," I said.

We sat there for a few minutes soaking in the atmosphere. This was an area where corporations used their buildings' anatomy to stake a claim on prestige and importance. Ascardi was clearly a titan at the game. We were in no hurry to commence our new career in breaking and entering. Besides, it didn't hurt to wait a while, until the city had truly bunkered down for the night.

"Well, we may as well get on with it," announced Greatrex.

I looked up the Safe-Tech shipping company in the Zona Farini industrial area, and we pulled back out into the street.

Fifteen minutes later we were sitting in front of another building. This time there was no overpowering sense of style. The building wasn't run-down; it wasn't really anything except nondescript. Solid walls of bland concrete acted as fascias and dividers for a series of small factories and warehouses. A row of meshed fencing ran along the front of each unit. It was about as inviting as Colditz. A little to our right, a locked wire gate led to a very solid-looking locked metal door. Above the door was an unimposing painted sign. In simple black lettering it read "Safe-Tech". To the left of the door was a loading ramp with a large, very secure-looking roller door. The only thing remarkable about the Safe-Tech building was that it was totally unremarkable.

The area could best be described as classic working-class industrial. Like most European industrial areas, it centered on the railway station just down the road. As we sat there with the windows down, we couldn't hear a sound. A good omen?

"Significantly down-market compared to head office," said Greatrex.

"Probably by design, I'm thinking."

"I don't think they're relying on street appeal here," observed Greatrex.

"You'd actually think they were trying to avoid it," I replied.

Greatrex began his visual analysis. "I see two cameras out

the front, one focused on the door, the other on the loading ramp. There's a keypad by the front door. We'd have to unlock the gate to get to it."

"Or go over the fence," I added.

"Over the fence would be better than breaking a lock," said Greatrex. "We may have a chance of them not knowing anyone was even here." Then he announced, "I'm gonna find the laneway around to the back. The security will probably be similar, but it's good to know."

I waited in the car, to keep watch. Ten minutes later Greatrex was back.

"Exactly the same, two cameras out back. You can bet the motion detectors will cover the inside area. I don't think they'd have them before the front door, or you couldn't access the keypad."

"Makes sense," I responded.

We sat there for another thirty minutes, just to ensure we were alone. When we'd run out of excuses to wait any longer, I said, "We can sit here all night, but our only concrete lead is an address on a piece of paper or computer sitting in that building. Let's do it."

We climbed out of the car; no one saw us, no one called out to us, no dog barked. We sidled up to the mesh gate. The big fella pressed his body against the gate to eliminate any sound and movement while I clambered over. Thanks to the Marines, this wasn't the first time we'd had to make a covert entry. Greatrex passed me a bag with his laptop and two flashlights, then followed me, levering himself over the fence with a fitness and grace that belied his size.

Keeping our heads down, away from the camera over the front door, we stole through the shadows the few feet to the entrance. As we reached the door, a security light came on, illuminating us like animals in a spotlight. We both jumped like amateur thieves. We should have known better.

"Should have expected that," said Greatrex. We waited in case an alarm followed the light. There was no sound.

I kept watch while Jack opened his laptop and opened Pro Tools. We'd have only one shot at this. If we got it wrong, we would have a lot of explaining to do. Before triggering the program on his computer, Greatrex pulled a cylindrical speaker out of his bag.

"State of the art," he said. "The laptop's speakers wouldn't fool any system." He then played the recording into the microphone next to the keypad: "Vittoria." It was as though Antonio Ascardi stood next to us. Then silence. We waited for an agonizing three seconds, and the machine purred back at us in a sultry female voice, "Voice recognized. Welcome, Signor Ascardi." We heard the faint whirring of a mechanical sound, a shudder, and then the slight metallic screech of creaking bolts as the front door unlatched.

As we moved forward, the flashlights revealed a very basic reception area. The floor was checkerboard vinyl, while a cheap and worn laminate counter split the room in half. Two aging metal desks sat behind the counter against the wall, both of them supporting untidy piles of documents. An older telephone system sat on a receptionist's bench immediately behind the counter. If there was money in the business, they weren't showing it off here. Greatrex's light stopped on another keypad just inside the door.

"Damn," he said. "That's a surprise." The keypad suddenly displayed a row of red flashing LED lights, as though warning us the world was going about to end. The speaker next to the keypad announced, "Per favore inserisca un codice." Neither of us spoke Italian, but we'd both read the *Da Vinci Code*. "Codice" meant "code," and we didn't have one.

We stood frozen as the last of the LED lights died. Again we expected the screeching of an alarm and flashing lights. Again, nothing. Then it occurred to me: a sonic alarm would be almost useless in a deserted industrial area like this.

"The system will alert the security company," I said. "How long do you think we have?"

"Five minutes tops," he replied. "They'll call whoever's number they have on file to check it's not a false alert and then send a team straight here."

"We better move fast." Nicholas Sharp, once again stating the obvious.

We moved through another door at the back of the reception area, which led to a small office. It looked dusty and antiquated, but two computers sat on metal desks and three filing cabinets on the concrete floor.

"You take the computers, I'll take the cabinets," I said. "Look for anything that says Ascardi or Venice."

We searched as though our lives depended on it. Mine did. I kept one eye on my watch. With two minutes to go, I asked, "Anything?"

"No."

We kept looking.

One minute to go, and I still had nothing from the filing cabinets. I moved to the piles of documents in the front office. Then Greatrex yelled "Crap!"

It wasn't what I wanted to hear.

"What's wrong?" I asked, dreading the answer.

"Another firewall; these machines have more security than ... somewhere with a lot of security."

I wanted to chuckle, but I was too busy searching for something that wasn't there.

"Come on," I yelled through the doorway. "We've gotta go, time's up. We'll find another way."

Greatrex didn't move.

"Move it," I said.

Nothing.

Then "Holy shit." Then a pause. "Holy shit" again. Then, "All right, let's go."

Greatrex was at the front door before me. I scooped up the bag and followed him out and into the cold night air, slamming the door closed behind us. The fence suddenly seemed like the Berlin Wall. Noise didn't matter now, only speed. Greatrex put a hand on one of the posts and heaved himself up, landing with a loud thud on the other side. I threw the bag and flashlights over to him and then clawed my way quickly over the wire. It's amazing what adrenaline can do.

As we climbed into the car, the sound of distant sirens pierced the air as the police grew closer. The Fiat's engine throbbed to life as Greatrex turned the ignition key. He floored the accelerator as we pulled sharply away in the opposite direction of the sirens.

Ten minutes and a couple of miles later, we both started to breathe a little more easily.

"That was too close," I said, "and for nothing."

"Define nothing," said Greatrex.

I turned and looked at him. "You found something, didn't you?"

"Maybe."

"Give it up."

"Well," said my smug friend, "as mentioned, omega-level security and firewalls protected that system. Way too much for a company that small, even if they do ship hi-tech equipment. Also, while the computer screens looked outdated, the computers themselves were the latest model, high-end Macs. I made my way through every barrier and was doing okay until I got to the last hurdle."

I was feeling very thankful for Jack Greatrex's skills. "Go on," I said.

"I tried 'Vittoria' as the password, but it wouldn't let me through. I tried adding her birthdate—nothing. Then I remembered the year Vittoria Ascardi died. I added that and got through."

"Inspired," I replied.

"I had minimal time, but I did find two things. One of them I was looking for, the other I just stumbled across. I think they both might be important."

I didn't want to kill the big fella's moment, but I wanted him to get to the point.

"The first thing was a shipping manifest with an address in Venice that wasn't Ascardi's house near the Grand Canal."

"Do you remember it?"

"Sure, it was a street address on the Lido."

"And the second thing?"

"This is where it gets a bit weird." Greatrex took a few seconds to think. "What was the name of the environmental group that claimed responsibility for the attack at the Cinaed power station?"

"I don't know anything about them, but they called themselves the Natural Earth Army."

"I thought that was it." This time Greatrex paused for a little longer. His expression was a picture of frozen concentration. Then he asked, "Why would Safe-Tech, a company associated with Antonio Ascardi, have manifests and paperwork connected to the so-called Natural Earth Army, a self-proclaimed eco-terrorist organization, hidden deep within its computer records?"

We both sat silently as Greatrex pushed the Fiat's engine to its limits. The streetscape of Milan whirled past in a blur.

Chapter 23

Once we'd cleared the outskirts of Milan, Greatrex drove into an Autogrill and pulled over.

"You drive," he said. "I want to get online and do some research."

I didn't argue. I was tired, but the three-hour drive to Venice was doable. Besides, I knew that when Greatrex said he wanted to do some research, that meant he was going to leave no dark corner of the internet unexplored. I wanted to see what he could find.

The drive also gave me a chance to think. We should have been relieved that we now had some firm evidence tying Antonio Ascardi into at least one of the events we were investigating, yet I was also disappointed. I had quietly hoped we were wrong about the man.

On the other hand, because we had to leave the shipping company's office so quickly, we had nothing to present to the authorities as proof.

"Couple of things are bothering me," I said.

"Shoot," said Greatrex, looking up from his laptop.

"What's Ascardi up to? I mean, if he has some sort of relationship with the Natural Earth Army and association with the power station break-in, then there's a strong chance he had something to do with Paris and perhaps even the assassination in London. What I'm still not getting is what he gains from any of this."

"Maybe you're assuming too much there. Maybe he's not looking to gain anything at all. Maybe he's agitating for something?"

"You mean a crusade of some sort?"

"Possibly," said the big fella.

I thought back to the conversation I'd had with Ascardi in his car in Paris. He was clearly wrestling with some major level of disillusionment. Maybe Greatrex's idea seemed plausible, or maybe the entrepreneur had something to gain that we just weren't seeing.

"Okay, question number two: Why me? Why is evidence mounting against me all over the place? If I'm being framed by Ascardi, what's his reason? I'm not seeing it," I said.

"I don't get that one either," said Greatrex. "You'd think that by framing you, an artist on his tour, he'd just be causing himself needless grief if you were killed or jailed."

"You'd think," I said.

A few more minutes and a few more miles went past.

"What if it's a case of keeping your enemies closer?" I suggested.

"That makes sense, except for one thing."

"Yeah, I know. Why am I Antonio Ascardi's enemy? What did I ever do to him?"

"And that, dear Watson, is something we have to find out," Greatrex said as he resumed studying his screen.

My phone rang through the car speakers.

"Nicholas." It was the General. "Is Jack with you?

"Yes, General, we can both hear you," I answered.

"Good, tell me, how did you go with your visit to Safe-Tech?"

I filled him in.

"You two do love to live close to the line, don't you?"

"We don't love it, General, but we always seem to end up there," I replied.

"Probably semantics. Now listen carefully. We've managed to do a little more digging around in Ascardi's early years."

We were listening.

"Apparently, he was a gifted young programmer while at university, quite outstanding. Several corporate heads were chasing him, but he declined all offers. The young Ascardi was clear in what he wanted to achieve, and no one was willing to bankroll his vision."

"There must be a lot of corporate headhunters who are kicking themselves now," said Greatrex.

"Yes, Jack, probably so, but also probably irrelevant," replied the General. Greatrex grimaced.

"What are you getting at, Sir?" I asked.

"Halfway through his second year, Ascardi just dropped out of his studies. He disappeared for several months. When he returned, he was cashed up and his future was assured."

"Do we know where the money came from and what strings were attached to it?" asked Greatrex.

"Good question, Jack, but no, not at all. No one has the slightest idea," said the General. "What does that tell you?"

"I don't have much experience in corporate finance," I said. "But it seems to me that if no one knows where the money came from, it didn't come from somewhere good."

"Precisely," replied our former leader. "Now, moving on.

It's interesting that you found a connection between Ascardi and the group claiming responsibility for the Cinaed break-in. It changes the ball game, doesn't it?"

"It sure does," said Greatrex. "I'm just doing some more research on the Natural Earth Army as we speak."

"Good," said the General. "Perhaps you can find some information on the Union of Islamic Fighters."

"The who?" asked Greatrex.

"The Union of Islamic Fighters," repeated the General.

I really didn't want to ask, but I couldn't help myself. "Why so, General?"

"Because they have just claimed responsibility for the assassination of Sir Phillip Morton, British Chancellor of the Exchequer."

This just wasn't getting any easier.

Greatrex and I drove on into the night. After finishing the call with General Devlin-Waters, Jack went back to his computer and I went back to my thoughts.

An hour out from Mestre, mainland Venice, Greatrex again looked up from his research. "I've tried every trick I know and invented a couple of new ones. I can't find any links between the Natural Earth Army in Britain, the Ghosts of the Revolution in France, and the Union of Islamic Fighters."

I thought for a moment. "Were you able to find out anything about any of the groups—who they are, where they came from, their manifesto?"

"Hardly anything. Normally, these sorts of groups have a strong presence in the murkier waters of the net and social media. They can be hard to locate, but if you know where to look, you'll find them."

"But not with this lot?"

"They just seemed to appear out of nowhere. There's a frenzy of online activity, and then they disappear again," answered Greatrex.

"But they definitely exist?"

"Yeah, they do. There's enough there to consider them genuine, but not enough to trace their history, membership, or anything more," he said.

"There you have it."

"There I have what?" Greatrex's tone had become terse. We were both tired.

"What these groups have in common is their lack of detailed historical presence on the internet. There's enough to identify them but not enough to find out much about them or where they've been hiding."

We slipped back into silence. I pressed down harder on the gas pedal and drove into the night.

"You may be onto something here," said Greatrex. "I'm going to try looking for links between the groups and common IP addresses. See if anything comes up."

Maybe it was time for a little Nicholas Sharp, historian of popular culture. "Think back all those years to the first Die Hard movie," I said. "Who was the bad guy?"

Greatrex thought for a moment. "Gruber, Hans Gruber. A classic villain."

I knew he'd know.

"When Gruber made his speech to the authorities about releasing political prisoners and comrades in arms around the world, some of whom didn't even exist, what was he trying to do?"

"He was distracting the authorities to cover up a robbery,"

said Greatrex.

"Exactly."

"You think Ascardi is a thief?"

"He may be or may not be; I don't care. But is he behind some sort of mammoth distraction or ulterior plan that we have no concept of?"

"Your worrying me," said Greatrex.

"I've been worried for a while. Now I'm moving into being really pissed. It's like this guy has written some sort of heinous score and we're all playing it for him, note for freakin' note."

We were entering the outskirts of Mestre when I announced, "I'm not going to Venice."

"You're what?" asked Greatrex.

"I'm not going to Venice, not yet."

My friend looked at me quizzically, his furrowed brow speaking volumes.

"I think you should arrive in Venice now, tonight. Check into our hotel and let everyone know you're there."

"And you?" he asked.

"Anyone asks, tell them you've spoken to me, but I'm not due in town for another day or so. Plenty of time for the show," I said.

"And where will you be?"

"Venice," I said, "but not officially. I'm going to find a little out-of-the-way bolt-hole and do some snooping around."

"Off the grid?"

"Yes, off the grid."

"Alone?"

"Yes, alone, but I know you'll be around."

"Nicholas Sharp, if I didn't know better, I'd think you had a plan and that you were keeping it from me," said Greatrex.

"It's not so much a plan," I said. "More a calculated improvisation."

"And what better way to sabotage a carefully written score than by improvising wildly over the top of it," observed Jack Greatrex.

"I think you've got the idea," I said.

Greatrex closed his computer and turned to look at me. "I'm not going to lecture you ..."

"But ..." I interrupted.

"But if Antonio Ascardi is up to half of the dreadful things you may be imagining ..."

"Yes."

"You may well be walking into a world of pain," warned my friend.

"Point taken and appreciated. But if I don't get my arms around this, all I have, at best, is a lifetime of you visiting me on Sunday afternoons in some forlorn European prison."

"I don't like to go out on Sundays," said Greatrex.

Chapter 24

Walking out of the modern Venezia Santa Lucia railway station and gazing down the concrete steps to the Grand Canal was like staring at a vibrant painting on a wall, and then stepping right into it. New gave way to old as I strolled onto the ferry wharf, the wake from passing boats splashing gently on the pilings underneath. On the far side of the waterway spotlights reflected off the distinctive and colorful Venetian architecture that lined the canal, just as it had for centuries. Even late at night the waterway was active. Cashed-up couples climbed in and out of gondolas or bought tickets for a vaporetto. Eager local vendors sought to make a sale to tourists before they'd even set foot in the old city. If any European city over-delivered on its reputation, it was Venice.

My immediate aim was to find somewhere to stay, somewhere close to the Grand Canal for ease of transport yet hidden down an alley or two. I also wanted to be walking distance from the Teatro La Fenice, where we'd perform. In any military operation access and intelligence were everything. The whole purpose of my clandestine arrival in Venice was to gain intelligence; to do that I would need good access to a variety of locations.

CHAPTER 24

It didn't take long to arrange some suitable accommodation through a tourist information kiosk on the wharf. I'd gone dark again, wary of advertising my presence in the city by using my cell phone.

Thirty minutes later, I stepped off a vaporetto at the Mercato stop, just near the Rialto Bridge. A few minutes and a couple of alleyways later I was outside the Vecchio Hotel Canal, a small hotel in a perfect location. It had frontage onto the Grand Canal but an entranceway off Calle dello Sturion. It also had twenty-four-hour reception, a requirement at this time of night.

I traipsed up an interminable flight of stairs and registered at the front desk. The downside to my plan was that I had to show my passport to register; there was no way around it. I was directed to my room at the end of a long, narrow corridor. As I walked its length my footsteps seemed abnormally loud, the mosaic floor and high ceiling providing a perfect echo chamber. At least I would know if I was about to receive any uninvited visitors. The room itself was all very classic and very Venice. A vivid, deep red-patterned wallpaper lined every wall and the wooden bed; two chairs and a desk were stylishly ornate.

I had a quick shower and put my head down. I was asleep within minutes.

I awoke at 7 a.m. I'd slept well, but Elena had taunted my dreams, as had a vivid image of Ascardi, standing over a smoking ruin. It should have been enough to unnerve me, but it just made me more determined.

After a few relaxing moments enjoying a light breakfast accompanied by piped classical music in the hotel dining room overlooking the Grand Canal, I felt as ready as I was going to for whatever the hell I was about to do.

I figured my first job was to locate the address in the Lido that Greatrex had found on the computer at Safe-Tech. Again I chose the vaporetto as the most discreet form of transport. Who remembers anyone they saw on a bus? For insurance, I wore the classic American disguise of a baseball cap pulled low over my eyes—clichéd but effective.

The vaporetto cruised along the Grand Canal and past the array of palatial homes and hotels that fronted onto it. The slow, throbbing engine gently propelled the craft eastward. Every type of water transport invented moved along the canal, from the long, thin barges used for transporting local freight to some slender timber Venetian speedboats guided by the hands of the city's elite. Sleek, low-profile water taxis were in abundance, carrying touristi to their destinations. As this colorful maze of humanity went about their business under the gentle glare of the warming morning sun, it occurred to me that in other circumstances I would have savored the frantic maritime atmosphere.

As we cruised past the Aman Canal Grande, where the rest of the tour personnel were staying, I decided to make a closer study of the Venetian architecture on the opposite side of the canal. No need to advertise my presence. A few minutes later, the vaporetto was out of the canal, past the Piazza San Marco and crossing the more exposed waters of the Laguna di Venezia to Lido.

Scores of vessels darted like water insects in all directions at all speeds. It seemed incredible they didn't collide. The scene was tempered by a vibrant blue winter sky aided by the morning sun casting a haze over the entire swarm. Even in my current state of mind, I couldn't ignore the spectacle.

As we approached the Lido ferry wharf, I noticed a number of small islands scattered across the water to the south. Some seemed heavily inhabited, with ancient fortified buildings and walls rising from the earth, others less so. Lido itself was a long, relatively flat barrier island protecting Venice from the incessant swells of the Adriatic Sea. The buildings coming into view seemed mostly as old as those in the main city but were more spread out. I was guessing this seven-mile sandbank gave its inhabitants more room to move than Venice itself.

The closest stop to the address Greatrex had given me was a fifteen-minute bus trip south to the Malamocco area. Another ten-minute walk through a run-down marine industrial area and I found what I was looking for, at least what there was of it.

The large tin shed in front of me made the Safe-Tech building in Milan look like design genius. Set in an environment of shipwrights and maritime workshops, I could barely believe this shack bore any relation to the prestigious Ascardi Group. Maybe it wasn't meant to. I couldn't see anyone in the vicinity of the building, so I risked a closer look.

The metal door was padlocked, so I didn't expect a reaction when I knocked. I'd prepared a vague excuse about looking for a boat-builder friend if someone had answered. No one did. Making sure I wasn't being watched, I pulled out my wallet. Secreted in a back compartment was a small cylindrical metal tool, around three inches long. I took it out and began to pick the padlock. As a sniper, I'd frequently accessed high vantage points in locked buildings. US marine training at its best.

Two minutes later and I was in. The interior of the shed

was in semi-darkness, and it took a moment for my eyes to adjust. Minimal light shone through a couple of small windows perched high on the walls; a little more glow seeped in from the cracks under the two doors. I looked around the dark space, but there wasn't much to see. Most of the dusty concrete floor was bare, but new-looking wooden boxes sat piled at the far end of the space.

I walked carefully toward them, trying to avoid any hazards in the dim light. When I got to the boxes, I tried to make out the writing on them. Most of it had been blacked out—odd. I shifted one of the boxes around, turning it in the direction of a faint beam of light from one of the high windows. I could just make out a few words. Whoever had been blacking out the shipping details must have been running out of paint at this point. I could just read a logo I recognized as that of a well-known IT company. I could also just discern the faint outline of another company name: the Ascardi Media Group.

It was then that I heard a scraping sound behind me, like a foot dragging on the concrete floor.

I started to turn around but I didn't get to finish.

There was only blackness.

When I came to, my head was pounding. I knew someone had hit me hard. My hands were tied behind my back, and I was on my side staring at a white wheel arch. I craned my neck to get a clearer view. I was in some sort of old van. From the rough ride, I gathered it was being driven along a road full of potholes to which the driver paid little mind.

I cursed myself for letting someone surprise me in a situation where all my senses should have been heightened. I was no longer an elite sniper, but I still had some professional pride. The bigger issue was that my clumsy break-and-enter could now expose my hand to Antonio Ascardi and his people.

Eventually, the van stopped. I pretended I was still unconscious, attempting to buy a little more thinking time. The rear doors creaked loudly as they opened. No one spoke. Probably there was only one man. I had come across too many professionals in the last few days not to expect the same here. It was a little late now, but I needed to be judicious.

Suddenly, two hands gripped my feet. They felt like metal clamps. I was dragged backward along the van's metal floor; there was no gentleness in the movement. I heard someone draw a deep breath, and then two arms enveloped my waist. In almost the same moment I was hoisted up into the air and twisted around. I felt myself being roughly slung over some sort of pivot point; feeling the hardness of bone pressed to by stomach, I assumed it was someone's shoulder. A stolen glimpse offered me nothing more than a face-to-face encounter with what I presumed to be the back of a man's coarse woolen coat. A short walk along a pathway, through a barn door, and I was thrown mercilessly onto a dirt floor, now with a greater understanding of what a sack of potatoes felt like.

Thirty seconds later I felt the full force of a blast of cold water on my face. I couldn't feign unconsciousness any longer. As I opened my eyes I coughed, spluttered, and gasped for air. I wasn't faking that.

The man in front of me was huge, a giant. He wasn't too much short of seven-foot tall and had a width of near half that. No wonder he'd picked me up so easily. He had long, straggly dark hair and a matching unkempt beard. My captor was probably in his late forties, but his weathered skin made an accurate guess hard. I looked hard into his eyes. They didn't appear to have the detached coldness of a professional killer's. An old and stained brown wool jacket failed to conceal his massive forearms, while his boots and pants were discolored and caked in dirt, suggesting of years of use. Judging from the giant's calloused hands, I would have guessed he worked on the land. More like a farmer than a henchman. I felt sure his name was either Ned or Hagrid. I didn't believe for a second that he was part of Antonio Ascardi's inner circle.

"Giusto, dimmelo ora. Cosa stavi facendo in quell'edificio?"

I knew then he wasn't called Ned or Hagrid.

"Parla Inglese?" I muttered.

The giant shrugged his shoulders, "A little. Tell me ... now. What were you doing in that building?"

It was time to lie. What happened in the next few minutes was going to have a big impact on how things played out here. I knew I couldn't beat this man in a fight, certainly not with my hands tied behind my back. I had to try and talk my way out, as slim a chance as I had.

"Norbert Fontana asked me to come down and check on the latest shipment, make sure it arrived," I said. I looked him straight in the eyes.

"You know Mr. Fontana?"

"I do. Very well, in fact."

"Why would he ask you to check on a shipment when he knows I'm here?"

"A fair question. We had word there was a break-in at Safe-Tech Shipping. Norbert wanted someone he trusted to come down and check," I responded.

"He doesn't trust me?"

I thought I may be gaining ground here.

"You know Norbert. He doesn't fully trust anybody."

The giant froze in thought. "Why didn't he tell me you were coming, and why didn't you have a key?"

I had no clue how to answer that, so I just started talking. I knew it was vital not to hesitate.

"Norbert tried to call you," I said. "He told me you were going to meet me there, with the key, but you didn't show up. Well—correction—you did show up, but way too late."

There it was, a glimpse of confusion on the giant's face. I pressed my point home.

"You know Norbert is going to be furious when he hears you knocked me out. I reckon you'll get no more work from him."

The giant rubbed his chin. "I didn't get a call, but I did leave my phone in the van earlier," he said.

"Well that might explain it," I suggested.

"I'll just go out to the van and get my phone now, to check," he said.

I couldn't have that.

"Yeah, do that," I said. "But first can you untie my hands so I can call Norbert and tell him all is well? He'll be waiting to hear from me."

"Are you going to tell him I knocked you out?"

I thought I had him.

"I'll cut you a break. I won't mention it if I can call him now," I said.

A further moment of hesitation. "I think it may be foolish to trust you. I don't know you."

"It would be foolish to cross Norbert Fontana."

The giant looked at me, his face screwed up, decision impending. There was no more I could do.

"Ho concordato—agreed."

The big man reached down and helped me up. I turned around so he could untie me. As he loosened the knots and removed the rope, I turned back to him, simultaneously kicking the front of his right knee and slamming my fist into the side of his head. If he came up again, I was done for. He didn't; he went down and was out cold.

I quickly tied my former captor up with the rope he had used on me. I found some more twine and bound his legs. I really felt sorry for the big guy. I was certain he wasn't evil to the core, more likely just a working man picking up some extra cash. I still needed him out of action, for at least a couple of days so he couldn't contact Fontana or Ascardi. That said, I'd have laid a bet that he didn't even know who Antonio Ascardi was.

I looked around the barn; there was a bucket in the corner. I found a tap, filled the bucket, and placed it within the giant's reach. I found some more rope hanging on a hook on the wall and tied him to one of the main posts supporting the structure, giving him enough room to move but not escape.

He'd survive, but he wasn't going anywhere. Nicholas Sharp, compassionate fugitive.

I walked out of the barn door into the afternoon sun. The building was on the edge of a once graveled yard, which now showed a lot more dirt than gravel. The yard opened up to a small, empty, poorly fenced paddock, whatever grass it once held overgrazed long ago. On the other side of the yard was a small cottage; like the rest of the property, it looked greatly in need of maintenance, its once painted facade now a mess of peeling paint. Several roof tiles were skewered at odd angles—makeshift repairs over many years. In front of the cottage a large black dog on a chain barked furiously.

I figured that if the giant had any associates in the cottage the barking canine would have alerted them by now. Just to make certain, I skirted the reach of the dog's chain and peered in though the cottage's dilapidated side window. There was no one in sight.

The old white van I'd arrived in sat in the middle of the yard. Again skirting the angry animal, I ran over to the van. The keys were still in the ignition. Before I climbed in, I looked once more around the old farmyard. The damn dog. I walked back toward it, trying to talk in a calming voice. I may as well have been singing Black Sabbath songs for all the effect it had. I ventured close enough just to check that he had enough water for a couple of days and then retreated. Despite my best intentions, he kept barking at me like I was Satan.

As I climbed in the van and drove off down the potholed road, it was hard to believe that this ramshackle farmlet was less than two miles from the refinement of Venice.

I grabbed for my cell phone in my pocket, feeling only my hand on my thigh. It must have either fallen out of my pocket when the giant slugged me back at the boat shed or the giant took it. Not searching him earlier had been a mistake, but I wasn't risking going back to do it now. That meant I'd have to make another visit to the boat shed. The problem was I still didn't know where I was.

Although cars were allowed on Lido, I figured there wouldn't be too many, especially in a remote area. The giant's car was probably known to locals. A strange man driving around in it may raise suspicions, so the driving had to be kept to a minimum.

The giant's phone! He'd said he left it in the van. I reached into the glove compartment, and there it was, laying in a mess of registration papers and half-eaten food. I reached for it as I drove. Fortunately, there was no passcode required. The giant was definitely not a professional. I brought up Google Maps, found my location, and headed back to the shed.

Twenty minutes later, after breaking into the shed again and locating my phone in a pile of dust by the packing crates, I was out and heading back to the ferry terminal. I briefly considered staying and staking out the shed, but I could have been there for days. I didn't have days. All I could do was go back to Venice proper, pack my bags, and officially arrive at the tour hotel.

Showtime.

Chapter 25

"That's it. I'm just not letting you out on your own anymore," said Jack Greatrex, his eyes narrowing.

We were sitting at a table in one of the private gardens owned by the Aman Grande Canal Hotel. A private garden in Venice is a rare luxury. This place had two. I had just told Greatrex of the afternoon's events.

"I'm beginning to think you're right," I responded. "My record for staying out of trouble isn't great."

I took a sip of the scotch in front of me and gazed out over the boats going about their business on the canal. The background soundscape of marine engines racing and waves splashing against the buildings permeated our conversation.

After leaving the giant's van near the ferry terminal at Lido, I had caught the vaporetto back to my hotel and packed half my bag, leaving some basic necessities in my room, paying in cash for three more nights, and heading to the Aman. It wouldn't hurt to keep my bolt-hole.

"Do you think the big guy you took out will remain undiscovered until all this is sorted?" asked Greatrex. "There'll be problems if he contacts Fontana or Ascardi."

"All we can do is hope," I said. "I tied him up pretty well. Besides, we may be coming to the point where running around behind Ascardi's back serves no purpose."

"You think he's on to us?"

"I've been thinking about that. I suspect that to some extent we came into this whole situation with him on to us. I appear to have been set up from the beginning, although I still don't know why. The only difference is that now we know I was set up." I could feel the blood rushing to my head as I spoke. It was my own little 'Hulk' thing. I don't turn green, but it usually doesn't end well.

"Then you think Ascardi knows that you know?"

"How could he not know?" I asked. "He must be aware of the break-in at Safe-Tech in Milan, and he's probably aware that I went to Füssen to meet Elena. He may well even be implicated in her death, and let's face it, Antonio Ascardi is more genius than fool."

"Then why the pretense of everything being normal between the two of you?"

"Look, I'm not sure, but it has probably suited him up to this point. For some reason, he has needed the tour to continue, although again, I have no idea why," I answered.

Greatrex looked lost in thought.

"Maybe Ascardi needed you to be in certain places at certain times," he proffered. "Maintaining the tour schedule may have been the only way he could guarantee that."

What Greatrex had suggested made a modicum of sense.

"You're right," I said, leaning forward on my chair toward the big fella, urgency creeping into my tone. No other answer made sense. "Damn, I should have seen that earlier. You have to be right."

I sat there looking out on the water, sipping my drink. My mind was jumping around like a cat on a hot tin roof, looking for a place to land, a place where everything fell into place.

A few minutes of silence stole past before I finally managed to corral my thoughts into a cohesive idea. "Assuming you're right, that means that we're here in Venice because Ascardi wants us to be here, and the real reason may have nothing to do with music."

Greatrex nodded.

I continued, "That means this is not over. Ascardi isn't done with us yet. No wonder he wanted the tour to continue." As the words spilled out of my mouth, I felt an arctic chill invade my core. The uncertain tremor in my voice reflected my growing concern as I pressed home my point. "Jack, based on past recent experience, it is likely that more people will lose their lives before this is done. That may well happen here in Venice. Not only will I probably be painted as the scapegoat for their deaths, but it will be our fault because we can't work this whole damn mess out."

We finished our drinks and stood up to walk into the hotel building. "One more thing," I said just before we reached the entrance. "I'm sure that boat shed near Malamocco is just a waypoint for Ascardi's tech equipment. We still have no idea of the final destination."

Greatrex opened the door into the hotel foyer and ushered me through. He stopped just inside the building and turned to me. "I agree. But I also think we can be fairly certain that Ascardi's house is not the destination. No point sending the gear to Malamocco first; it's out of the way."

"I suspect you're right," I said. "There remain two probable endpoints: offshore or a location close to Malamocco."

We began to cross the foyer as we continued talking in

hushed tones. "We need to find that location," said Greatrex. "If we can get a look at what's going on there, I think we'll find out what this is all about."

"Well, so far, the deeper we dig, the further away we seem to get," I said. "Maybe we should change tack. Maybe it's time to get a bit more aggressive. Instead of following the equipment's trail, maybe we should start following some of the players."

"Risky," said Greatrex.

"I think we're way beyond worrying about that now. We either go for it, or more people die and I—or we—go to prison."

"We have no choice," said the big fella.

"No, and what troubles me the most is Antonio Ascardi knows that."

"Nicholas, it's so good to see you." Aislinn Byrne's voice sounded as soothing as a fine Bordeaux as we sauntered up to our table.

I leaned down and kissed her cheek.

"Mate, you do look one step the other side of dreadful," said Patrick Jay Olden as he got up to shake my hand.

Jack and I had just been shown into in the hotel's restaurant. As great as it was to see the two of them, I was distracted by the sheer lavishness of the room we had just entered. Rococo artworks lined the walls; ornate gold leaf framed them. The ceilings were well over double height with matching grand windows overlooking the waterway.

Aislinn seemed to read my thoughts. "This is some place, isn't it?"

"It seems more like a palace than a hotel," I said.

"Apparently, it once was," added Patrick.

"And all on Antonio Ascardi's tab," added Greatrex with a wry smirk.

It did seem strange that we were chasing down the man who was footing the bill for our splendid, if temporary, lifestyle.

"So, what's the story, Nicholas?" continued Patrick Jay. "You look like a Christian who's just taken on the lions and not fared so well."

Interesting analogy.

"Well, I guess the bombing in Paris has hit us all pretty hard," I said, trying to make up ground. "I've also had a couple of issues to deal with." Not very convincing, but it would have to do.

"As devastated as we all feel," said Aislinn, "we're here to do a show, make some beautiful music, and lift the spirits of those who come to see us."

Aislinn was already lifting my spirit. The music. I had almost forgotten about the music.

"We're playing the day after tomorrow," I said, even though they all knew. "Has anyone been to the venue yet?"

"Yes," replied Aislinn. "Patrick Jay and I had a private tour this afternoon. Teatro La Fenice. It is spectacular."

"That being said," began Patrick, "I'm starting to become acclimatized to spectacular being the norm."

"Do these venues compete with a campfire at Uluru at sunset?" asked Greatrex cheekily.

Patrick Jay smiled. "Not quite, but the drink service is better."

We laughed. Laughter was good.

"Have you heard about the press conference tomorrow afternoon?" asked Aislinn.

I felt my unease rise in tandem with my eyebrows as I looked questioningly at Greatrex. "Sorry, I hadn't gotten around to mentioning that yet."

The others looked surprised, but I was all too aware that both Greatrex and I had other things on our minds.

"Yes," continued Aislinn. "Tony has planned for us to meet the Italian press at the opera house tomorrow afternoon. There is an equally spectacular smaller room there called Sale Apollinee."

Patrick Jay took over. "The idea is for is to play for around twenty minutes and then answer questions."

I looked across the table at Greatrex. Ascardi must have a reason for calling the impromptu presser and performance. I just had no idea what it was.

"Let's order," said Patrick, as an impeccably penguin-dressed waiter with a bow tie and white jacket moved toward us, bottle of wine in hand.

After we'd ordered, Greatrex said, "I've been doing some research. Do you know what 'la fenice' means in English?"

We didn't respond.

"The phoenix," he said.

Prophetic.

"To the phoenix," I toasted. Three of us raised our glasses.

Greatrex raised an eyebrow.

Chapter 26

"Signore e signori della stampa, benvenuti, Aislinn Byrne, Nicholas Sharp e Patrick Jay Olden … Ladies and Gentlemen of the press, please welcome Aislinn Byrne, Nicholas Sharp, and Patrick Jay Olden."

The bilingual announcement was met by polite applause. Members of the press were never as enthusiastic as the ticket-buying public. Their job was to remain cool, aloof, and, with regard to the music industry, frequently judgmental. We didn't know the MC, who'd introduced himself to us earlier as Roberto Bianchi from a local music society. As we swanned through the tall double doors that led to the small stage, he turned to us, applauding and smiling. He'd done this before.

La Fenice's Sale Apollinee held about one hundred and fifty people sitting on carefully aligned pink and gold chairs. We gazed around the room as we took the stage. Apart from the fashion, you'd be forgiven for thinking you'd walked into the eighteenth century. Cream walls with yet more gold leaf were decorated with oversized gold-framed mirrors. An ornate balcony surrounded the room, its balustrade another example of the intricacies of Venetian design. The few bits of technical equipment that enhanced a modern performance were kept as hidden as possible. The stage on which we were about to perform was simple and unobtrusive, but clearly not part of the original design.

Sale Apollinee was a room in which you would expect to hear a Vivaldi string quartet rather than a didgeridoo. Nevertheless, here we were. Looking out at the faces of the Italian music press, I wondered if they were thinking the same thing.

As was our way, we began our short performance with Patrick Jay's haunting introduction. The didgeridoo had a different quality in this room, but it was still captivating and challenging. I joined in, playing the magnificent full-size grand piano before me. When Aislinn began to sing, I was sure several members of the press were suddenly jerked into paying attention. Yet again, she had won hearts, in this case some very tough ones.

One long piece and twenty minutes later, we were finished. The applause from the floor was noticeably more enthusiastic than it had been at the start.

A stagehand moved up and put three chairs in a semicircle at the front of the stage and indicated we should sit. It was time for questions.

"Buon pomeriggio a tutti. Good afternoon, everyone," said Aislinn. More applause.

Roberto Bianchi rejoined us on the stage to compere the questions, all of which were to be in English.

It took all of two minutes to realize that the reporters and journalists in front of us were not just the Italian music press.

"What was your reaction to the bombing at the Palais Garnier in Paris?" asked the first reporter, in a distinctly British accent.

Before anyone could answer, another voice: "Aislinn, how

did you feel when you realized so many people had died right in front of you?" This time the accent was French.

Bianchi tried to exhort some control. "Ladies and gentlemen, Signorina Byrne, Signor Sharp, and Signor Olden have graciously agreed to answer questions about their music. That was made perfectly clear to you in your invitation."

I turned to Aislinn; her upper lip was quivering and she clutched at her chair, her knuckles like talons. I reached out for her hand. Patrick Jay had done the same on the opposite side. Despite Roberto Bianchi's words, the barrage didn't stop.

"Mr. Olden, what do you say to those who have said the bombing was an attack on multiculturalism?" The questioner had a German accent.

At the back of the room, two large double doors opened. Antonio Ascardi strode purposefully through the doorway. He was flanked by two very large men with short-cropped hair. Even from where I was sitting, the bulge in their oversized jackets indicated that they were each carrying a firearm. That was new. Ascardi stood there in his trademark black suit and tieless white shirt. His arms were crossed, face drawn tight in concern ... or was he just a better method actor than me?

The MC looked at us. I shook my head and began to stand up, trying to give Aislinn and Patrick Jay a lead.

Then another question, an Italian accent, "What do you say, Signor Sharp, to reports that you had something to do with the Palais Garnier bombing?"

The room erupted; people were calling out everywhere. I began to lead the others off the stage. As I turned, I was sure I saw a curt smile sneak onto Ascardi's lips. Then it was gone.

Amid the chaotic cries emanating from the press, we marched across the small stage, climbed down two steps, and exited the room through a pair of oversized double doors. Our refuge was the large ornate chamber that acted as stage wings. I waited till the others had passed and then slammed the doors closed behind us. Tears were streaming down Aislinn's face as Roberto Bianchi apologized and tried to comfort her.

I marched over to Jack Greatrex, who'd been waiting for us.

"That's it then," I said quietly. "That was the whole reason for this press conference. Public suspicion has now fallen on one Nicholas Sharp." I was furious.

"Get ready for the ride," said Greatrex. "This is going to be tough."

I thought for a moment and then turned to Bianchi. "Who organized the press passes for those people out there? You?" He took a step back, his back arching as he recoiled at my anger. I didn't care.

"No, Signor Sharp, it wasn't me. As I just said to the reporters, I was told that the discussion was to be all about your music."

"Then who organized this?"

"Well, sir," replied Bianchi, "my understanding was that the press list was organized by Mr. Norbert Fontana and Mr. Ascardi himself."

I looked over at Greatrex.

"Here comes that world of pain," I said as I turned to see Aislinn crumpled in a chair, her tearful face a portrait of anguish. My thoughts went to Elena lying murdered in the snow, the wretchedness of the people who senselessly lost their lives in Paris, and finally the desperation of my own predicament. "Whatever that bastard has in mind, I'm ready to roll."

We remained in the same room for another twenty minutes while Bianchi and the opera house staff cleared the Sale Apollinee. As we prepared to leave, the heavily framed door at the opposite end of the room opened, and Ascardi's two armed offsiders walked in.

"Signor Ascardi would like the room please, said the man on the right." It was a demand, a polite demand, but definitely a demand. "Signor Sharp and Signor Greatrex, please remain."

One of the men held the door open as Aislinn and Patrick Jay turned toward it; at the door Patrick Jay turned around to look at me. I just nodded in affirmation. Things were about to get interesting; our friends were best gone.

We sat there in silence. The two henchmen didn't say anything more. Greatrex and I just looked at each other. Finally, after keeping us waiting for several minutes, the door opened again, and Antonio Ascardi strolled casually into the room.

"Nicholas, Jack," he began, "this gives me no pleasure; however, I think it's time we dispensed with any charade of cordiality and transitioned directly to the truth."

I nodded.

Ascardi continued. "I thought I had generously provided everything you needed to immerse yourselves in our little tour. Yet perhaps I failed to cater for your incessant curiosity. The two of you have been nauseatingly determined and persistent. The break-in at Safe-Tech, so many enquiries behind my back, and, Nicholas, your latest escapade in Malamocco."

So much for that going unnoticed.

"If you can forgive the rather clunky musical metaphor, I'm thinking the two of you suspect I have punctuated our musical adventures together with a slightly edgier, perhaps even Machiavellian counterpoint." Smiling and gesticulating as he spoke, Ascardi seemed delighted with his sobriquet. It was almost as though he was describing one of his own rare wines. His mouth widened, rising at the edges through pursed lips. The man's eyes, however, remained impassive and disinterested, as though there was a level of emotional detachment going on here that was even more worrying than his words.

Greatrex and I looked at each other. "To be honest, yes," I said.

"Well, I am here to put your minds at rest," he said. "I think that this is an opportune time for you to know you are completely correct."

A cutting silence filled the room. We weren't expecting that.

"Tony, are you admitting to being responsible for the trail of death that has followed us around Europe?" I asked. Even though we had been almost certain of his involvement, I still felt a blood-pumping fury envelop me as the conversation developed.

"Yes," he said. "I am telling you exactly that. Now, before you start asking a series of questions that I have no intention of answering, let me just say this: it has given me no pleasure at all to pursue this path of tasteless violence. To be honest, the whole situation really has me pissed. I have, however, deemed it necessary."

"No pleasure?" said Greatrex. The big fella's fists were clenched and his neck was pulsating. His frustration radiated across the room. "No freakin' pleasure. Innocent people have died!"

I knew my friend too well. The manner in which his shoulders kicked back and his arms tensed in anticipation told me an explosion was imminent. The two henchmen shifted on their feet, preparing themselves.

"Oh, I can surely see your need for self-righteous anger," said Ascardi. "I would probably feel the same if I didn't know about the other pressures at play here. Sadly, you will never see what I see. All I will tell you is that what I do, I do for the good of our fragile little world. People don't know how to help themselves; I *can* help, so I do. I've told you before, I search for alternative solutions. In this case, that is exactly what I have found."

Greatrex glanced at me, tacitly expressing surprise at the level of Ascardi's escalating ramblings.

"The expression on your face is so readable, Nicholas. Yours even more so, Jack. No, I am not a madman. As in everything I do, from the day I wrote my fist line of code, I see ahead of the game when others can't. The world will be thankful one day."

I'd had enough; so had Greatrex. Without thinking I rushed forward at Ascardi, knowing Jack would be right behind me. If we moved quickly enough, we would have the element of surprise ... but we didn't make it halfway across the room before the two henchmen had withdrawn their guns from underneath their jackets, pointing them directly at us.

"No," said the man on the left, "you would be dead before you could touch us."

He was very calm, very cool. Yet another professional—it seemed Ascardi had an unlimited supply of them. We stopped.

"There is no need for that sort of behavior. Get a grip, guys," said Ascardi. "We shall sort this out together, as adults."

I couldn't believe what I was hearing. This man's grip on reality seemed to be tenuous at best.

"At least tell me one thing," I asked. "Why have you gone to so much trouble to implicate me in the eyes of the authorities? Why am I your scapegoat?"

"There are a couple of reasons, Nicholas, but as I said, I'm not going to elaborate on my motivations now."

Ascardi's demeanor was calm, almost friendly. He had just admitted to murdering numerous people, yet now he spoke as if discussing online gaming

The entrepreneur then grew silent, absent in thought. I noticed the skin on his neck tighten and his forehead furrow as tension slowly enveloped his face. It was the same look I'd seen in the car in Paris.

"It's time to talk business. There is something I need you to do. You won't like it, so I will give you some choices. Nicholas, I believe you left the military because you wanted to make you own decisions, your own choices. Well, here I am, trying to help you out."

This was going nowhere good.

Ascardi spoke again. "As you know, tomorrow evening you are scheduled to perform here at Gran Teatro La Fenice, in the main concert hall. You have seen the concert space; it is a remarkable room. Unfortunately, that performance will not be taking place. The reason is simple: at best, Nicholas, you will be in prison; at worst you will be dead. If that is the case, I shall offer the press a moving obituary outlining what a wonderful man and musician you were and how surprised we all were to learn about your subversive activities. I shall ask the world to remember the best of you, and all that you brought to the arts. I will insist that the demented condition that led to your violent demise was not an indication of who you really were."

Ascardi paused. His facial muscles seemed to relax and his eyes softened momentarily. "I must say that I really do believe your death would be a loss to the music world. You play beautifully, and the sound that you, Aislinn, and Patrick Jay have created together is irreplaceable. You *will* be missed."

The man's feigned empathy defied belief.

"Are you done yet?" I asked. "Nothing you can say or do will make me help you. As soon as we're done here, Jack and I are heading straight to the authorities to give them all the information we have." I hoped I sounded convincing, but in my gut I knew I didn't.

"All the information," said Ascardi smiling. "What information do you really have? What evidence? You are the man under suspicion. The press is calling for your head—or they will be after this afternoon's press conference. I imagine your name will be all over the late news. Who would then believe anything you said?"

He had a point.

"Now let's get into the fine print. Tomorrow afternoon the Italian prime minister, Angelo Mancini, will visit the Basilica San Marco here in Venice. Some recent restorations were financed by a generous private benefactor: me. I will accompany the prime minister as he inspects the finished renovations. As we leave the basilica and before we walk back across the Piazza San Marco, the prime minister will stop to talk informally to the press, giving him an opportunity to express his gratitude to me, as a well-known supporter of

European culture. That is when you will assassinate him."

"Not going to happen," I said defiantly.

Ascardi raised his hand, as though to stop me wasting my breath. "Now, Nicholas, here are your choices. First, you do as I ask, shoot Prime Minister Mancini and attempt to escape. You won't escape, of course. You will be seen; in fact, I may even point you out myself. Obviously, you will be arrested. Given the current rumors in the press about your unsavory activities, no one will be particularly surprised that you were 'caught in the act,' so to speak. In time, you may even grow to enjoy prison life."

The henchmen either side of Ascardi allowed themselves a wry grin.

He continued. "Your second option is to choose not to take the shot. The prime minister will live, and this will be inconvenient to my plans but not catastrophic. There is, however, a consequence for this choice. On the other side of the piazza, Norbert Fontana will be sitting at an outdoor table having a coffee. He will be joined by Aislinn Byrne; that has already been arranged. Also joining him will be Domenico here." The henchman to Ascardi's right nodded at the introduction. "Now, here is the kicker for option two. Norbert will have a cell phone with him. It will be on the table but out of your sight. If you fail to carry out the assassination, he will dial an encrypted number that will detonate a bomb planted somewhere in the piazza. You will not know where. I would caution you to think carefully about this option. There will be an untold number of families and children scattered around the square. You will have no idea which ones you would be about to murder," he said.

Greatrex's body language spoke volumes. His shoulders

sagged as he stared down at the polished marble floor. The tiredness rippling over his face was like a torrent of defeat. I knew it was the thought of kids being harmed that had hit him. In contrast, I was feeling a little more optimistic. As a sniper, I had always looked for alternative courses of action to achieve my kill. An idea was already forming in my head. What if I took out Fontana? Then ...

"I know what you are thinking, Nicholas. If you shoot Norbert Fontana, I can assure you it will be no effort for Domenico to reach over and press the key on the cell phone."

What if I take out Domenico first? I thought to myself.

"Of course, as we are supplying the rifle, we will also supply the only ammunition available to you ... one bullet."

"Shit," I thought.

"Finally," said Ascardi, "there is a third option, which I suspect you may find tempting. You may decide to assassinate me. I have lived a committed, if slightly flawed, life. It may be my time is up. If that is your choice, so be it. I should warn you, however, that the consequences for this third option are the same for that of the second. Norbert will detonate the bomb and many innocent people will die."

Three choices. No choice.

"Oh, one more thing I might add. If you decide to be a hero and use the gun on yourself ..."

"The bomb," I said.

"Exactly."

I thought again about making another lunge for this deranged bastard, but the abrasively stern look on the two bodyguards' faces told me my effort would be wasted.

"Well, that's it then," said Ascardi. "We'll be in touch in the morning for the final arrangements. In the meantime, you have a choice to make. I suggest you choose wisely. Oh, and, Nicholas, you know that I put great import on precision. I cannot stress enough the importance of timing in this situation. Your window is limited; there will be no opportunity for hesitation." With that, he nodded at his two offsiders, turned around, and marched out the door.

"Shit," I repeated after they had gone.

"Exactly," said Jack Greatrex.

Chapter 27

Jack Greatrex and I must have sat in that room for another forty minutes going over every option available to us. We couldn't go to the authorities; no one would believe us. There was no going back. I was in so deep now, not even the General could dig me out.

All the options Ascardi presented would result in unjustified bloodshed. It even occurred to us to just leave town, but we realized Ascardi would probably kill those innocent people in the Piazza San Marco just to make his point.

We had nothing. It couldn't get any worse ... and then it did.

Eventually, we decided to head back to our hotel. At least we knew Antonio Ascardi wasn't staying there. While the tour was in Venice, he was based at his own palatial home just off the Grand Canal. But he was more likely at his undisclosed location.

Although the tour was the least of our problems, it was with sadness that I realized it was over. Performing with Aislinn and Patrick Jay had been a great experience. We knew taking them into our confidence would only endanger them.

As we left the room and walked to the top of the Grand

Staircase in the opera house foyer, it occurred to me that I may have performed my last show. Whatever happened tomorrow, I could tell myself I left in style.

"Mr. Sharp," came a voice from the bottom of the stairs.

I looked down to see the distinctive blond hair of Jasper De Vries from Europol. A bad day just got worse.

We descended the stairs, but not by choice. De Vries was accompanied by three uniformed officers I assumed to be local police. De Vries himself conveyed no more warmth than he had in our first meeting in Paris. His eyes still radiated the warmth of a snowstorm, perhaps this time with a glint of self-satisfaction.

There was no offering of hands. "Mr. Sharp, this is Ispettore Davide Romana of the Polizia di Stato."

De Vries eyed off Greatrex. "Mr. Jack Greatrex, I presume."

Greatrex just nodded.

"Sharp, I was told I might find you here. Since we last met, I have been digging into your background a little more deeply. I have also received further information regarding some of your more recent activities. Perhaps you would care to explain these."

De Vries then produced his beloved tablet, flicked through a couple of screens, and passed it to me. No wonder he had looked so smug. The image on the screen was not of high quality, but it was clear enough to be used as evidence in court. It took less than three seconds for me to realize it depicted part of the Cinaed Nuclear Power Station. In the lower left corner of the picture, backdropped by an array of pipes and machinery, was the image of a man looking up at the camera. His body language suggested that he was uncomfortable and didn't belong in that mechanical environment. The man's face, however, was easily identifiable. It was me.

"Well?" asked De Vries.

Silence.

"I can't begin to explain," I said eventually. Nothing had occurred to me that would in any way get me out of this. "But again, you've got this all wrong," I continued, in vain.

"You leave me little choice," said De Vries, clearly not concerned with finding another.

Ispettore Davide Romana of the Polizia di Stato stepped forward. He nodded to his two colleagues, who also stepped forward, taking their place either side of me. "Signor Nicholas Sharp, I am placing you under arrest for your involvement in terrorist activities at the Cinaed power station in Scotland, the murder of Sir Phillip Morton in London, the bombing of the Palais Garnier in Paris, and a murder in Füssen, Germany."

Again silence. Then Greatrex grunted. It was his raspy, low-pitched "what the?" grunt, denoting extreme vexation.

If I was taken into custody, innocent people would die in the Piazza San Marco the following day.

I looked directly into the cold blue eyes belonging to Jasper De Vries of Europol.

I said, "I'm sorry, De Vries."

"For your crimes?" he asked.

"No, for this." I balled my right fist and, attempting to feign a relaxed stance to conceal my intent, I sucker punched him on his right cheek just below his eye.

I knew that I had no time to wait for any reaction, not with police officers surrounding me. Taking advantage of a millisecond of confusion, I used all my weight to shove the officer to my right, placing my foot behind his ankle. He went down.

The officer on my left was quicker, reaching into his buttoned leather holster for his weapon. Greatrex stepped forward to block him. I yelled out "No." I needed Greatrex on the right side of the law.

In that same moment I raised my left foot and kicked the officer hard with the heel of my shoe. The powerful blow landed on his hand as he fumbled for his gun. I heard the sickening crunch of breaking bone. That left only Ispettore Romana on his feet. To reach his service pistol he had to cast aside the charge sheet he had just read to me. His complete surprise at my reaction and the second he took to cast the paper aside it gave me the opportunity to charge. There was no technique, just sheer force as I ran straight over him. Continuing my lunge across the pink carpet and onto the hard stone floor, I heard the first bullet ricochet off one of the huge marble pillars in the foyer. The missed shot provided me a vital extra second. More gunfire peppered the glass surrounding the front door behind me as I ran into the night.

Now it was official. I was a man on the run.

I had to keep moving. Several alleyways branched off the small piazza in front of the opera house. I chose one for no reason other than it was close, and belted toward it. People and buildings flashed by in a blur as I attempted to put as much space as I could between me and the officers following me. My senses focused on the voices behind me and the enveloping sound of my own rapid breathing.

I just ran, as fast and far as I was able.

At any turn I could come to an unpassable dead end, and it would all be over. The shouting voices and the clatter of running feet behind me seemed to swell and recede as I turned each corner. My strained, heavy breathing remaining my one constant companion. I just kept running. The only saving grace was the many streets, alleys, and laneways that allowed me time and opportunity to change direction undetected.

It made some difference that it was dark, and several shadowed doorways offered some potential refuge. Where possible, I chose the dimmer and less populated alleys to aid my escape.

It was proving difficult to break free of my pursuers. Although there were people all over the place, no one seemed too fazed by a lone man running. That would change, of course, when they came across the police who were chasing me. I had no doubt fingers would be pointed and directions given.

I just kept changing direction where I could. It was easy to give the impression I was running in no specific direction because I *was* running in no specific direction. Within minutes I had no idea where I was. Suddenly, I heard my pursuers way too clearly, they were close behind me, threateningly close. I turned a corner and stepped into the shadow of a large locked doorway. I held my breath waiting to be discovered. Two polizia in uniform dashed by. I didn't recognize them; obviously, De Vries had called in backup.

I stepped out of the shadows and turned down the next alleyway. I was beyond lost. At first my only aim was to avoid the big piazzas, where I would be too easily exposed. As I ran it became clear to me that I couldn't keep this up forever. Eventually, I would come around a corner and the lawmen would be there, waiting. They were in front of me and behind me now. I could feel myself being hemmed in. Still I kept moving.

I looked upwards toward the evening sky, but I couldn't see enough sky to gauge any sense of direction.

More feet, more yelling, another doorway in shadow. My luck couldn't hold out much longer.

I decided my only chance was to make it back to my original hotel room. The bolt-hole. There was a chance that De Vries and the polizia didn't yet know about it. I figured they would find out about it soon enough, but in the meantime, it could provide a temporary safe harbor and get me off the streets. The trouble was I had no idea which way to go.

I found myself running down a singularly narrow alleyway and over a tiny low-slung bridge that crossed a small canal. I was surprised that even in this confined space there were gondoliers hawking for passengers and the tourist dollar. I was halfway over the bridge when I heard, "Signor Sharp, fermato ora per favore—stop now please!" I glanced behind me. Damn! It was the Ispettore, what was his name … Romana. "You have caused us a great deal of angst, signor," He aimed his service-issue revolver at me. I stopped. Romana spoke into his phone, I assumed giving directions to our location.

There was no point pleading with the man; in his mind I was guilty, and I couldn't really blame him. To my left there was a young couple climbing on board their gondola; they were laughing and smiling in anticipation of their romantic ride. They stopped laughing when they saw Romano's gun.

"It's all right," he reassured them. "I am with the polizia."

He momentarily turned to the couple as he spoke. That was all I needed. I reached down into the gondola, wrenched the oar out of the gondolier's hand and swung it across the bridge toward the policeman. He tried to move sideways but there was not enough room to get out of the way. I caught him hard on the side of his torso. The force sent him over the edge of the bridge and into the canal. I turned and sprinted off down the alley. Another friend gained.

I was getting desperate. That was too close, and time was on everyone's side but mine.

Then I saw it—so simple I should have thought to look before. A yellow sign with black writing and a long thin arrow. It said "Per Rialto"—*for Rialto.* My bolt-hole was not far from the Rialto Bridge. All I had to do was follow the tourist signs.

Twenty minutes and two more close calls later, I was at the Rialto Bridge. Three minutes after that I was passing through the front door of the Vecchio Hotel Canal and bolting up the long stairway. I was out of breath and looking decidedly disheveled when the receptionist looked up from his desk. His eyes seemed to bulge in surprise when he saw me.

"Next time I think I'll just walk up them."

The receptionist relaxed a little, offering a professional smile.

I took my key, panting and trying to appear every bit the stupid turista he'd decided I was. "Those stairs are going to kill me one day."

Chapter 28

I lay on my bed, trying to slow my breathing and quicken my thinking. As far as I knew, only Greatrex knew about this location. How safe was I in this hotel room? The answer depended on how quickly the authorities got my picture out though the press and the effectiveness of their processes for scanning registered hotel guests throughout the city. Given the reaction at the press conference earlier at the Sale Apollinee, I figured the media would lap this whole scenario up, meaning I'd have well less than twenty-four hours of sanctuary here. But in twenty-four hours this whole thing would be over, one way or another.

Then there was the prospect of the next day's events. That was troubling me big-time. The idea of what was expected of me cast an impenetrable cloud that I couldn't seem to cut through. I had no doubt that at some point, however reluctantly, I was going to find myself, rifle in hand, scanning the Piazza San Marco for my target. Who would be that target?

There had to be another way through this, but for the life of me I just couldn't see it. I lay on the bed and let my mind wander, praying a solution would present itself.

I must have dozed off because it was just after midnight

when I looked down at my watch. I was hungry, but nothing could be done about that. I wasn't going back out onto the streets.

I wanted to call Greatrex. If he hadn't been arrested, and I couldn't see any reason why he should have been, he'd be back at the hotel. I knew with certainty I couldn't risk using my own phone; the authorities would track it the moment it was turned on. I couldn't use a hotel phone for the same reason; they could well be monitoring the big fella's calls and would track the line to this location. Then the penny dropped. The giant from the Lido. I reached into my pocket. The phone I'd acquired from him hadn't dropped out during the chase.

"It's me," I knew he wouldn't recognize the number.

"Are you safe?"

"For now. I've got to be brief. Any update?" I asked.

"Ascardi now knows the police and Europol are trying to arrest you. He contacted me. If you're arrested, he'll still detonate the bomb in the square."

"Then I'd better stay free," I replied.

"He gave me instructions for tomorrow," said Greatrex.

Two minutes later I knew what was expected of me. The gist of it was that I needed to find my way to the roof of the Basilica San Marco by 1 p.m. No problem for the most wanted man in Venice.

Greatrex finished with, "Are you going to be all right tonight?"

"If they knew where I was, I would have been arrested by now, so I think so," I responded. "I'd better go. This call has taken long enough." I hung up.

In the military I'd been trained to figuratively sleep with one eye open. A sniper often had to set up his hide well before the target arrived at the expected location. When the time came, you had to be alert enough to take a clean shot. Sometimes that meant sleeping in an exposed position. One eye open.

I awoke just before sunrise. My half-sleep had been restless, disturbed again by images of Ascardi and the trail of death he'd left in his wake, and mine.

I was particularly tormented by dreams of Elena. It was as though she was trying to tell me something, but I had no idea what. Whatever we'd had, and I didn't understand what that was, had moved me. We'd shared a closeness that seemed to appear and disappear behind a veil of her making. She'd had so much to give; on the other hand, she was way past mischievous, more like devious really. Either way, she had been needlessly killed, and the anger I felt devoured me like a cancer.

I was angry for all who had died at Ascardi's hand, but with Elena, the fire of fury burned much closer to home.

As I lay there on the bed, I consciously allowed the twisted bitterness to grow within me. Bullies and manipulators were the cesspit of humanity. Ascardi was both. Resolve overtook fatigue as I felt my outrage call me to arms. I would use my anger to make Ascardi pay for Elena's death, and the deaths of the other victims. I would team my hunger for vengeance with my professional skills and stop him. Decision made.

Suddenly, I heard excited voices and the movement of running footsteps resonate down the corridor. My bolt-hole had been discovered.

I leaped off the bed. The room was at the end of a long corridor, and there was only one door out. Always a planner,

I'd figured out an escape route the night before. Opening one of the bedroom windows, I heaved myself up and climbed out onto the window ledge, closing the casement behind me. The rooftop of the adjoining building was a manageable leap away, not more than two yards, but a fall down the cavernous space between buildings would be debilitating at best. I coiled my body and vaulted across the space. The strained scraping sound of the window behind me reopening added an unneeded motivation as I landed, cracking some terracotta tiles and crabbing across them, turning the skyline into an escape route.

Because Venice was so crowded with buildings, it was easy to move across distances while maintaining height. I had frequently done the same thing in Iraq. It was all about balance and judgment. I rapidly put a decent space between me and my pursuers. I had probably done more rooftop work than they had. That would give me a small advantage and a chance.

Then I heard them ... the faint sound of airborne engines. Then the throbbing of rotating metal blades growing louder. Helicopters.

It shouldn't have come as a surprise. With the severity of the charges against me, the authorities would have put the city under lockdown. That meant bringing in all the resources they could muster, including the choppers. Now I was totally exposed. Once they saw me, I felt certain they would shoot. From the sky I would be an easy target.

I ran over the pitch of the nearest roof and slipped behind a large red-brick chimney. It was wide enough to conceal a man and thick enough to stop a bullet. As the first chopper flew over, I moved back around the chimney, keeping the structure between the aircraft and me. The helicopter flew past without deviating. I'd got away with it.

Then came a second chopper. Damn, I was now totally exposed. I had no choice but to slide back to the other side of the chimney again. I hoped no one in the first chopper was looking backward. As it approached, the first kept a straight course. I was safe … then I wasn't. The first chopper had swung around toward me. Worse, the crew had obviously radioed the second bird, which was now slowing down to a hover not far from where I hid.

The first round impacted the chimney just above my head. Shards of shattered bricks rained down on my head. The people shooting at me were clearly not trying to take prisoners. The second round hit an inch away from my shoulder. I had no choice; it was time to move.

I ran down the steep incline of the roof, slipping as some of the old tiles gave way. Shots rang out behind me. I was seconds away from a bullet. I scanned the skyline, desperate for a way down. Then I saw it. Two rooftops away a glass skylight reflected sharply in the morning sun. I would be heavily exposed if I went for it, but if I could make it and then get down through it, I'd be out of sight of the airborne marksmen. The rooftiles just behind my right foot disintegrated as another round hit. Go.

I zig-zagged my way across the next roof, trying to make the police snipers' job as difficult as possible. Bullets splintered the rooftiles either side of me, kicking shards of porcelain into the air. I made it to the end of the roof, dove and rolled over the edge. A round of gunfire echoed across the rooftops as the capping I'd just arched over shattered into pieces. The second roof, the one with the skylight, was lower. As I landed,

I pressed myself up against the wall of the higher building. It was temporary cover at best. The helicopters would need to swing around to get a clear shot. That movement might give me one brief opportunity.

As the choppers began to swerve, I sprinted to the skylight, bending down to rip an old tile off the roof as I ran. The crews in the two helicopters must have figured out my plan. They were coming in fast, spraying bullets from the sky.

I raised the rooftile above my head and smashed it down on the skylight. The surface cracked but didn't break, and the tile bounced off. I wasn't going to make it. I grabbed the tile and raised it again. As I began the downward motion, I felt my skin tear as pain shot through my arm. I dropped the tile. It was simply luck that it landed on the cracked skylight and crashed right through it. It took me all of two seconds to jump through the open space, land on the floor below and roll away from the barrage of airborne gunfire to claim protection under the solid roof.

The polizia would quickly work out the street address of my refuge, but I had to prioritize my wound. Blood was seeping steadily from my upper left arm. Spasms of pain shot through my nervous system as I wiped it away. It could have been worse. The bullet had only grazed me. It needed a wash and a bandage, but that would have to wait. I took off my jacket and ripped the sleeve off my shirt. As I tightened it around the wound, the waves of pain increased. For a moment I felt my consciousness wane. A minute later I was okay, and the bleeding appeared to have slowed.

My next priority was an extraction plan. I didn't know where I was going, but I knew I had to keep moving. I was in some sort of attic. Steep stairs led down to the next floor. I took them two at a time. It would be too late for the front door. The polizia would be on the street by now. Fortunately, the house was empty, so there was no one to say, "He went that way." Small mercies.

I found the back door. It led to a small courtyard. Windows from neighboring houses backed on to the space, sheltering it from the street. In other circumstances it would be a place to relax and share a glass of wine under the vines. To me it looked like a potential kill zone. I ran to the opposite wall and chose a window that would be large enough to climb through. The glass shattered into thousands of small pieces as I drove my foot through it. A moment later I'd cleared some of the jagged remnants away and hoisted myself through.

I needed to get out of the area, but I figured I wouldn't survive long back on the streets. With only about four hours to lay low before Ascardi expected me at the Piazza San Marco, I headed out the front door, straight into a dark, narrow laneway. That was good. There was no one in sight. I jogged slowly toward what I thought was the laneway's northern end. When I got there, I stopped and stuck my head around the corner: a wider alleyway smattered with small shops, street vendors, and a thin crowd.

I ventured out and made my way east. An idea was starting to form in my overtaxed brain.

The alleyway gave way to a small piazza at the eastern end. Two polizia stood on the piazza corner opposite me. I ducked back into the shelter of a doorway, wondering if they'd seen me. I counted ten seconds. No reaction. Stepping back out into the alleyway in the direction from which I had just come, I walked straight into the sightline of a group of four uniformed polizia who seemed to be searching door-to-door. The group of law officers saw me as soon as I saw them.

"Smetta, Lei e in arresto!" Then in English, "Stop, you are under arrest!"

Without thinking, I turned and ran across the piazza. I knew the polizia behind me would be drawing their guns and giving chase. I'd have to chance it with the two officers already in the piazza. People scattered as I ran across the space and turned down the first laneway I came to. I heard the officers call out; they couldn't fire a shot with so many people milling around, so I just kept running. All I could do now was run.

I had one hope. Attempting to maintain a northerly direction, I belted down three alleyways before I saw sunlight streaming onto a broader section of footpath ahead.

I burst into the open, recognizing the Riva del Vin on the Grand Canal. I had inadvertently doubled back close to my hotel. The paths beside the canal hosted a plethora of humanity. Restaurants were busy serving breakfast to locals and tourists alike, and early shoppers were making a start on the day. I wanted the polizia to see me—that was part of my ill-considered plan. I ran in the direction of the Rialto Bridge. The clomping boots and barked commands told me the officers were close. I was counting on the crowd to continue to keep the cops' bullets at bay. People seemed to be calling out and pointing at me. If my plan was to have any hope of success, I had to be noticed.

I ran up the steps leading onto Ponte di Rialto, the most famous bridge in Venice, pausing for a split second to make sure everyone saw me turn right onto the bridge. I sprinted up the next lot of steps toward the center of the bridge's arc.

Five paces in, before any of my uniformed pursuers saw me, I ducked to the left behind a vendor's clothes stand. I grabbed a bright red coat and a woolen hat off one of the racks and moved back down toward the steps, putting the clothes on as I went. The vendor didn't notice what I'd done, and no one on the bridge seemed the wiser.

The polizia rounded the corner onto the bridge. I bent down behind a stand selling tourism trinkets, trying to look like I'd dropped something. Again, no one seemed to pay me any attention; they were too busy gawking at the officers running past.

I waited a few seconds for the first wave of polizia to pass by, my nerves strained to breaking point. I figured there would be a second wave in the next minute or so, then a swarm.

I took advantage of the break and slipped unnoticed back down the bridge stairs and swung to the right. I probably only had a minute, two at the most, to make my play. Another cobbled laneway opened up to a small waterside piazza by the canal. It was signed as the Campo Erberia. There were fewer people here. The small piazza was surrounded by buildings on three sides. At the far end there was an old wooden pontoon where a couple of gondolas were tied up alongside an unattended barge. From the way their arms gesticulated wildly, I assumed the two brightly dressed gondoliers were heavily involved in discussion. They were fifteen yards away, with no customers in sight. Fortunately, their eyes were focused up the canal as they chatted. I quietly padded over the stone space and down onto the pontoon, stepping unnoticed onto the barge. The freezing water enveloped me as I slipped quietly over its side and into the canal.

The Grand Canal's cold waters enveloped me like a freezing liquid coffin. Every painful stroke up the waterway took me a little further away from the chaos I'd hastily created to mask my exit. I was driven by the hope that the authorities would be searching the streets around Per Rialto rather than the canal itself. Even in the extremely cold water, the wound in my arm felt like searing hot coals were pressing against it, the constant pain reminding me that this was a short-term strategy.

Keeping mainly under the cover of moored boats, pontoons, and pylons, I swam slowly up the canal. At best I only had around fifteen minutes in the water before being debilitated by hypothermia. I knew what I was looking for, but I didn't have long to find it.

Ten minutes later, my initial burst of energy began to subside. Each stroke required more strength than I had to give; each kick screamed in painful futility. Two minutes further on and my aches had turned into debilitating numbness, my body demanding immediate submission. Then I saw what I'd been searching for. A pair of giant wooden double doors rose out of the water. The canal water ran under the doors, presumably into an upmarket boat shed of sort. I swam to the doors, grabbing desperately for the support their brass handles offered. Pausing to take a couple of painfully deep breaths, I mustered what energy I could and dove underneath them.

I came up in a dark cavern. A small shard of light filtered through the gap in the doors, allowing me to make out the shadow of a stone landing and the shape of a hull looming above me. I treaded water as I listened for sounds inside the space, hearing nothing.

Slowly making my way around to the stern of the boat, every tired muscle crying for relief, I fumbled around in the dark. No ladder—that would have been too easy. As my right foot gained purchase on the shaft of the craft's submerged propeller, I heaved myself up, grabbing a cleat on the transom to stake my beachhead. Instantly, my slippery fingers lost their grip on the smooth metal and I slid downward, falling silently back under the water. Seriously short of strength and energy, I willed my way back up, kicking as hard as I could with increasingly failing legs. Frantically gasping for air as I broke the surface, I regained my breath for a minute, clutching at the boat's rudder before endeavoring to escape the bone-chilling water again. I knew I'd only have the strength for one more attempt. Using the submerged propeller as a lever one last time, I lunged upward. My fingers found the cleat but immediately started slipping off again. I dug deeper, my hand like a frozen claw on the metal. The wound in my arm shot stabbing pain through my torso as I pulled myself slowly toward the transom. For the second time that morning I thought I would pass out, then suddenly I was over, somersaulting chaotically into the boat. Relief beyond words.

Shivering on the deck, I felt waves of warm blood oozing down my arm. I was well aware that too many people's lives depended on me pulling myself together and not bleeding out where I lay, but awareness isn't everything.

A minute or two passed before I found the mental clarity needed to assess my situation. The craft appeared to be some sort of luxury launch. Not unusual around Venice. If you could afford a large home on the canal, you could afford a luxurious boat.

Crawling my way painfully along the vessel's deck through the unlocked cabin doors, I half clambered, half fell down the couple of steps onto what I assumed in the dim light to be some sort of lounge area. In the darkness my hands groped around, eventually finding the plush softness of the craft's padded seats.

I leaned against one of them and untied the knot in the shirt that was wrapped around my injured arm. The blood began to flow freely. Ignoring the throbbing spasms, I refolded the shirt and tied it back around the wound. Stripping off my sodden clothes, I wrapped myself in an old picnic blanket that had been left folded on the seat.

It was exhausting work, so I laid down ... just for a minute.

Chapter 29

When I came to, I was shivering uncontrollably. My whole body was so blindingly numb it was difficult to even raise my arm to look at my watch; two hours had gone past.

If moving a limb was difficult, getting to Piazza San Marco undetected would be near impossible. Even if I pulled myself together physically, every law enforcement officer for a hundred miles would be centered on bringing me to justice.

I wanted to contact Greatrex and the General, but I couldn't give the authorities any opportunity to track my location. As I struggled for clarity of thought, I became all too aware that the coldness that racked my body was slowing my thoughts. Nicholas Sharp, befuddled arctic lone wolf.

Despite my haze, I knew the only way I could prove my innocence was to prove Antonio Ascardi's guilt, and I only had a few hours to do it.

Belatedly, I gritted through the pain and forced myself to move, feeling my way around the cabin in the near darkness. I desperately required dry clothes and nourishment—biscuits, chocolate bars, anything. Maybe even a first-aid kit. My arm needed to be properly bandaged, and something to mute the pain would be helpful. As I groped through the small cupboards and gear stowed under seating, my fingertips became my eyes.

Ten minutes later, my plunder lay on the seat next to me. Halfway through my search, to my relief, I'd found a flashlight. Using the light, I'd easily located dry biscuits in a galley cupboard. I had also found a first-aid kit and some drinking water. That was a savior. After washing my wound out, I wrapped it in a clean bandage and downed some ibuprofen. The arm still throbbed, but it was functional, and the pain was dulled.

My surprise discovery was a spare set of keys to the boat. I suppose it made sense to have a spare set in case the originals went overboard. Their discovery got me thinking. Perhaps ...

A short time later I had a plan that would succeed brilliantly or fail miserably. There would be nothing in between.

My confidence grew as I climbed up onto the bow to confirm that keys for the craft also unlocked the doors that opened onto the canal. I left the two doors closed, but a nudge from the boat would now push them open.

Further rummaging below decks had produced a dry, warm jumper, track pants, and a plastic weather jacket. Turning the ignition key, I was rewarded with a low-pitched purr from the boat's powerful inboard engine. I prayed the dock's walls were thick enough to mute the rumbling noise from the house above.

I didn't wait around to find out. Edging the throttle slowly forward, the boat clicked into gear and began sliding gently through the water. When the bow made contact with the large wooden doors, they swung open.

As the harsh daylight tortured my eyes, a collage of color

and chaos revealed itself. Narrow-beamed canal barges carried their first deliveries of the day. Gondolas and water taxis ferried eager tourists to their destinations, enjoying the uniqueness of the city as they cruised the waterways. Some private craft, many not dissimilar to my own, swept along the waterway with a sense of purpose and direction. Under the watchful eye of the warm winter sun, the scene appeared jubilant, almost festive. I just felt apprehensive.

Using the boat to get to the piazza was my only chance. Plan A was to blast out of the dock and roar down the canal. People would turn, the polizia would notice, but I may have a chance of making the piazza, abandoning the boat, and disappearing into the crowd. I dismissed the idea as too risky. There were just too many polizia in the area, and the distance was too great for a quick sprint.

Plan B. It would take a bit of nerve, but there was no way around it. As I left the darkness of the pen and moved into the daylight, I swung the helm to starboard and joined the other craft on the canal, keeping my pace leisurely and measured.

For the first time I could see the splendor of my temporary transport. Long and narrow, the sleek craft was constructed of glistening polished wood with cream-colored plush vinyl cushioning on the seats. The helm sat in front of a long, low cabin area midship. The opulent cabin opened out to a small rear deck. It clearly belonged to someone of means, so that was the role I would have to play.

I positioned myself as low as possible in the driver's seat while maintaining a clear view ahead. As a former marine, I knew boats, so handling the craft was not a problem. Maintaining this gentleman's charade in the center of Venice was a different game. It was a long way from beaching a six-man marine inflatable in enemy-controlled territory. To help me along I had found an Italian straw hat under the boat's dashboard, which I wore low over my face. Combined with my new upmarket woolen jumper, I hoped my outfit gave me the look of a man who belonged on this craft. My appearance, at least from the waist up, had changed considerably from the description of the man the polizia were chasing.

I pinned everything on the fact that an affluent gentleman cruising the canal in open daylight wouldn't register as unusual. My natural instinct was to regress to plan A, shove the throttle to full, and make a run for it. I had to dig deep for enough self-control to fight the urge. It was difficult to look relaxed and carefree when every nerve in my body was drawn tight as a piano string.

As I motored under the Ponte di Rialto, my apprehension almost swallowed me whole. Numerous polizia still roamed the busy areas either side of the canal and on the bridge above. I'd noticed at least two helicopters circling overhead, crews with binoculars hanging from their open cabin doors. My heart rate skyrocketed as I passed an oncoming polizia boat, but the officers onboard didn't even give me a second look. For a reckless second I was tempted to wave to them—stupid idea.

The canal widened after I passed under the Ponte dell'Accademia. Then the Piazza San Marco, in all its splendor, appeared on my left.

I had a chance here.

But where would I moor the boat? If I appeared uncertain or lost, my movements would attract the attention I was endeavoring to avoid. I eased back on the throttle to drift past the piazza without stopping or losing the momentum needed to steer. I surveyed the waterside facilities.

Gondolas and water taxis queued in their multitudes along the southern edge of the piazza. Any strange craft there would be noticed.

I motored further along the lagoon. As I headed east, fewer boats lined the waterfront. A little way further along, and further away from the piazza, I nudged the boat to the shore and tied it to an available bollard on the stone wharf, where I hoped it would remain undiscovered for at least a few hours.

I climbed up onto the landing. Several people milled around, but far fewer than in the piazza itself. Law enforcement in the piazza would be on high-alert and extremely attentive to anything out of the ordinary. They would have the dual role of searching for me and protecting the Italian prime minister, whose visit I could only assume was going ahead. Ascardi's instructions would have me in position a couple of hours before the prime minister's visit to the basilica, but he hadn't advised me how I could get to the building undetected.

I walked along the waterside pathway, discreetly hugging the buildings. My wound wasn't visible, and I'd lifted my appearance above conspicuously scruffy.

It didn't take long to make it to the Palazzo Ducale just before the entrance to the piazza. I'd been instructed to find my way to the basilica roof, but I couldn't go in through the front; my limited knowledge of Italian history would have to get me in through the back.

At the entrance to the Doge's Palace I lined up to buy a ticket. It being winter, the queue was short. The one security guard on door duty seemed uninterested in anyone who wasn't an attractive female turista. I felt a little guilty taking advantage of his lecherous mind. As I waited, I kept my face glued to a map of Venice that I had picked up on my walk along the waterfront. First rule of fitting in: look like you have a purpose.

My shoulder muscles slackened with relief when I'd bought my ticket and entered the palace. I didn't join a tour; I wanted to be free to roam as much as possible. A map of the palace had come with admission. I studied it. If I remembered my history, the Basilica San Marco had been designed as the Doge's personal place of worship. The basilica structure virtually adjoined the northern wall of the palace.

Time. I glanced at my watch. It had taken me far too long to get down the canal to here. I had less than thirty minutes to make it to the roof of the basilica by 1 p.m. Ascardi had been very specific about the timing, his attention to detail unsurprisingly exact.

Get the timing right, get it wrong. Either way, people were going to die today.

Chapter 30

Massive archways standing tall like stone sentries surrounded the space as I passed through the Porta della Carta and entered the Palazzo courtyard. The roofless quadrangle was vast, and the multi-stories of functioning rooms in the Doge's Palace revolved around it. Groups of tourists wandered around, guidebooks in hand, soaking up the iconic building's checkered history. Keeping my hat low and my head down, I studied the map in front of me. It looked like I'd have to make my way up to the next floor. Tourists and tour groups loitered, absorbed in their studies of the building's art and architecture. One more fascinated soul would fit in. All the security guards seemed preoccupied giving directions to tourists and monitoring the inquisitive hands of children touching things they shouldn't.

I made my way across the palace courtyard to an imposing set of steps. According to my map they were called the Scala dei Giganti, the Giant Steps. It made sense; they were huge. I climbed them, ascending to a long, majestic gray-stone balcony, following the crowd along and through a pair of imposing double doors. The excessive grandeur made today's wealthy look like they were living on struggle street. Intricately ornate gold leaf edging framed massive frescoes on the walls and ceilings. Vast polished stone floors reached like runways from wall to wall. I briefly gasped at the splendor but was too worried that I wasn't going to make my deadline to appreciate it. I pressed on. There was little doubt the basilica was close, but I couldn't yet figure out how to get to the roof to access it. What I really needed was a Robert Langdon type to show me the way.

I headed toward the Doge's apartments, sniffing out access to the roof. Too many people roamed the area for me to break a window unnoticed. Then Robert Langdon appeared; I heard the words, "Secret itinerary tour people, follow me please."

About fifteen eager tourists followed an English-speaking Italian guide. "And now we will leave the public section of the palace and inspect the Piombi, including the cell where Giacomo Casanova was imprisoned. The cell is up this way, just below the roof."

"Below the roof" was all I really heard. I dawdled a moment and waited for the tour to pass me by. Then I joined on at the end, hoping the group was large enough for me to assimilate unnoticed. The guide led us through a door with a sign reading "No public access."

I was in.

Ten minutes later, as we ambled along a wooden corridor high up in the building, we passed a window through which I saw an enormous domed roof arched like a massive conservatory just a few yards away. At the roof's peak, where there could have been a telescope, there was a cross. This was it, the basilica.

I paused until the rest of the group turned the next corner in the corridor. No one noticed me stop; I didn't think anyone had noticed my presence at all.

Reaching across the wide stone sill, I tried to open the small double window. It didn't budge. Pulling my faithful lockpick from my wallet, I worked the lock, running the tool's sharp edge around the window frame and along the gap between the two panes. Then I reached in, grasped the window handles and pulled hard. They opened toward me so quickly I nearly lost my balance. A solid-looking wire grating was the next hurdle. Although once sturdy, the grating now felt rusted and weakened to the touch. The cement that joined the metal to the stone window surrounds had also deteriorated. Again I used the lockpick to work the rim of the grating where it joined the cement, digging it out as much as possible. Acutely aware of time, I climbed up onto the sill and kicked out with both my feet. The grating fell away, clattering down to the roof below.

I paused to listen for any reaction to the sound. Two seconds later I heard the clatter of footsteps approaching down the stone corridor. Someone investigating the noise, another tour group, or my group returning? Because of the echo effect on the stone walls and floor, I couldn't be sure which direction they were coming from, but the loudness of the footsteps suggested they were only seconds away.

With people so close, I couldn't afford the extra noise that would be created by my feet impacting the loose terracotta tiles of the next-door roof. I rolled over the edge of the window ledge, swung myself down and hung precariously by my clenched fingertips. I counted to thirty, hoping whoever was in the corridor would just pass by disinterestedly. My injured arm throbbed mercilessly under the pressure of my weight.

As I counted thirty-one, my hands gave way.

On the basilica roof, I waited another minute, my back pressed against the wall of the building I had just left, waiting for a cry of discovery. I heard nothing.

The basilica's roofline revealed itself as a world above a world. Dips and pitches, curves and stone half walls rolled out before me like a disorderly maze. I felt the heat of the new afternoon's sun radiate from every exposed surface. My biggest immediate problem was once again being spotted from the air. I would need to find some cover quickly. Ascardi had told Greatrex that police and security personnel would take up positions around the building and on the balcony high above the piazza at 1 p.m. Police helicopters would patrol until the prime minister had left the area. He was not due to arrive until three, but if I wasn't in position by one, I'd never make it. I glanced up at the clock tower across the piazza: ten to one ... probably the same odds of me succeeding.

A walkway spanned the basilica's rooftop, presumably for maintenance crews. I ran quickly along it, staying low, melting into the shadows of the roof's domes where possible. I'd have to remain up here undetected for over two hours. That was a big ask.

My first job was to locate the scaffolding that Greatrex had told me would be near the stonework at the base of the center dome. I found it easily. As expected, a long, thin package wrapped in a folded builder's sheet was stowed under the lowest scaffold. I reached down and picked it up, immediately feeling the all-too-familiar shape of an M40A5 sniper's rifle in my hands. The outline of the chunky McMillan stock and slender length of the 25-inch stainless barrel were almost comforting as I ran my fingers along the coarse material. They were also proof that Ascardi's financing of the building's restoration gained his people unrestricted access.

Suddenly, I heard the distant sound that had plagued me all day. A sniper's worst nightmare. The beating of the chopper blades was getting louder, each rotation doing my head in a little more. I had a sense of being hemmed in by the deadly birds of prey that hunted overhead. Climbing under the scaffolding, I lay down flat on my stomach and waited. If they spotted me, I would have no means of defense. Vulnerability defined. I waited some more. Eventually, the chopper passed above and the threatening sound of its roaring engines and palpitating blades faded.

Feeling exposed, I climbed toward the eastern edge of the roof, overlooking the Piazza San Marco. The elaborate facade on this side of the building rose above the edge of the rooftop, providing good cover from the balcony and piazza below.

I looked down at the balcony. Four armed polizia marksmen lined the balcony's width. All of them held high-powered rifles, but their eyes scanned the piazza below rather than the rooftop above and behind them.

I turned back and inspected the area behind me. A professional shooter's greatest concern was being ambushed while lying in wait for his prey. This environment did not encourage me in any way.

If I was lucky enough to evade the choppers overhead and the marksmen on the balcony below, there was still every chance the roof would be inspected before the prime minister's appearance. Directly behind me, steep steps climbed to a door into one of the mammoth domes, allowing access to the roof and a plain view of my back.

My only hope was that security services had already secured the building roof and then locked the door from the inside. Hopefully, no one would see the need to open it again to reexamine the skyline. Either way, I'd still have to take precautions.

With a little under two hours to wait, I needed to find a position that allowed me a full view across the piazza without being seen. To my left I saw that the contour of the roof contained two smaller pitches. I crawled up over the first section and kept going until I was in the shadow of the second pitch. From there you could still overlook the piazza below but not be seen from the dome doorway. I had found my hide.

I climbed into position. The first job at hand was to check my weapon. I pulled the rifle out of the old builder's sheet, inspecting the parts I could access. The gun appeared well serviced and maintained. I hadn't expected otherwise. I removed the detachable Schmidt & Bender Police Marksman 16 x 50 scope, which would act as my binoculars without exposing the gun's barrel until necessary. I then pulled out the box magazine: one round. Ascardi had stuck to his word.

Again I heard the familiar beat of helicopter blades. Now was a good a time as any to test the camouflage capability of my hide. I laid the rifle into the gutter a little way back from the facade. Positioned in the shadow of the gutter, I hoped that from the air the gun would look like one long line among a series of other long lines. Shrinking into the corner behind the facade, I covered myself in the white builder's sheet, its color closely matching the iron roof and the stone building. I was about to see if it matched enough. If the chopper crew saw me, I had nowhere to go.

Once again I heard the helicopter coming closer. Thirty seconds later it hovered directly above me. The bird's downdraft pumped air down, causing the edges of my hide to begin to flap; I grabbed at them. Between its pulsing blades and whining engine, the chopper's piercingly loud presence resonated menacingly across the rooftops. I could hear nothing but the bird's mechanical caterwauling as I pulled myself tight, bracing myself for bullets to enter my body. Surely, they'd seen me.

From under my sheet I glanced toward the balcony below. One of the marksmen raised an arm, signaling something—I couldn't tell what—to the chopper crew above. I clenched my fists and huddled further into a ball; any second now the pain would come.

A period of somewhere between a few seconds and an eternity dragged past, then I heard the pitch of the helicopter engines change. At first the throbbing noise grew even louder, deafeningly so. Then I realized, as the sound grew deeper, that more power was being applied. The bird was slowly moving off. The marksman must have been giving them the all clear. Nicholas Sharp, invisible man.

There was nothing to do but wait … and pray. Just as well I was at church.

Chapter 31

Now it was a game of patience. Snipers often wait hours, minimizing movement and staying alert for their prey lest they become someone else's. The real challenge, however, was to retain focus and tranquility.

Once I had scoped out the piazza below, I formulated the distance and trajectory to different locations around the square. I didn't know exactly where my target would be positioned, so I had to cover all possibilities. Truth be told, I didn't even know who my target would be.

I calculated the wind's velocity. The breeze blew directly off the Adriatic Sea, across the lagoon, and between the buildings either side of the northern section of the piazza. The distance wasn't huge, but the wind was erratic like that of an inland lake. This would not be an easy shot.

Having taken every precaution, my mind began to wander as I looked down at the crowded piazza.

Everyone has a tipping point. The line where logic descends into emotion. What had pushed Antonio Ascardi over the edge to the point he would condemn many of these innocent people to death?

The entrepreneur had achieved success beyond most people's imaginations. If you believed him, he'd done it his way. Not many can say that. His obsession with technicality and detail buttressed his talent for seeing a bigger picture. Together with his savviness for business, this unique skill set formed the foundation of his vast empire. What more could a man like that need?

Yet something had triggered him or perhaps triggered a dormant psychosis within him, or maybe it was never particularly dormant, just concealed, like a privacy setting hiding some forbidden content away from public view.

Could a man live with being that conflicted?

I laughed to myself. Take a look in the damn mirror, Sharp.

There must have been a trigger. Financial? Possible but unlikely; the man was obscenely wealthy. Who could touch him in that way? His sister's death? That seemed possible, although I didn't understand why that would have driven the light away so completely.

I thought about everything that had happened up to this point. Sure, Ascardi had instigated some dreadful events and laid the blame at my doorstep, but there was more to this; it wasn't just about me. I knew it. Men like Ascardi conventionally have a higher purpose, yet Antonio Ascardi wasn't, and had never been, a conventional man; his words at the Teatro La Fenice revealed that his goals were certainly skewered, unconventional, obscured.

No matter what angles I considered, all the hypothetical deliberation in the world boiled down to one thing. I needed to stop him. One moment, one bullet.

I fought to refocus on the view before me. The piazza was filled with color and vibrancy: families with kids running around enjoying themselves; older tourists, taking the trip of a lifetime, savoring every moment in an exciting and unique environment; locals earning their living, performing the tasks they performed every day, serving coffee, selling tickets, guiding tours. A litany of life's stories. I wanted to yell down to them, "Run now and keep running." Abruptly, a vision flooded my reality—an explosion, desperate screams, blood splattered chairs and tables, mutilated corpses.

There could be no warning anybody.

The decision. I had to decide where to consign my bullet. Ascardi was a clever man; whatever I decided he would find a way to make his plans come to fruition. I was sure of that. So, the logical choice was to take Ascardi out, put an end to it.

I looked down across the piazza. Which families, which children would I be sentencing to death by doing that? I couldn't do it ... I wouldn't do it. Anger and frustration seethed through me like poison from a viper. What could I do? Murder an elected prime minister? No, not in me ... or was it? If it meant saving lives ...

Was there a way to take out Fontana and his sidekick? I could see several cafés and ristorantes. I didn't know which one Fontana would be seated at. I was certain he'd be in view, so he would have a view. I'd get a clean shot, but only one bullet ... for two men, Fontana and Domenico. It wouldn't work that way.

Again, let the anger grow. I would control it, but it would also empower me. How dare this malfeasant force me into this position?

I realized I was so focused on doing what I couldn't do that it prevented me focusing on identifying what I could do. Think forward. I scanned every corner of the piazza. An answer would be out there. I just had to find it.

Minutes went past. Helicopters flew overhead three more times. Each time I grew more confident about my concealment. With each passing moment I could feel the pressure rise. Keep scanning.

The crowds were building now. Word was out. Groups of people were milling around hoping to get a glimpse of the prime minister as he entered or left the basilica.

Then there he was, Italy's top politician, surrounded by men in dark suits—I guess it's the same the world over. The prime minister strode across the piazza toward the basilica. Antonio Ascardi was walking beside him. My instructions were to shoot after the inspection of the restorations, not before. I still had time, but if there was an answer out there, it evaded me.

The crowd thinned out a little after the PM entered the building. From my position, I could see thirty yards in front of the basilica but not the entranceway itself. Ascardi would know that and position the prime minister accordingly when the time came.

Sure enough, ten minutes later security personnel were laying out sections of sturdy metal fencing, each section linked to form two opposing L shapes. They created a laneway and staging area for the VIPs and crowd control barriers for the media and public in preparation for the "impromptu" press conference.

I raised my scope, still covered by the builder's sheet, and scoured the cafés and restaurants around the piazza's perimeter. It took three minutes to locate Norbert Fontana and Domenico. They were at a café at a forty-five-degree angle across the piazza from me, on the north side. It was a fair shot, around four hundred feet; I could make it, although there was no point. Two men, just one bullet.

Don't get frustrated. Think.

Fontana was pulling out a chair for Aislinn. She'd have no idea what was at play here. Then Patrick Jay appeared from the shadow of a nearby portico and pulled up a chair at the table.

The scene was set. I was about to become the lead actor. I kept searching. There must be a way … look, think, imagine.

The makings of an idea trickled into my head. It wasn't much, but maybe there was a chance, a tiny, remote possibility that I could turn this around.

Remote as it was, there was nothing else.

I knew what I had to do.

Chapter 32

I looked at my watch yet again. It was nearly time. If everything was running on schedule, there was only about ten minutes to go. I studied the position where I estimated the prime minister and Ascardi would be standing. Thanks to the barriers, the location was obvious and I'd be able to get a clean shot.

I raised my scope to have one last look across the piazza where Fontana was sitting with Domenico, Aislinn, and Patrick Jay. Fontana had been smart. He was positioned on the side of the table furthest from me. I couldn't see his phone. I assumed it was either in his pocket or positioned in front of him on the table. Domenico was sitting across from him. So, although I could see Fontana's head quite clearly, Domenico's body was between me and the phone, if indeed the phone was on the table.

Aislinn and Patrick Jay were seated either side of Fontana. I assumed he thought them to be some kind of insurance. If so, he'd underestimated me, and my accuracy. Nevertheless, Domenico's presence at the table was the insurance.

I studied the dimensions of the table and distance between chairs over and over again. Then I closed my eyes and saw the picture in my head. I opened them again and checked my accuracy. I repeated the process twice more. I did the same for the position on the piazza just behind the security barriers where a microphone had now been set up. The media was gathering behind a barrier around ten feet away, but my shot was still clean.

I had a clear shot at everyone.

With five minutes to go, I reaffixed the scope to the rifle. I drew the rifle under the cover of the builder's sheet and pointed it toward the piazza. I kept the barrel back, hidden behind the facade. When the time came, in a couple of minutes, I'd rest it there, but there was no need to expose myself in that way yet.

I moved the rifle backward and forward, scoping the barriers, then the café. I couldn't help but notice the hundreds of people across the piazza as I scanned. The innocents.

Then it was time. The rise in noise of the crowd immediately below me told me something was about to happen. The prime minister and Ascardi strolled into view. The PM was smiling and shaking hands as he walked toward the microphone, ever the politician.

I pushed the rifle out and rested it on the ledge of the facade, still scanning my targets. Ascardi had been meticulously explicit; there would only be a small window to make the shot. The café, the PM, Ascardi, Fontana, back and forth.

I let the builder's sheet slip off. I needed to feel the breeze to fine-tune my calculations.

I slowed my breathing, found my rhythm.

"Sharp, don't move, not even a bit." I recognized the voice of Jasper De Vries.

Shit.

"I'll need to put the rifle down," I said. My brain was jolted into turmoil, urgently scrambling for a solution.

"Slowly, then turn around, again slowly."

I laid the rifle down, slowly, and turned around.

De Vries stood in a variation of the Weaver stance: feet wide apart, one perched slightly forward, an allowance made for bridging the roof pitch. His pistol was held in a two-handed grip, the trigger hand slightly forward. The barrel pointed directly at my torso. I'd used the same stance before. Textbook.

"De Vries, if I don't take a shot here, innocent people—civilians—are going to die." I knew there was zero chance of him believing me, but I had to try.

"I am not a fool, Sharp. Do you think I will stand back while you assassinate this country's head of government?" he replied.

"I can only tell it like it is," I said. I figured he was around six feet away from me. It always seems much further when someone is pointing a gun at you.

"Carefully climb slowly to your feet and move toward me, away from the rifle," De Vries instructed.

"As you say." I followed his instructions. The seconds were ticking away, too quickly. If the prime minister and Ascardi stepped out of range, the next sound we heard would be an explosion.

"One last time, man, listen to what I'm saying. Ascardi has a bomb planted somewhere in the piazza. People will die!" My voice sounded terse and reeked urgency, but the agent just didn't get it.

"Keep moving slowly toward me." I felt the harshness of his stare almost challenge me to act. Defiance. Clearly, he believed nothing I said.

I didn't know what to do. One unexpected move and I'd be shot.

So, I made an unexpected move.

Trying to appear like I slipped on the steep angle of the roof, I fell forward. As I went down, I pushed back with my feet on the gutter that ran between the two rooflines and sprung forward toward the agent. It was a desperate move, but desperate was all I had. De Vries adjusted his aim, but before he could fire, I wrapped my hands around his right ankle and yanked hard. Despite his professional stance, he had balanced himself precariously with a foot either side of the pitch, so he went down quickly, hitting the hot surface of the roof with a massive thud.

The agent's gun slipped from his hands. For a fraction of a second I was tempted to reach for it when I felt the force of a freight train pound the side of my face. Except it wasn't a freight train, it was a well-calculated punch from a professional who was trained to do this for a living. The blow left me dazed, but high on adrenaline, it would take more than one punch to stop me. Then he did it again. The agent connected with the same spot on my face, sending waves of sharp pain through my head. My only remaining semi-coherent thought was Don't let him get the gun.

Through my blurry fog of vision, I saw his outline rise above me, a dark silhouette against the bright sun. His elbow was drawn, fist clenched. I knew then he didn't need a gun; his fist was going to be the weapon that neutralized me.

As the punch powered toward me, I rolled frantically to the right. De Vries' fist glanced off my left arm. Normally, that would have been a win, but he connected with my wound, sending another round of agony my way.

The last blow had cost De Vries his balance. Things had suddenly become messy, both of us sluggishly trying to land a definitive blow and struggle for a foothold at the same time. We rolled over the roof together in a clenched embrace. De Vries' face was a picture of intensity, and I expected mine looked like an abstract portrait soaked in blood. I managed to free my right arm and lunge a panic-driven blow to his left temple. I didn't wait for a reaction and hit him in the same place again. The agent hadn't been able to get either arm out from under me to retaliate. He grunted in frustration. Suddenly, the grunt turned into a war cry as his right arm broke free. I made a grab for it, but he swept it out of my reach, leaving me no chance to block his impending blow. The war cry ended with De Vries' elbow landing a crushing blow to my windpipe. Gasping desperately for air, I tried to break free.

I couldn't breathe, I couldn't find air. Now on his knees, De Vries wrenched his other hand free. He was on top of me and punching each side of my head, my face turning to rubber. I found what little strength I had left and headbutted him between the eyes. He looked startled. The expression spurred me on. I punched the side of his face quickly, three times in succession. De Vries was moving slower now; he started to roll off me, not by choice. I punched him again and then shoved my palm into his shoulder, wrestling his body off mine. He put out an arm to stop himself but must have miscalculated. His head hit the roof with an almighty whack.

Not wanting to repeat the agent's previous mistake, I immediately hoisted myself up and over him. The movement shot pain from my wound into my shoulder, but I knew if

I stopped now this man wouldn't give me an opportunity to start again. I balled my fists and hit him hard in the face, again and again, alternating hands. He was too stupefied to react meaningfully. A few light blows glanced off me. I was sure each blow I delivered with my left hand caused me as much pain as him. He continued to struggle under my weight, clearly surprised that our roles had been reversed. I suspected the blow to his head from the roof had done me a big favor, but I wasn't stopping to assess the situation.

I honestly don't know how many times I hit De Vries, but I was certain I stopped when he lost consciousness.

I wasn't far from that state myself, but there was no time for self-pity. The fight with the agent had taken too long, yet I hadn't heard the expected explosion. Wondering if there was a chance the PM may still be in sight, I clambered down the roof, grabbing the rifle with one hand. I cautiously peered over the edge.

The PM and Ascardi were still talking to the press, but they looked like they were finishing up. The politician was stepping away from the microphone, and his minders had moved in closer, preparing to surround their charge. Ascardi looked nervous. He even risked a glance up in my direction.

I rested the rifle on the top of the facade. No choppers yet. Unable to fly low and interrupt the press conference, they may have missed my tango with De Vries. My head was throbbing, my vision was still blurred, and I was breathing heavily. A deadly trifecta for a sniper attempting to take a shot.

I got back into position. I had the prime minister in my sight, then Ascardi, then the table where Fontana sat. Nothing had changed.

After three deep breaths I concentrated on slowing my erratic breathing into a steady, even rhythm.

The prime minister began to move away from the press. Ascardi looked worried. I figured I had less than ten seconds to make the shot. Keeping the PM in sight, I reached into my pocket and pulled out my phone. I fumbled with the pad as I searched for the number I wanted. I found it and pressed dial. Then I put the phone on speaker and sat it down on the roof next to me.

Now I had both hands on the rifle. My breathing was slower; I had some control. It was all about control. Deep breath in, pause, out, pause, repeat.

The phone stopped ringing and a familiar voice answered. "Sharp?"

I had banked everything on this moment, and on the curiosity of human nature.

"Sharp, what the hell? Why haven't you ..."

I moved my sight from the PM to Fontana's table.

I saw Fontana doing exactly as I'd hoped. As he spoke into the phone, he looked up over Domenico's shoulder toward my position. It was the natural thing to do. As he turned toward me, the phone that he clutched to his ear came into view.

Breathe out, pause, squeeze the trigger.

The shot reverberated across the piazza as I felt the rifle kick back. Some people turned in my direction, others ran or went to ground. I kept the rifle to my eye long enough to see the phone shatter in Fontana's hand, taking parts of his hand and ear with it.

I paused for less than two seconds to take in the chaos below me. The PM's security had instantly surrounded their master. In a huddle, they began to cross the piazza away from the basilica. Ascardi was left behind, his face creased with fury. I wasn't surprised he was so visibly upset that I had messed with his carefully detailed plans. In truth, his reaction pleased me. Experience had taught me that angry people were more prone to mistakes, and I needed him to start making some. I didn't look back to the table at the café; I'd heard the screams.

People were starting to point toward the basilica's roof. Interestingly, Ascardi was not one of them.

I looked up; the helicopters had turned around and were heading in my direction. I was now way too exposed. I had almost no chance of making it off the rooftop alive and even less of escaping the polizia and security swarming the piazza.

My only faint hope was misdirection. I moved over the pitch of the roof to where Agent De Vries was still lying unconscious. I pocketed the Sig Sauer P226 that was laying close to his unmoving body. Frisking the agent, I took his Europol ID out of his wallet and put it in mine. I felt bad for him as I laid the rifle down and placed it in his right hand. For De Vries' sake, I hoped the marksmen in the choppers wouldn't shoot an unconscious man.

One last glance down at the piazza. Ascardi ran toward the water's edge on the western side near the Doge's Palace. I turned and clambered across the basilica roof.

The chase was now on. Nicholas Sharp, the hunter, back on familiar ground.

Chapter 33

I sprinted toward the doorway leading from inside the basilica. After climbing the ladder, I opened the door and entered the building. It was vital for me to get to the polizia before they got to me. As I stood on the internal walkway looking down into the church, I heard the clatter of boots making their way up to my position. It was time to take the initiative. I looked like I'd just been in a fight, so I'd make that work for me.

I yelled, "Up here! At the door leading to the roof!" I ran toward the row of uniformed men who had just come into sight and were running toward me. Their stern faces and determined expressions suggested they were there to do a job, no matter what or who got in the way. I held out the Europol agent's ID in front of me. "De Vries, Europol. There was a fight. He's out there on the roof, unconscious."

The polizia stopped for a moment. Their weapons were drawn, but they hesitated.

A tall, broad-shouldered officer, clearly the man in charge, moved to the front of the group. He eyed me up and down. This wasn't going to go my way.

"I'm working with Ispettore Davide Romana of the Polizia di Stato. Call him now," I continued. I then pointed to the door. "The suspect is out there, go … now, before he comes to!"

Nothing.

Then the radio on the officer's shoulder crackled, "Target down, up on the basilica roof. He is armed but appears unconscious."

That seemed to do it. "You stay here," said the senior cop, poking me in the chest. "Rossi, you stay with him," instructed the officer to one of his younger subordinates. Then the group swarmed past me toward the door.

I waited until they were out of sight and then turned to the young officer. "Rossi, is it?" I asked.

"Yes, Sir."

Not for the first time in the last few days I looked a law enforcement officer directly in the eye and apologized.

"I'm so sorry, Rossi," I said. I clenched the Sig Sauer in my pocket.

His face expressed bewilderment as I flipped it around so the butt was pointing out of my grip.

"What for, Sir?"

"This, I'm afraid."

In one swift movement I produced the weapon and brought it down hard on the back of the young officer's head. I caught him as his knees buckled and lowered him to the floor. I didn't like cold cocking anybody, never mind a law officer. He would certainly have a headache when he came to, maybe even concussion. I guiltily prayed for nothing more.

Without further hesitation I bolted down the basilica stairs and out the giant front doors, waving the Europol ID ahead of me as I ran.

I couldn't believe that no one stopped me.

Ascardi had a head start, and he was aided by the fading evening light and public confusion. The piazza was in disarray; no one really knew what had just happened, so people were panicked. Parents were clutching their kids' hands and heading out of the area, and a blue stream of polizia swamped the vast space as shopkeepers and restaurateurs closed their shutters. I was halfway across the piazza, running toward the water, when I caught a glimpse of the entrepreneur through a gap in the panicked crowd. He was way too far ahead. Standing at the southern end of the square, at the edge of the stone quay by the water, he was embroiled in an intense-looking conversation on his cell phone. If he turned right, he would be heading for either his house or the Aman hotel. If he turned left, I figured he would head toward the unknown location we'd been looking for.

He did neither. An expensive-looking launch, not dissimilar to the one I had arrived in, pulled up in front of him. He stepped off the dock, straight onto the boat's stern.

I kept running, but I knew I had no chance. The launch took off as quickly as it had arrived. The boat was a hundred yards out by the time I got to the water's edge. In the half-light I could just make out the figure of Ascardi's other offsider from La Fenice at the wheel.

I turned and ran along the quay toward the place I'd left my boat a few hours earlier. I yelled and shoved and pushed people out of my way. This would come down to a matter of seconds.

Thankfully, the boat was still there, waves lapping at its sides. I jumped down, pulled the keys out of my pocket, and started the engine. Running frantically back to the stern port cleat, I slipped the rear rope. Climbing back into the cockpit,

I leaned over the windscreen and threw off the forward line. I then pulled back hard on the throttle, reversing quickly, making the boat's stern cut into the chop behind. Once turned about, I centered the wheel and pushed the control forward to full.

As the waters of the Bacino di San Marco opened up before me, it was clear that I had a lot of distance to make up. I powered forward, my boat jumping onto a fast plane over the waves as they sprayed showers of saltwater around me. Ascardi's boat was now just a speck in the distance.

Five minutes into the chase my confidence began to grow. My boat's speed across the water was rapid; the previously purring engines howled in mechanical stress. It was hard to be certain, but I seemed to be gaining on the craft ahead.

Then I looked up toward the horizon; what I saw in the distance eliminated any hope I had felt.

A thick bank of fog had descended right down onto the water. It was as though a dark, gray fortress wall had appeared out of nowhere and Ascardi's boat was headed straight for it.

For a good seven or eight minutes we remained in formation, my boat's engine still screaming as I pounded across the waves. Spray lashed my eyes, but I kept focused on the boat ahead. Distances across water can be deceptive. I was uncertain how far away the wall of fog really was. I pulled De Vries' gun out of my pocket. I steered with one hand as I lined up my shot with the other. If I could get close enough to make the shot, I could maybe even just hit the fuel tank and slow Ascardi down. Probably another minute or so and I would have a chance ... thirty seconds ... I raised the gun ... the stern was almost within range ... I would make it.

Then Antonio Ascardi's boat disappeared. All I saw ahead

of me was the gray wall of rolling mist. I had lost him.

I shut down the throttle and turned off the engine, hoping to catch the sound of Ascardi's motor to guide me. Nothing—only the lapping of waves on the boat. I must have sat there for several minutes. I saw no reason to do anything else.

The quiet was broken by the sound of a ringing cell phone, mine. I'd forgotten that I'd left it on after calling Fontana from the basilica rooftop. "Yeah," I said. It was Greatrex.

"Well?" he sounded anxious.

"I'm fine," I said, "but it's over, and not in a good way."

"What do you mean?"

I told him all that had happened.

"Are Aislinn and Patrick Jay all right?" I asked.

"Yeah. I did just as we discussed. I was close to Fontana's table but out of sight. It got interesting after your shot. Blood everywhere, Fontana screaming his head off. The only calm person was Domenico. When he realized the cell phone was out of action, he grabbed Aislinn by the arm and led her to a side alley."

"So, as we thought, Ascardi wanted her there for insurance in case something went wrong," I said.

"Yep."

"I'm assuming from your calm demeanor that you took care of Domenico and that Aislinn is safe," I said.

"Well, yes and no. Don't worry: Aislinn is fine and Domenico is having a long rest, tied to a mooring pole under a bridge."

"But?"

"But it wasn't me who took him out. Do you have any idea of the power behind the swing of a long wooden didgeridoo when swung by a very upset Australian?"

"Patrick Jay?"

"Indeed. When he saw the way Domenico manhandled Aislinn, he didn't hesitate," said my friend.

"That's great," I said, imagining the scene in my head. "But still, we've lost our man. There is no way to find him. I think I'd better just turn the boat around and go back and turn myself in to the authorities."

"Bullshit," said Greatrex.

"What do you mean?" I asked.

"I mean, I've seen you do some pretty stupid things, but I've never seen you give up."

Greatrex was right. Giving up had never been my way. Still, I just sat there, staring into the darkness.

"So, I have no idea where the hell Ascardi has gone. There is Lido, there are islands all over the place, or he could have doubled back to the mainland." My voice sounded tired and empty. "Suggestions?"

The phone was silent.

"Who could possibly know where Ascardi's base may be?" asked Greatrex eventually.

I said nothing, I had nothing.

"I'll get onto the General," said Greatrex. "We'll see if he can source any ideas of a location that Ascardi is tied to in some way."

"Okay," I said. "I'll head to Lido and make myself scarce until I hear from you—" I stopped mid-sentence. "Lido, the shed ... I know a man who will know Ascardi's place," I felt hope rise in my gut. It was a welcome sensation. "He may not want to tell me, but he'll know."

"Nicholas, are you all right?" asked the big fella. "Nick ..."

"We'll talk," I said. I reached down, restarted the engine, pushed down on the throttle, and headed, far more quickly than was safe, in the direction of Malamocco.

Chapter 34

"Cosa vuoi, what do you want?" said the huge man opposite me, his tone agitated and aggressive.

We were standing in the kitchen of the small farm cottage on Lido. I had burst through the door and surprised him while he was preparing his evening meal. Half-sliced vegetables were scattered across the table, and water bubbled on the primitive stove. The knife in his hand and the boiling water on the stove were potential weapons, but I still felt confident, if only because I was pointing Jasper De Vries' Sig Sauer directly at the big man's chest.

"I need information, quickly," I said. "Put the knife on the table and sit down over there." I motioned with the gun to a chair at the end of the large kitchen table, away from the knife and the stove.

The giant sat down.

"Why should I tell you anything? The last thing you did to me was smash me unconscious when I untied you. Go to hell, cretino!"

The big man leaned forward, looking as though he was going to stand up.

"Just after you did the same thing to me. Now sit. I don't want to shoot you, but I will. Lives are at stake."

The man in front of me stared straight into my eyes, as if he was making his mind up. He scratched his beard, tilted his head to one side and then announced, "I do not trust you."

I didn't blame him.

"And I don't trust you," I replied.

A moment of silence.

"Look, I'm sorry about what happened before," I said. "There was no choice. I meant you no harm, but I couldn't let you contact Norbert Fontana."

After docking the boat in a small canal at Malamocco, I'd spent the fifteen-minute ride here on a stolen bicycle thinking about how to approach this meeting. Deception had worked when we'd met, less than forty-eight hours ago, but honesty was now my best chance. "I don't blame you for not trusting me, but you need to know I'm not the bad guy in all of this."

"I will give you two minutes to state your case. After that, gun or no gun, I will upend this table and deal with you."

I could tell he meant what he said, so I explained everything. Ascardi, Fontana, the explosion in Paris, the nuclear power station in Scotland, the assassination of the British chancellor, the murders in Füssen, and the shooting in the Piazza San Marco. I left nothing out.

The big man sat in silence, but the kitchen table was still on its legs.

Again, his head tilted, and he stared straight into my eyes. Judgment day. "That's quite a story. I suppose it may even be true." The big man paused. Then he said, "I never liked Fontana. When he came here and found me tied up the way you had left me, he was angry, more than angry, enraged. He didn't give a shit about me. My dog wouldn't stop barking at him, so he kicked the dog, hard."

I could see the anger flaming in the giant's eyes.

"The dog is still at the vet, but he will be all right. I don't trust people who are needlessly violent toward animals. You will think that stupid. Whatever ..."

I sat silently. If I made any platitudes, this man would see right through them.

The giant seemed to be talking to himself now, as if I wasn't there. "I suppose you did show some concern, some humanity—the water and all that."

More silence.

"All right, I will take the risk and trust my gut." The giant reached out his hand, "I am Giuseppe Santoro. American, you can call me Joe."

I stood up, feeling the relief coursing through my veins. I put the gun down on the table between us and offered him my hand. "Nicholas Sharp."

"Now, Nicholas Sharp, you think I know where Fontana and his boss, this Antonio Ascardi, have their hideout?"

The term "hideout" was a little too Wild West for me, but all I could say was, "Yes, I'm hoping you do."

Joe Santoro then offered a wry smirk, the mistrust in his eyes had vanished. "Well, you're in luck, my new friend. I know exactly where your Signor Ascardi will be, but you are not going to like it."

"What do you know about the Black Plague?" asked Santoro. He was making us both a strong coffee. I was acutely aware of time pressing down on me, but I couldn't push him. I knew Ascardi would react badly to Fontana's shooting. With all his resources, both technological and financial, he would have a plan B. I had to get to him quickly, but any competent marine gathers intelligence before acting.

Besides, I needed the coffee.

"I know the plague wiped out huge parts of the population of Europe, including Italy," I replied.

"Well, in this area everyone who had the plague or was even suspected of having the plague was shipped off to Poveglia Island."

"Poveglia?"

"It's about half a mile that way," said Joe Santoro, gesturing with his thumb over his right shoulder.

"That's where you believe Ascardi has some sort of base?"

"I know it. I know it because I have seen Fontana and his men head directly to the island from the shore near the shed where they store their equipment."

"Tell me about the island," I asked. "I presume you've been there?"

Joe's laugh was hearty but brief. Then his face grew taut, his expression serious. "Very few locals have been to Poveglia," he said.

"Why? It's so close."

"There is a lot more to the island's troubled story," continued the giant. "As well as a plague graveyard, the place was also an insane asylum. It is rumored that doctors performed illegal lobotomies, experimenting on and torturing patients. They say sometimes you can still hear their screams at night."

I couldn't help but chuckle to myself. "This sounds like a scene out of a B-grade horror movie," I said. "Surely, no one takes it seriously."

Joe Santoro's face seemed strained. He brought a huge hand to his jaw and rubbed it, as if wiping away the tension. His eyes became focused and intense.

"Nicholas, I can see why you would be skeptical, but you must trust me. What I say is true. Over 150,000 souls have died on that godforsaken island. They say the soil is fifty percent human remains. Poveglia is the most haunted island in Europe. It is illegal to even set foot on it. Only a fool would try."

I was taken aback by the conviction in my new friend's voice.

"Who owns the island?" I asked.

"A few years ago, the government sold it off to pay down debt. It has changed hands a couple of times. Once they've been to the island, no new owner wants to hold onto it."

I sat back in my chair and sipped the much-needed coffee. It was smooth but with an unexpectedly raw bite. I waited, hoping Joe Santoro would laugh and tell me this was all a joke at my expense. But he didn't.

The more I thought about it, the more it made sense. What better location for Antonio Ascardi than an island protected by a sinister history. It was the best security available … fear.

"I need to go there," I said. "I need to go to Poveglia."

Santoro was silent. He was a man who thought before he spoke. His face etched with concentration, I could tell he was making up his mind about something.

Eventually: "Hell," he said, "I will take you. We will go in my rowboat. A quiet approach. I'm not having you get lost in that mist."

"I can go alone," I said.

"From what you have told me about these people, it would be foolish to go alone. I will come," he responded.

I thought of Greatrex, but he wouldn't get here in time.

Then the giant surprised me. "If I have inadvertently helped them, then I need to help you take them down."

I nodded.

"Besides," Santoro continued, "for the last twenty-four hours, ever since Fontana paid his last visit here along with that brute of an offsider and the girl, I have been trying to figure out a way to make him pay for injuring my dog. Perhaps he will be there, if he is out of hospital," the giant laughed.

I didn't laugh. "Girl, what girl?" I asked.

"Didn't I mention that? Yes, they had a girl with them. I hadn't seen her before. She was actually quite stunning, you wouldn't forget her. They took her to the island with them."

"Can you describe her?"

"Of course. As I said, she was the type you would remember. Long dark hair, a warm, sensuous face, but more than anything I remember her eyes. They were a deep, deep green. They were eyes that a man could get lost in."

Chapter 35

The mist hung low over the water. We couldn't see ten feet ahead of the bow. Joe Santoro was rowing in quiet, powerful strokes. I sat at the stern of the small boat, the passenger. Almost all sound was muffled by the thick fog. We could have been in the middle of the Atlantic.

"I hope you know where you're going," I said.

"You get to know your way in the mist," Joe responded. "Keep the waves at the same angle as they hit the boat and you're basically going in a straight line. We're headed directly for the island."

I was glad Joe had insisted on coming. I could have rowed around in this fog all night and gotten nowhere.

"How long till we get there?" I asked.

"About ten minutes."

I tried to focus on the task ahead. There was no certainty here about anything. Joe's description of the girl he had seen had only added more confusion. I tried to put it out of my mind.

Quietly, we slipped through the fog. Symbolic.

A few minutes later a shadow started to loom out of the misty darkness ahead of us. I could just make out the shapes of a low tree line, a long building, and then a tower. Their gradual revelation though the surrounding murkiness added mystery to the image. As we drew in closer, an even more foreboding sight was given form by the neglected appearance of the buildings, half fallen walls and whole sections swamped by vines from the surrounding bushland.

"There's a canal that runs between the two main sections of the island," said Joe. "We'll put in there, on the eastern side, furthest from the buildings. Do you expect any sort of guard?"

"There's a strong chance," I said. "Keep your eyes open."

We followed the island's misted silhouette to the east, low trees and thick scrub looming in the darkness. Joe maneuvered us into the canal, and the boat bumped against a stone bank that appeared from nowhere. We'd arrived.

I put a hand to my lips, motioning for Joe to be silent. The two of us sat there quietly, listening to a soundscape of rustling bushes, the unnervingly low-pitched whistle of a developing breeze, and waves pummeling the bank. Joe Santoro's stories of mass death and screams in the night hadn't spooked me, but I was now entering a zone beyond exhaustion. As I stumbled out of the boat onto the canal bank, I began questioning my ability to trust my senses. Was that crying voices I heard in the wind? Could I see the shadows of gaunt, skull-like faces staring back at us from the undergrowth? Nicholas Sharp, needing to get a grip.

Joe climbed up after me. He tied the boat to a large rock, and we both stood on the bank waiting, listening.

My cell phone vibrated in my pocket. I pulled it out: Greatrex.

"Nicholas, are you all right?"

"As safe as can be expected," I whispered, not wanting to

advertise our presence.

"I have news," said my friend. "The General did some digging. It appears he's got some very thorough researchers at his disposal."

"Go on."

"Well, they searched a litany of shell companies for any real estate linked to Ascardi. What they found was well hidden, but I think we've struck gold."

Greatrex paused, as though expecting a reaction. I just listened.

"It appears," he continued, "that Antonio Ascardi recently bought—"

"Poveglia Island," I interrupted.

"... How?"

"I'm standing on it." Nicholas Sharp, smart-ass.

"Hmph."

I looked up. Joe Santoro had moved along the water's edge, pointing with his flashlight to indicate he'd explore inland. He shone his beam over a narrow opening in the bushes and he slipped out of view. I let him go.

"Nicholas, there's more," said Greatrex.

"Okay, what have you got?" I asked.

"As you suggested, we've been looking for connections between Ascardi and the groups claiming those attacks. We found them: URLs connected to them, and money transfers to each group, all in Bitcoin and almost untraceable."

"Then we've got the how but not the why," I said.

"Yeah, but that's not all," replied Greatrex. The call was starting to fade a bit. Santoro had told me reception was bad on the island. I could only just make out what Greatrex was saying. "It appears that Ascardi also has URL links and funding arrangements with a host of other radical groups. A heap of them, right across the world."

"That can't be good," I said.

"No, not at all, especially when you factor in that, according to the General's people, traffic has heated up considerably between Ascardi and many of these groups over the last ninety minutes."

"That's worrying," I said.

"Nick, the General believes Ascardi's next move is going to be decisive, perhaps even catastrophic."

"Just as well someone's on the job," I said, feigning confidence I didn't feel. "Now, Jack, listen carefully, this is what I want you to do—"

The line died.

Nothing else for it, we were on our own—best keep moving. I made my way along the water's edge and turned left along the path I'd seen Joe take.

I quietly called the giant's name. No reply, just the unnerving low growl of the wind.

I walked along a little further down the gloomy track. "Joe, can you hear me?"

Nothing.

A moment later my heel caught something solid, the light ping of the sound suggesting it was metallic. I knelt down and shone my flashlight's beam on the object. Joe's own light was lying smashed and half buried in the ground. I flicked my beam off, welcoming the darkness.

Joe Santoro had just disappeared.

I left what there was of a path and started moving through the undergrowth, thinking the cover would make my detection more difficult. In the distance, the tower we had seen from the boat gradually appeared as a shadow through the mist. Using the top of the tower as a marker, I made my way toward it. Another lower building to the right of the tower appeared a couple of minutes later. I waited under the cover of the edge of the bushes, gazing fixedly at the buildings.

I was trained to use the darkness to my advantage, but without night-vision goggles I'd have to wait for my eyes to adjust. It took several minutes, but slowly the view before me materialized out of the shadows. The buildings were ancient and derelict. Vines had woven their way through crevices and along the crumbling walls. Nature was reclaiming this tragic settlement.

I could neither see nor hear any human activity.

I made my way carefully along the side of the first building and around the tower. A stone walkway ran between the next building and the water's edge. Someone had erected scaffolding along the wall, presumably to reinforce it. Briefly stopping to listen, I could again make out the now familiar slapping sound of the waves' persistent attack on the shoreline. The growl of the wind had strengthened and now whistled eerily through the scaffolding, but there was no other sound. At least nothing human.

Time was against me. I risked discovery if I moved too quickly now I'd left the cover of the woodlands. Nevertheless, in a few minutes I'd cleared the next two buildings and rounded a corner to the western side of the island.

I found nothing.

If Joe Santoro hadn't vanished, I might've given up at that point and returned to the boat. Nothing else suggested I was on Ascardi's trail.

Either way, the point was moot; I had nowhere else to go.

Logic told me the only approach was a methodical search through the buildings. Easy to say, but between the fog, the darkness of the ruined buildings, and the increasingly distracting tone of the wind, I was feeling decidedly uneasy. I forced myself to mentally discard Joe's stories about the island. But if there was nothing to those tales, why had the Italian government banned visits to the island?

It looked like the fog was beginning to wane. I pressed on.

I entered the closest building, feeling my way through the doorway and along the walls. It was a large structure, lined with crumbling brick walls. What little light there was came through the caged windows. The shadows of the bars punctuated the growing streams of moonlight that guided my search. The bars told the story—this must have been a prison at some point.

I searched from one end to the other, regularly tripping over fallen stonework and discarded furniture. There was no sign of human habitation. As I passed through a large doorway at the far end of the building, I found myself again surrounded by trees. I could make out another building almost totally overpowered by vines and undergrowth about ten yards away. I glanced at my watch and moved toward it. I had been on the island for around thirty minutes; this was taking way too long.

Speeding up as I pushed through the undergrowth, I almost bumped into the side of the next building. As the fog receded, the moonlight gradually intensified. A little extra light helped my search but also left me exposed. I stepped through the doorway into the building, again pausing to listen. The soundscape hadn't changed, and my nerves hadn't improved.

Moving along the side of the wall, I came to a large arched doorway. The old wooden doors hung precariously on their hinges. Because the roof was virtually non-existent, the moonlight shone on some broken framework, a couple of upturned chairs, and several piles of rubble.

Stepping through the doorway, I could make out a decrepit stone stairway to my left. I shuffled into the room. At least now, under the moonlight, I could avoid the obstacles scattered around the floor. Despite every effort to tread lightly, the sound of my feet crunching on broken stone resonated like splintering glass through the space.

The next room was large and wide. A pile of metal bed frames lay stacked untidily in a corner. I suspected this was the infamous asylum building. Pausing between steps, I made my way slowly across the length of the space.

Then I heard it, a scraping, metallic sound from a small room adjacent to the one I was standing in. I stopped and listened. A moment later I heard the sound again—no mistaking it. Choosing my foot placement carefully, I moved closer. Reaching the door, I poked my head around the corner.

The space before me appeared to be some sort of chapel. In the moonlight I could make out religious frescoes on what was left of the ceiling. The room was mostly empty and just as abandoned as all the others. Then I heard the metallic sound again.

I felt a cold chill on my skin as my senses jumped to attention. At the far end of the room, the shadow of a hooded figure slowly materialized out of thin air. The ghost of a lost soul?

Nicholas Sharp, losing the plot, again.

I stood, transfixed. The figure I was watching wasn't

appearing out of thin air, it was passing through a floor-level wooden trapdoor whose hinges voiced the cry of twisting, scraping metal as their unoiled components fought with each other for movement.

I welcomed back reality and backed out of the doorway, flattening myself against the stone wall that shielded me from the room.

Suddenly, a blinding white light flooded my vision; I couldn't see a damn thing.

Chapter 36

"Nicholas, you just don't give up, do you?"

I recognized the insistent tone of Antonio Ascardi.

I could just make out several shadows standing on the other side of the bright lights. One of them was obviously Ascardi. The two outer shadows made their way around the edges of the light and approached me. Each figure grabbed one of my arms.

Ascardi continued to speak. "Sadly, your penchant for curiosity has become unaffordable ... for both of us. Disarm him and bring him downstairs." He disappeared into the chapel's shadows.

One of the men moved behind me and held both my arms, the other one frisked me, removing my gun and knife. They pointed their powerful flashlights toward the doorway.

"Move," said the man behind me as he shoved me on my way. I had no chance of attempting an escape.

I was led into the old chapel and across to the trapdoor. No sign of the hooded figure. The man who had searched me reached down and opened the wooden door in the floor, revealing a steep ladder.

"Down," he said. Reluctantly, I descended.

The room I entered, a basement of some sort, was nearly the size of the two large rooms above us. Modern overhead lighting revealed three rows of computers and electronic equipment neatly organized into workstations. Several oversized screens strategically placed on stands around the room displayed a myriad of perpetually changing data. High-level technology contrasted with the aging stone walls and the enormous wooden rafters supporting the ceiling. Ascardi had put a great deal of thought and effort into creating this environment. It wasn't quite in the class of a Bond villain's lair, but it wasn't far behind.

There were four people in the room, spread out across the rows of computers, each focused on their work. Across the room stood Antonio Ascardi, absorbed by the tablet in his hand. No one looked up, no one said a word. It was as though I hadn't even walked in.

Eventually, Ascardi raised his head and spoke. "Nicholas Sharp, you have been a pain in the ass for much too long." Not for the first time the man smiled broadly with his mouth while his eyes retained the stony aloofness of a man detached from his emotions. "Your irritating efforts this afternoon have caused me some inconvenience, nothing more. You know I get really pissed on the rare occasions someone or something unforeseen disrupts my precisely conceived arrangements. I suspect you thought your wits had saved lives at the Piazza San Marco today. Now you are going to see that your recklessness will unwittingly cause the deaths of many more people. Absolutely unnecessary, if you ask me. If only you'd just done what you were told."

Unexpectedly, Ascardi's shoulders slumped. "You know, it's a shame, Nicholas. This is all so sad." The contrast in the man's demeanor was so severe it was like there were two life forces existing within him.

Just as abruptly as it arrived, the brow furrowed and the brief glimpse of light vanished from Ascardi's eyes as he spoke again. "Why don't you take a minute to savor your failure?"

I had no intention of taking a minute.

"Whatever you're planning, Ascardi, you must realize you now have no chance of achieving it." I refused to use the term "success." "After today, the authorities will be on to you. They will hunt you down. It's over." My words spoke more of bravado than confidence.

"Why? Why will they be after me?" he asked. "Surely by now, you understand that it is you that the authorities are pursuing, Nicholas. It is you who have been blamed for everything. Who would believe the word of a murderer and terrorist on the run?" Then he added, "That is if they had a chance to speak to you ... which they won't."

"By now Jack Greatrex will have spoken to the police and Europol," I said. "He will have told them about your location here, and whether they believe him or not, they will come to this island to check it out." I was on a roll here, quite the actor.

Ascardi hesitated, but it was just a show. He then allowed himself a smile. "About that," he said. Reaching into his pocket, he pulled out a cell phone, tapped on the keypad, and threw it to the henchman standing next to me. "Take a look," was all he added.

I looked down at the screen being held up before me. It showed Greatrex lying unconscious on a pile of ropes, presumably on a ship or boat. Blood seeped from his ear. I allowed myself no emotion.

"Is he dead?" I asked.

"Not yet, but he soon will be. He is on his way here to join you as we speak."

I felt a modicum of relief but didn't let it show.

"So, you can see, Nicholas, no one is coming to your rescue."

"What about the man who was with me, Joe Santoro?" I asked.

"Yes, that was unfortunate. He bumped straight into one of my patrols. He is also alive, albeit temporarily. Sadly, the three of you are all going to be sharing the same sad fate this very night."

I saw no need to ask what that fate was.

I felt my chest tighten as I fought to mask any external reaction. It wasn't fear but rather the familiar sensation of pungent acrimony flooding though me. "You're full of shit, Ascardi," I said.

The sides of his mouth drooped as his eyebrows raised in a feigned look of indignity.

"Men like you always end up the same way," I continued. "Dead and discarded. I may not be around to see it, but it's all going to end badly for you, eventually." I had made my statement.

This time Ascardi's face betrayed genuine despair; at first his lips pressed into a thin line, and then he momentarily dipped his head, avoiding my gaze. When he raised it again his jaw sagged noticeably as he tilted his head to one side—perhaps some sort of quizzical acceptance. "You may well be right, Nicholas, but I don't care." His response sounded despairingly genuine.

I didn't know what to say, so I said nothing.

"I can tell you are surprised by that, but you are probably

astute enough to know from my tone that I mean what I say."

I thought for a moment. I could see no real way out of this. Certainly not for Jack Greatrex, Joe Santoro, or myself. All I could do was play for time and hope something would turn up.

"All right, have your moment," I said. "Why don't you explain to me what this is really all about?"

Ascardi just looked at me, as though he was processing a decision, considering all options. He turned to the young tech-head working the station on his left. "Ricardo, how long do we have?"

The young man glanced up from his computer, his face masked with concentration. "We have at least ten minutes, Signor Ascardi," he announced.

Ascardi turned back to me. "All right, Nicholas, it doesn't really matter now, not from your viewpoint anyway. I can afford to spare you a few minutes more of my time; after all, you have tried *very* hard."

Talk about condescending.

"It may even be good for me to share," he continued. "I suppose that's what a therapist would say ... if I had one. You Americans love your therapy, don't you? I always thought the process a futile exercise in self-pity."

For a moment I thought back to my own therapist. She was waiting for me in my apartment overlooking Venice Beach in L.A. She only saw things in black and white, but her rigidity was delicately balanced by her ability to listen. Her counsel had proved effective in letting me purge my emotions and move on. Sadly, I thought it unlikely I would ever see her again. It was a shame: she was the best piano I'd ever owned.

Ascardi's words snapped me back to the present. "All right, so let's call this a morbid bedtime story about one man's disappointment and betrayal, if you catch my drift."

Bedtime story, I got it.

"Vincenzo," he said, speaking to the man beside me, "bring Sharp over here, where he can see the screens more clearly." He indicated a chair to the right of where he stood.

Vincenzo pushed me in that direction. I walked over and sat down.

"Elia," said Ascardi, looking at the man who had held me by the arms upstairs, "Please keep your gun trained on our visitor. It would appear that he is a sneaky one. Vincenzo, do the same."

So, I sat there, two weapons pointed at me, both out of reach—an impossible situation.

Ascardi began to talk.

Chapter 37

"Years ago, when I was young, it became clear to me, and to countless others, that technology's rapid development was going to provide a runway from which humanity could soar to new heights. The possibilities bouncing around in my head seemed endless. I knew there were pitfalls, but I thought that advancements in communication across the globe would save us from ourselves. The sixteen-year-old me imagined a space where people understood each other, the way each other thought, the way each other lived. Can you see it, Nicholas, a world where our differences—politics, religion, artificial borders—receded to the background, and our common goodness prevailed?"

I saw it, but I said nothing. John Lennon had seen it too.

"A few months into my university studies it became obvious to my teachers that I was gifted well beyond my peers, not only in my ability to write code but my capacity to envision and create what others thought impossible. Eighteen months into my studies I created a gambling algorithm that was failure-proof. Of course, the university shut me down. That type of creativity was unacceptable to them."

I just remained silent and nodded, knowing we would get to the point in the end.

"Stay with me, Nicholas. You need the backstory to understand the man, and I am trying to help you understand." After a short pause, the entrepreneur continued. "Word got out about the young genius studying in Rome. The corporates came after me. The money they offered was staggering for such a young man, but in the end the money was why I turned them all down."

My face must have shown my confusion.

"To explain a little further, it was these corporate jackals' obsession with money that repulsed me. I wanted to make a difference, not cash in. I presented my ideas to them; the concept of such a high level of technological communication in the hands of the people seemed worthless to them. There was no profit in it. The few who saw the potential viewed it as a threat to their own structures. In retrospect, my naivety was laughable."

I nodded, just wanting to keep him talking.

"Then, at my lowest point, I was approached by a man. He had heard about me and wanted to talk. More to the point he wanted to listen. I made my pitch, expecting nothing, of course, but his reaction caught me by surprise. He saw what I saw in the potential reach of social media platforms and offered me the seed funding to create a start-up. Without boring you with all the details, I disregarded my studies immediately; I already knew more than most of my teachers, so I began my journey."

Ascardi looked at me directly, again his head tilting and his smile becoming lopsided. "It was probably twelve months before I realized that my backers were the mafia. Even then it didn't bother me that much. I grew up in Sicily, where the mafia were often referred to as the Cosa Nostra. Did you know that the term translates as 'our thing'? That's exactly what many of my contemporaries thought of them as. A sort of people's shadow government. Again, the naivety ... Anyway, within two years it was obvious that my backers were only humoring me regarding my work on social media. It had been my gambling program that had caught their attention, and that was the area in which they wanted me to work. By then it was far too late—no one leaves the organization. I decided to do as they asked but still use their money to pursue my vision as a side project."

That certainly explained the General's questions over where Ascardi got his funding.

"Fast forward many years, Nicholas, and we come to the crunch. I had continued to appease my backers and had made them a great deal of money. The decision-makers high in the mafia hierarchy are not stupid people, but they are set in their ways, the old ways. Some of the younger leaders saw the potential of my work and encouraged it. The older dons, not so much. By the time they realized that my own personal power had reached a level that threatened theirs, I was ordered to shut down."

Once again Ascardi paused, gazed down to his feet, and then raised his head to look at me. It was almost as though each pause of conversation and downward turn of the head was a new act in the play, a costume change. In Ascardi's case, however, they were mood changes. When he looked up, his eyes were wide, his bearded chin projected forward, and his voice was low and menacing.

"The poor fools had no idea, not a clue. My power and influence had usurped theirs years earlier. They couldn't touch me. Obviously, I refused to comply. I was approached over and over again, each time steadfastly refusing to subjugate myself to them. At one point two of their most influential leaders, the capomandamenti, came to see me personally. They argued their case well and finished the discussion with a direct and ominous threat. But I mean really, what could they do to me?"

Head down, mood change.

"Vittoria," began Ascardi, "was a beautiful girl. My beloved sister had no malice and bore no one any animosity. She was not part of my business; she had no relationship with my sponsors. She had done nothing."

Another pause, deeper into the darkness.

"These bastards kidnapped her. They told me what they'd done and made the usual threats to bring me into line. I ignored them. I had the power and resources to find my sister. I was beholden to no one. I had complete confidence. A week later my beautiful Vittoria's body was dumped on my doorstep, like a pile of unwanted garbage."

Ascardi stopped talking and again looked to the ground. I could barely hear the man as he muttered "the arrogance."

I didn't know if he was referring to his or theirs, but there it was, the tipping point.

All I could say was, "I'm sorry."

The entrepreneur stared absently across the room. I couldn't guess what he was seeing. Then he resumed. "So, through the fog of my debilitating grief I began to strategize. There was no chance I was going to roll over for those cretinous morons who murdered my sister, but I had to consider my response. That was the hardest bit. I realized I would have to appear to acquiesce to their demands to give myself time to plan."

Again there was a pause in the story. I assumed Ascardi was

deciding how much to say. I'd assumed *incorrectly*.

"Ah, yes, I see from the pathos in your eyes that you now think this to be a case of an emotionally injured man whose grief has sent him into a downward spiral."

Ascardi had assumed *correctly*.

"I'm afraid that's only part of the story. You see, like anyone in deep mourning I began reflecting on my life and achievements. Looking at my success, you would think my self-assessment would have been positive. Sadly not. For the first time, my grief allowed me the clarity to see the way the world, people, had embraced my work. The sheer influence over millions, if not billions, of lives was gratifying. The effect of that influence was mortifying.

"People hadn't used the platforms I had given them to improve the world, to reach out to others. They used my technology and my vision to inflame their own vanities. Where people once sought success, they now only seek notoriety and attention. My social media platforms are full of people who have achieved absolutely nothing, displayed no talent, yet through me they stake a claim on celebrity and build influence over others. A complete moron expresses an ignorant opinion on social media, and suddenly it's a movement. A talentless model snaps a couple of stylish selfies, and suddenly they're an icon. Society has peaked, and we don't seem to realize. Every tower humanity has built will come crashing down in a valueless sea of moral corruption, and not only will it be our fault for doing nothing about it, it will be my fault for enabling it!"

Ascardi's breathing was becoming labored, and his voice fell into a deep rasp as he spoke. The man's thoughts spilled out of his mouth with an increasing tempo, such was the urgency of his passion.

"Then there's the politicians," continued the entrepreneur. "Our leaders. Our society, apart from a few glitches, has mostly sprouted strong leaders who had the integrity, passion, and fortitude to counteract those who breed evil. Leaders with vision—do you remember them, Nicholas? Churchill, Obama, Ardern. With despair in my heart, I tell you: that time has passed."

I was unconvinced, but I wanted Ascardi to keep talking. "In what way?"

"Power! Today these pissant leaders are only about power and optics. Politicians seek only to win the twenty-four-hour news cycle. There is no forward thinking, nothing beyond today's popularity and the next election. And of course, it is not lost on me that I was one of the entrepreneurs who empowered that same news cycle. I helped create the massive warping of reality we've currently labeled fake news, and now we can't tell what's real and what's not. If a politician decides global warming doesn't exist, that becomes his reality and that of his or her followers. That's the worst part, Nicholas. I've enabled a world of deception; we took the filters away and allowed ourselves to be our worst. You don't have to be a genius to realize the endgame here will be the destruction of the planet."

Ascardi was now breathing rapidly, his forehead glistening in a film of perspiration.

"So, there you have it. The one person I have ever truly loved, my beautiful Vittoria, died through my self-obsessive neglect and the duplicity of my colleagues. My life vision of a world enriched by communication is now on the verge of destruction, ruined by those to whom I had gifted my dream.

This is my legacy. Betrayal and disappointment ... beyond repair."

A moment's silence.

"I sought to protect, but in reality, I destroy. I think you know a little about that, don't you, Nicholas? Kindred spirits, perhaps?"

Sucker punch.

Chapter 38

The sound of the technicians pecking away on keyboards resonated in the background as I thought about all Ascardi had said. If the man before me hadn't murdered so many innocent people, I could have felt empathy for him. Even with that, it was hard not to feel something.

"I get it," I said, although I really didn't. "But how does everything that's happened over the last few weeks connect? I get the why but not the how."

"I have spoken too much already, so I'll be brief," replied Ascardi. "The attempt to trigger an explosion at the nuclear power plant in Scotland was simple. It also displays a pleasing duality. The company that owns the plant is largely underwritten by my own Italian backers. They have many hidden investments around the globe, including a great deal of money in fossil fuels and nuclear energy. Thirty years ago, the fools thought it would be a way to hold the future to ransom. The Cinaed explosion meant I would damage them financially. More to the point, it would have damaged the nuclear industry. The disaster would have been felt around the world, as with Chernobyl. One step forward for the planet."

And hundreds if not thousands of deaths, I thought silently.

Ascardi chuckled. "You know, even though, thanks to you, the detonation failed, there was a bonus outcome." He raised an eyebrow. "My media group was able to report the details of the attack before anyone else because I knew what was happening in advance. Food for thought, don't you think, Nicholas? Don't just report the news, create it as well. The ultimate media saturation."

I didn't respond.

"The rest is relatively straightforward. The British chancellor, the French politicians, the Italian prime minister, they were all hell-bent on curbing the powers of social media ownership. The fools were attempting to introduce regulations that would force the two or three most powerful influencers to divest interests, weaken our strength. They also wanted us to take some responsibility for the content on our platforms. As if we could change human nature."

"But if you wanted to make some restitution for what you'd created, wouldn't those regulations have helped you?" I asked.

"Way too little, much too late. The regulations would have only hampered me. This war needs to be waged by someone more powerful than mere countries. My plan involves a certain amount of public havoc, and yes, Nicholas, there will be some collateral damage. But your country knows all about that, doesn't it?"

I ignored the jibe. "So, the politicians who impeded your plans had to be murdered. Even your friends?"

"For heaven's sake, define 'friends'? In that sordid little world, every friendship has a purpose. My relationship with those men had become vacuous. In all honesty, I suspected their altruistic approach had little to do with good intentions anyway. A little covert digging, and it turned out all but one of them had either taken bribes from or were blackmailed by my mafia friends in their bid to diminish my influence."

"Even Gabriel Arquette?"

"No, he was the one exception. It was a shame. I'd known Gabriel for a long time, but he was a talker. Thanks to his perception of my success, people were beginning to question how I got started."

Brutal.

"Now I think I'm over-bragging here, Nicholas, but I've got to share the real kicker with you. I had invited the two senior mafia leaders, the capomandamenti, to meet me in Paris. Peace talks, if you like. I wanted them to think I was declaring a truce. We had a lovely dinner just before—"

"Just before you escorted them to box five at the Palais Garnier, the night of our concert."

Ascardi produced a glacial smile. "If that didn't send a message, nothing would."

I was starting to feel like Atlas with the whole damn world sitting on his shoulders.

"But what about all this?" I asked, waving my hand across the room.

"As is my way, I have sought and found alternative solutions. I really thought you and Jack Greatrex would have worked it out by now. Apparently not," he shrugged.

"By murdering people?" I asked.

"There is no other way."

I must have looked like an unbeliever, so Ascardi explained.

"Tonight, Nicholas, tonight will see my plans elevate to the next level. Take a look at that first screen." Ascardi indicated a large screen in front of the stone wall behind him. He tapped his keypad, and a list of names appeared:

THE NATURAL EARTH ARMY
THE UNION OF ISLAMIC FIGHTERS
THE GHOSTS OF THE REVOLUTION

"You recognize the names, I presume," he said.

I nodded.

"Yes, they are the groups who have claimed responsibility for the attacks in Scotland, London, and Paris. Of course, they are all my groups. When I say 'my', I should add that they all existed before I found them. I have spent two years scouring the world for malcontents whose ambitions exceeded their capabilities.

"I have supplied them with money and means. I have primed them for action. All this, of course, without them knowing their benefactor's identity. These three groups were my test run. It has gone well, I think."

I maintained my silence. Ascardi pressed his keypad again. The groups multiplied. He scrolled down. There were far too many to count.

"Over two hundred insurgent organizations around the world, Nicholas, all under my control, financially and operationally. These vigilantes have two things in common apart from my sponsorship. They have all been overactive on social media, calling for some sort of revolutionary change, be it political or environmental. All are extreme in their views, accepting violence and bloodshed as necessary. That's why they had struggled for support, support that I have given them."

"I'm not understanding how ..." I began.

"Let me explain," Ascardi responded. "Tonight, several of these groups will act; some political leaders at the highest levels around the world are now living their final few hours. I believe there is a senator from Utah who has been strongly advocating reducing global emissions targets. He seems to be gaining some momentum not only in Washington but through spreading ignorant lies on his social media platforms. Tonight he will be assassinated by a car bomb outside his office after a meeting with oil company executives. Responsibility for the attack will be claimed by a group known as the Tribunal of Penance." Ascardi scrolled down his list. "Ah, here they are."

The entrepreneur continued. "A similar purge will occur in Greece, where three cabinet members are meeting secretly to discuss dismantling environmental safeguards in order to encourage more productive business relationships with the rest of Europe. Incidentally, all three politicians have received enormous financial donations for their upcoming election campaigns from companies controlled by the Cosa Nostra. Their deaths will be in a motor accident. The group responsible: the Alliance of Diminishing Light. You've got to love some of these names."

There will also be two major environmental catastrophes over the next twenty-four hours: there will be an enormous fire at India's largest open-cut coal mine in West Bengal. It will take months to control and will incapacitate the site. We can't ignore the developing countries. They do a lot of environmental damage in the name of economic growth. Anyway, that fire will be started and nurtured by the Ek Mauka—One Chance." Again, Ascardi scrolled down his list to find the group.

"Finally, there will be a nuclear detonation in the state of

New Jersey on America's heavily populated eastern seaboard. It will be initiated by the People's Solar Coalition. Of course, this final event has been imposed on us by your interference at the Cinaed facility. You see, Nicholas, you saved a few thousand Scots only to cause the deaths of several thousand more of your compatriots."

I was certain someone had driven a pile driver through my stomach.

Ascardi seemed to search my face, gauging the effect of his words.

"Don't look so mortified, Nicholas. This is a rolling campaign over many months. There will be many, probably thousands, more civilians who will die in this multitude of tragedies. We need the deaths of innocents to provoke the outrage.

"If the world will not wake up by itself, I will wake it up. You must see where we're going here, Nicholas? Valueless, corrupt leaders and organizations removed and incapacitated to create a vacuum for change. In one sweep I can mute the power of those who act only for themselves, including my mafia tormentors, and leave the world better placed to survive. I will save us from ourselves.

"For my finale, once my arrows have been fired and my little war of influence has been waged, I will destroy what I have created. Over the last few months, I have developed some powerful malware. A powerful virus—a superbug, if you like—will be injected onto my own media platforms and those of my remaining competitors. Over time it will render all privacy settings dysfunctional. Around the globe every individual's private information will be exposed for all to see. This crisis will make the Cambridge Analytica scandal look like a small inconvenience. All social media platforms will collapse under the weight of the world's distrust."

"But that will destroy your own business."

"Regrettably, Nicholas, I will achieve through physical and social violence that which could not be achieved through peaceful advocacy. A familiar historical story, I believe. If I have to destroy myself to do it, so be it."

At first, I was speechless as I took it all in. Then I found my way. "My God, man, you have turned your grief into guilt, and your guilt has become an insane passion for revenge. Can't you see that?" I offered.

"No, Nicholas. All I see is the transformation of my legacy, possibly inspired by the depth of my grief; I grant you that, but nothing more. I am engineering a correction of the past. It is what must be done."

And I couldn't see a way out.

Chapter 39

For several minutes Ascardi was distracted by his tablet. I assumed he was issuing instructions, commanding each cell of his militia. Eventually, he looked up, as though he had forgotten I was there.

"You will need to go now. Vincenzo will make sure you are secure," he instructed.

"One last question," I said. "Why me? Why did you drag me into this?"

Ascardi looked at me like I was an annoying child who needed placating. He lowered his pad. I had his full attention again.

"It's complicated, Nicholas."

I held his eye.

"All right. First, let me say the recording deal with you, Aislinn, and Patrick Jay Olden was all aboveboard. I was excited when I heard you together and thought you would be perfect for the Vittoria label. Amid the chaos of life, it is the role of the arts to be the tranquil healer. Truth be told, I think Vittoria would have loved your work as well.

"It was after that when things went a little … 'off-kilter.' I was having trouble accessing some of the resources I had targeted, particularly those with paramilitary experience.

These were essential to my plans. Coincidently, Vittoria's lover, who shared my grief and my determination to effect social change, had some contacts. She had worked for a network that had connections and influence all over the world. She put me in touch with them."

The term "network" gave me an uneasy feeling. I had heard it before.

"These people made it clear they could help me out, but the help had a price ... you."

"I'm not following," I said.

"You will, you definitely will," said Ascardi.

Apparently, you had recently done a disservice to these people and caused some major upheavals in their planning. To put it simply, you really pissed them off."

I didn't like where this was going.

"They mentioned something about Iraq, the Isle of Wight, and a man called Giles Winter. I presume you know him."

Pile driver again. I remained silent as I processed what I had just been told.

Finally, I said, "I knew him, but he's dead. I killed him." It was too late to be anything but honest.

"There you have it," said Ascardi. "That's why these people required me to implicate you for my test run. That explains it all. Of course, although I was slightly reluctant, I did agree to their terms ... for the greater good. I must say that these are powerful people, Nicholas; they have a broad reach. They seem to function far more like a shadow government than the Cosa Nostra could."

I was reeling from the fact that this situation had anything to do with my previous interaction with Giles Winter and his people. It did, however, make a modicum of sense.

As I sat there, putting it all together, Ascardi returned to work on his tablet. A few minutes later I heard the now familiar metallic scraping. I looked toward the trapdoor at the end of the room. Ascardi looked up from his work.

"Ah, here we are," he said.

The hooded figure I had seen earlier seemed to float down the stairs in effortless movement.

"Nicholas Sharp, I would like you to meet my partner in our quest for justice. This is Vittoria's lover and friend. Do take off your hood, my dear," he instructed.

The figure turned away from us and slipped the hood down around her shoulders. She flipped out her long dark hair and let it cascade down her back. Then she turned around.

"Hello, Nicholas ... now, don't be angry."

She moved across the room while I sat there like a dumb shmuck. There was no sign of injury or a bullet wound. I had been played. Nicholas Sharp, victim. That label didn't sit well with me.

Elena walked up to Ascardi and kissed him on the cheek. Then she turned to face me.

"I'm thinking we should talk," she said, her eyes unreadable—just the eternal Atlantic swell.

The schmuck just nodded his head.

"I'm sure Tony has filled you in on my relationship with Vittoria. I was devastated when we lost her. She brought out the best in me; sometimes that could be very hard to find. I miss her every day."

I said nothing.

"That being said, Nicholas, I want you to know, my feelings for you were genuine."

I was sure Elena wanted me to respond. I was wound too tight to say a word.

"I once told you that you would be angry with me if I revealed the truth about Marina del Rey. You will be angry, but I will tell you.

"I came to see you on behalf of Giles Winter. He wanted to know if you were still the man you once were. We had to test you. Unfortunately for you, you passed. I did tell you I worked in recruitment, of sorts. That was the last work I did for him. I then returned to London and the arms of my beloved Vittoria. As I said, she brought out the best in me. I decided to leave that world behind."

I was ready to leap across the room as a deep anger swelled within me. Then logic took hold: I was clearly outnumbered by Ascardi's men.

"I know," she continued, "you are unhappy with me. As things turned out, when we lost Vittoria, I needed to step back into my covert world one more time, for her. You know how that feels, don't you, Nicholas?"

I ground my teeth.

The girl in front of me continued her speech. "London, Füssen, yes, it was all real. But I had to disappear. Tony received word that the mafia were sending a professional assassin to kill me as a way to get to him. Vittoria all over again. Besides, you and I were getting too close; our relationship was clouding my perspective. I needed to die for you *and* the Mafia assassin to give up. But Tony and I underestimated you; we should have known better. You never give up, do you?"

For a few seconds, she just stood there, her dark hair cascading recklessly down the sides of her face as she stared me down. Her clenched jawbone suggested an anger that matched her words, but I was also certain there was some level of regret in her eyes.

"It was never my intention that you die. We didn't realize the mafia hitman would come after you when he realized I was already dead. I could live with you going to prison. I always thought that was the worst-case scenario. It turned out I was wrong."

"What about Cinaed?" I finally asked, if only to prove to Ascardi that I had one more question in me.

"Yes, that was my moment of hesitation. It had taken me a long time to come completely on board with Tony's plans. My emotional devastation equaled his, but I was uncertain whether destroying a nuclear power station was the right strategy. So I led you there, knowing you would stop it. You always do the right thing, don't you, Nicholas?"

Elena looked at Ascardi; her expression softened, her eyes almost glazing over in a reluctant acceptance. "Of course, now I understand the lengths we have to go to ... realize Tony's vision."

Ascardi smiled.

Chapter 40

I stared vacantly through the bars at my new Italian friend. Despite Ascardi telling me he was alive, I was relieved to see it for myself. Vincenzo had brought me to the first building I'd searched on Poveglia, the old prison. The henchman stood behind me, far enough away that I couldn't touch him. Even if I could reach him, my hands were zip-tied in front of me, nullifying any chance of engagement. Vincenzo's left hand gripped a handgun, a Beretta M9, his right a flashlight pointing into the cell in front of me. On the other side of the bars, exposed by the light's beam, was Joe Santoro. He lay on an old metal bed frame, his mass extending far beyond it. There was no mattress, and his right hand was handcuffed to the bedhead. His face was cragged with dogged frustration.

"Nicholas," he said.

"Joe, are you all right?" I asked.

"A mite pissed off at these cretini, but I will live."

"In all honesty, I don't think that's their plan," I said to him.

"Enough talk!" said Vincenzo. "Step aside."

I took a step to my left and watched as the henchman pulled a key out of his pocket.

"Further."

I took another step and then watched Vincenzo use the key

to unlock Joe's cell.

"In," he instructed.

"What if I don't?" Nicholas Sharp, petulant child.

"I'll either shoot you as you stand or throw you in there and then shoot you," he responded.

Joe raised an eyebrow. I gave a small nod that I hoped Vincenzo wouldn't see. I also hoped Joe and I were understanding each other.

I turned back to Vincenzo. "Do what you've got to do," I said.

He grunted then raised his gun, pointing it directly at my head. I tensed up. His finger started to squeeze the trigger when he said, "No, this is too easy. I think I will hurt you a little first."

Vincenzo said it like he was going to enjoy it. You can always count on a bully to want to make it personal.

He then took a step closer to me and shoved me hard in the back. I offered no resistance and fell forward into the cell. Vincenzo followed me in, holding the gun in front of him.

He made it about three feet into the cell when there was an almighty roar. Joe the giant sprung to his feet, his speed belying his enormous size. Before Vincenzo could react, Joe had grasped the bed's head with his cuffed hand, it's base with his free hand, and swung the metal frame around toward the henchman, knocking the Beretta out of his hand in the process. By the time Vincenzo realized Joe's plan and moved forward to defend himself, Joe had pushed the frame against Vincenzo's torso, pinning the henchman's body and arms between the bed frame and the cell's bars.

"Nicholas," called the giant.

I knew my cue. Running back into the corridor, I turned

and slid my zip-tied hands between two of the bars just beside Vincenzo's head. The henchman turned his head toward my hands and snapped at them. Joe was using all his strength to maintain the pressure of the bed against him so he couldn't move his body at all. The henchman was lashing out angrily with his teeth, at one point grabbing part of the zip-tie with his mouth. I struggled to pull it free. Joe reacted by letting out another deepthroated scream. Vincenzo turned toward him just as Joe headbutted him on the bridge of his nose. The henchman momentarily slumped, his eyes glazed over but still open. I took the opportunity of his brief stupor to slip my hands over either side of his head, the zip-ties forming a necklace around his throat. Before he could react, I pulled hard with both my hands, the tie cutting into his neck as his head pressed hard against the bars. Vincenzo struggled with the adrenaline-boosted energy of a man facing near-certain death. He kicked at Joe under the bed frame; Joe grunted in pain but didn't let up applying pressure with the bed to Vincenzo's chest. I pulled harder. Vincenzo struggled desperately, somehow getting an arm out from under the frame. He tried to pull my hands off but couldn't get a grip. He then took a swipe at Joe, but it was too late—his strength had deserted him.

I felt his body go limp as Joe released the bed frame and the henchman quietly slipped to the ground.

"Nice work, my friend," I said.

"I've had a little time sitting here, stewing in my anger. Anger breeds fortitude," he responded.

I nodded, bending down to search the henchman's pockets for another key. I found it and unlocked Joe's handcuffs. His arm looked strangely twisted, but all he did was exude the now familiar grunt as I released it. The giant could evidently stand a lot of pain.

Joe used the key's jagged edge to cut through the binding on my hands. I leaned down and grabbed Vincenzo's Berretta.

Five minutes later we were both outside the cell, and Vincenzo was locked within. I briefly filled Joe in on my conversation with Ascardi and Elena.

"What do we do now?" he asked.

"I want you to go down to the water, find the spot they're most likely to bring their boat in. I have a friend arriving, and he'll need help." I told him about Greatrex and the situation he was in.

"What will you do?" asked Joe.

"I'm going back to Ascardi's control room to stop him."

"On your own?" he asked.

"I'm sure you and Jack will be along soon, but when I left him Ascardi was ready to act." I said.

I gave Joe the flashlight and directions to the asylum's chapel.

"You'll also need this," I said, passing him the Beretta.

"So will you, my friend."

"I'll pick something up on the way—now go."

The tightly drawn features on Joe's face told me he wasn't pleased. Still, he reluctantly took the weapon and we separated.

I cautiously retraced my steps back to the asylum building. I wasn't sure if Ascardi had stationed more men around the island. I was counting on he and his people being focused on their work in the control room.

I made it back to the building and edged my way along the outer wall until I reached the old wooden doors. Keeping my back to the wall, I craned my head around to peer inside.

Once again, the room seemed totally empty. I felt the same level of apprehension as I had the first time I'd stepped into the space, only this time it wasn't past ghosts or the eeriness of the room that was causing me to sweat on a cold night.

Suddenly, the world exploded as the first punch hit me straight on the face. It was a hard, painful blow that immediately caused my vision to blur. The second blow collected the side of my head; it felt like a hand grenade had just detonated inside my brain. The onslaught had surprised me completely, rendering my mind virtually incapable of a quick reaction. Peering through my stunned haze, I made out two tall and solid figures bearing down on me.

I was already close to losing consciousness when the third punch loomed through the clouds of my impeded vision. All I could do was duck down, uncertain if I would make it back up. With relief I heard my attacker groan sharply as his hand crashed onto the edge of the solid wooden door where my head had just been.

Flailing on the ground, I reached for a fist-sized piece of stone that was lying a couple of feet away. Despite my brain sending a message to my body to give up and rest, I climbed unsteadily back onto my feet. While one man was clutching his obviously injured hand, the other turned toward me. The lowered eyebrows and intensity on his face said anger; the way the muscles in his arms tensed and his fists were balled said revenge. If he connected with me, it would be over. Desperation and anger make dangerous bedfellows. Focusing all my energy on the rock held in my right hand, I waited a second for my attacker to maneuver back in close enough to strike me again. He drew his fist back ready for his final shot when I brought my hand up and rammed the stone into the side of his head. I didn't even stop to assess the damage. I just ran like hell out the doorway.

It had been my own stupid fault. Of course Ascardi would have had people watching. They had simply been smart enough to stay out of sight. I hadn't. I ran out of the building and turned toward the thick undergrowth, the camouflage of the trees beckoning.

The greenery enveloped me as I left the path outside the building. I ducked left and weaved right. I had no plan; I just needed to be unpredictable. Behind me voices yelled frantically through the wind. Beams from flashlights roamed haphazardly, lighting up the scrub around me. I lowered my head and kept moving forward.

It came as no surprise when I heard the first gunshot. It didn't come anywhere near me; my pursuers were firing blind, but with the scrub so open they would soon get lucky. More gunshots, too many. I hit the ground, making myself the smallest target I could be.

The gunfire stopped. My assailants had changed strategy.

Suddenly, there was movement through the trees not far away from where I lay. A flashlight beam bounced erratically across the branches, pausing only inches away from my position. I could hear only one set of footsteps rustling heavily through the bushes, and they were coming toward me. I couldn't hear a second set of steps. They had split up.

I raised myself into a crouch. If my stalker came within reach, I'd have him. I looked around. The moonlight dissipated in the thick undergrowth, casting only random shards of light. I couldn't make out anything I could use as a weapon.

It didn't take long. A branch snapped a few feet away. Then I made out the shape of a man silently working his way through the scrub directly in front of me. It was Ascardi's sidekick Elia. As the henchman passed just ahead of me, gun in hand, I vaulted forward out of the undergrowth. I opened my arms to reach around his thick neck. With momentum and surprise on my side we both hit the ground with an awkward thud. As we went down his gun flew out of his right hand into the bushes. I landed two quick jabs to the back of his head before Elia's physical prowess came into play. He was large and strong and managed to elbow me sharply in the kidney and push me backward into the brush. I stumbled momentarily. As I regained my footing he turned toward me, pulling a knife out from his jacket. They always seem to have a knife.

Before he could get the blade completely clear of his coat to launch an attack at me, I did the only thing I could do. I charged directly at him, throwing my body aggressively into his. The big man's face radiated surprise as my body weight sent him back to the ground. His fist tightened around the knife. I grabbed at the weapon but couldn't shake it free of his hand. Holding my forearm across his throat, I used my leverage to beat his knife arm against the ground. The henchman used his free left hand to punch my ribs, and then the back of my head, each blow sending me deeper into a numbing fog. I kept pounding the knife arm on the ground. Finally, it spun out of his hand. I stretched my arm, clutching desperately for the weapon. My fingertips finding the handle, I swept the knife into the air. The henchman landed one more powerful blow on the back of my head as the metal glinted in the moonlight above him. His eyes opened wide as he struggled to break free.

With all my remaining strength I plunged the knife down between his ribs and into his heart. I held it there as the life seeped out of the big man. He gurgled, then he was gone.

Now I had a knife.

A second flashlight beam peppered the trees with light: the second henchman. As the beam pushed to my right, I moved to intercept it. Two minutes later, the light flicked past ten feet ahead of me. I slipped out of the bushes and onto the track just behind the dark figure. Raising my right hand, I began to plunge the knife toward the back of my pursuer's neck.

He must have heard me because he flipped around in an instant. Suddenly, we were face to face, but my knife hand was still in motion. In a textbook response my opponent did exactly what I had just done to Elia and grabbed the wrist of my knife hand. As he did so, he brought up his gun with his right hand. In an instant my role had changed from attacker to victim. The gun was everything. As the henchman leveled the weapon at my chest, I coiled my legs to use them as a spring. Before he could squeeze the trigger, I leaped up, kicking out with my left foot. The soul of my shoe connected solidly with the handle of the gun and the fingers that gripped it. My attacker cried out in pain as his wrist cracked and the gun flew out of his broken hand. The gun was now out of play, but the move had come at a price—I had dropped the knife. Sensing I was off balance, my attacker then lunged at me with all his weight and sent me to the hard ground. It was as though he was playing from my song sheet.

On the ground we wrestled and punched at each other, clawing for the knife. I'd received way too much battering over the last thirty minutes; my relationship with consciousness was now fragile at best. Each of my opponent's punches gave him more advantage and caused me more grief. Fifteen seconds later the henchman found the weapon first. Before I even realized he had it, his left arm was silhouetted in the moonlight as he raised the blade above me. Even with the adrenaline flowing I could feel the energy of my tired body waning. I reached for his neck and wrapped my hands around his throat. His neck was too thick, and my hands weren't large enough to have any effect. I could smell the liquored stench of the man's breath as the knife began to come down. My only chance was to minimize the damage. The henchman's arm had almost completed its arc when I rolled desperately to my left, knowing I couldn't fully avoid the blade. I felt its sharpness pierce my side to the right of my ribcage. The pain seared through my body as though a hot poker had been plunged into me.

My opponent withdrew the knife and raised it for a second blow. I had almost nothing left in me.

I frantically rolled again, straight into the bushes. I was flailing wildly, reaching for anything, when my hand struck a metal object on the ground. I rolled again, clutching for the object as I went. I almost passed out with the pain as I rolled onto my wounded side. Then suddenly I was on my back and my attacker was on top. His knife arm was coming down again; I had nowhere to go. I wrapped my fingers around the metal object—it was the dropped gun. I raised it and fired blindly, but the knife still headed toward me. How could I have missed? I gritted my teeth waiting for the pain, but the knife bounced off my chest. My assailant hit the ground beside me, dead.

I lay there for several minutes as my lungs screamed for air. Eventually, I reached down through my blood-soaked shirt to the knife wound. It wouldn't be fatal, but the pain was debilitating. Somehow, I ripped the shirt from the body next to me for a makeshift bandage to match the one on my arm.

The improvised first-aid treatment had consumed too much of my remaining energy. Forcing myself upright, I dragged myself to a nearby tree and leaned against it, gasping erratically. I looked around. No sign of Joe or Greatrex. No surprise, given the odds they had to overcome.

I knew I couldn't wait for them either way. Using the tree as support, I clawed my way up its trunk until I was standing, if you could call it that. Hunched over with acute pain striking lightning bolts through my body, I took a first step. It didn't kill me. I then began the slow stagger through the bushes toward the asylum.

At least now I had a knife *and* a gun.

Chapter 41

Both times I had tried to enter the asylum building I had been compromised. That couldn't be coincidence. Now I clung to the shadows, sheltering in their protection. I moved slowly and carefully until I came to the doorway with the precariously hanging wooden doors.

I stopped at the door. Through the moonlight and shadows, I couldn't spot any cameras or laser intrusion detectors. Getting down on to my knees, I started feeling around in front of me for anything that didn't seem to belong. A minute later I found it. My hand had touched a rubber LED sensor mat under a light layer of dust and gravel. Previously, I'd walked straight over it. I may as well have rung the doorbell.

Running my hand lightly around the edge of the mat, I identified a narrow pathway, about six inches wide, between the edge of the sensor mat and the wall. I hoped pressing myself against the stone wall and following that track with my feet would allow me to enter the building undetected. Once through the doorway, I stayed on my hands and knees, sticking to the perimeter walls and sweeping the ground ahead of me with my palm.

At the chapel entrance I detected another sensor mat in the doorway. Again, I felt my way around it and crawled toward the trapdoor at the far end of the room.

I could think of no safe or effective strategy for entering a room full of armed soldiers through a roof. I likely wouldn't descend the ladder before being cut in half by a hail of bullets.

I would have considered alternatives, but there weren't any.

I couldn't see how this could end well, but neither could I just walk away. If I did, I was committing an untold amount of people to an early grave.

The only way I could figure this was to make an outright one-man assault.

I ran my hands around the trapdoor's perimeter. There were no wires and no sensor pad on top, but Ascardi may have been using LED sensor tech on the approaches to his control room. I needed to be able to drop down through that hole in the floor quickly. The few seconds it would take to open the door after giving him warning of my presence could make all the difference between a successful infiltration or a futile death.

As I pulled the knife out of my pocket with my right hand, I gently lifted the trapdoor with my left, just enough to run the knife around the perimeter. Halfway along the opposite side of the hatch, I felt it with the blade's tip: a small sensor button that when released would probably trigger an alarm if I lifted the trapdoor any higher. Trying not to move the door any more than I had to, I eased the blade over the button to hold it down.

Now: to move in one quick advance or go the stealth route and try and get down the ladder unnoticed? Success depended on where people were looking when I entered. I decided to try the stealth approach first. I could always change strategy mid-stream.

Keeping the knife on the sensor button, I cautiously lifted the trapdoor open, trying to minimize the metallic scraping of the hinges that I had heard earlier. The workers below made enough noise that the door's quiet creaking went unheard. The darkness of the chapel also meant that no light would be noticed from inside the control room. I risked a look down into the room. It appeared to be populated, as before. If anything, the tension and focus of work in the room had increased. Ascardi's deadline was looming, so everyone was hunched over the computers with conversation kept to a terse minimum. While I was thankful for their distraction, their heightened level of activity also reminded me that time was an issue.

I pulled my head up. Stealth it would be. Swiveling around while still keeping my knife on the sensor button, I placed my first foot on the top rung of the ladder, pausing nervously to test the waters. There was no reaction. I lowered myself another step down, focusing entirely on keeping my movements slow and noise to a minimum. I continued step by step, biting my tongue to avoid crying out in agony from bolts of pain generated by the knife wound as I stretched my torso to pull the trapdoor back down. As the door came down, I slid the knife quietly back off the sensor switch.

When I reached the floor, I lay down flat so I wouldn't be seen over the banks of computers. There was no sound, no alarm. I had a chance.

Ascardi and one of his henchmen were a good twenty feet away from where I lay. It was too great a distance to cross without being seen. The four computer operators were closest. Elena was at the nearest bank of computers with her back to me, looking over one of the operator's shoulders.

My biggest threat was Ascardi's henchman. He would be a professional, trained to react in emergency situations. I would need to take him out first. Then I'd go for Ascardi and deal with the computer operators as required. It was my own weakness that I couldn't really judge how much of a threat Elena was.

I quietly maneuvered myself to an upright position, holding my newly acquired gun in front of me. I paused to gauge my chances. The knife wound in my side was causing me grief as spasms of pain invaded my body without warning and my arm throbbed consistently where the bullet had grazed it earlier. I was also so far beyond physically exhausted that I couldn't trust every message my brain was sending me. Perfect.

Ascardi's man began to turn around. Act now or give it up.

I leaped to my feet and fired. My bullet took the man straight through his heart. Ascardi turned and spat out one word: "Sharp!" I turned toward him and began to squeeze the trigger a second time.

Another of Ascardi's men stepped out of the shadows on the left-hand side of the room. He was holding a pistol pointed directly at me. I had no time to re-aim. This was it. Then Elena, who had turned to look at me when I shot the henchman, turned back to the man with the gun and screamed "No!"

I braced for the impact of the bullet, but then Elena, the unpredictable enchantress, stepped between the gunman and me. She was too late to stop him. I heard the sound of the gun firing, but I felt nothing. For a second Elena just stood there with her back to me. The gunman must have missed. But he hadn't. Elena slowly started to buckle and then fell to the ground.

Ascardi lost it completely. Before I could react, he had produced a pistol from his pocket, turned to the gunman while shouting "You fool," and then shot him between the eyes.

I looked up to see that the four men who had been sitting at the computers were now all on their feet. Each held a small revolver aimed at me. I hadn't counted on them being armed. They didn't fire, but they didn't flinch either. I put my gun down.

Both Ascardi and I ran to Elena. I got there first. She was struggling to breathe, and blood wept from her mouth. I looked down at the wound in her chest. Too much dark blood pouring onto the stone floor.

She looked at me; those deep Atlantic-green eyes were fading. "Nicholas, I'm so sorry." She tried to smile, but all she could do was flinch.

Ascardi kneeled next to her, cradling her head in his arms. "Tony," she gasped.

And with that, she was gone.

It was a surreal picture, Ascardi and I kneeling on the ground next to her. Then he looked up at me, his face contorted with rage. "This is your fault, Sharp," he snarled.

He looked around, obviously realizing he'd dropped his gun as he rushed to Elena's side. He got up, walked over to one of the armed computer technicians and grabbed his revolver.

I knew what was coming, but despite having nowhere to go, I wasn't going to stay there and wait for it. I sprang to my feet. I couldn't outrun four armed men, but I might have a chance to take Ascardi out before I went down.

The man closest to me hesitated, as if waiting for orders. I knocked him out of the way and lunged for Ascardi. I was too slow. Ascardi raised his weapon and aimed. I was still eight feet from him; I'd have no chance. Still, I would die trying.

It was then that the earth shook. An explosion echoed through the room, so loud that it felt like my ears were imploding. The roof started to collapse. Stone and wood showered down upon us.

Ascardi lost his footing and fell to the floor, disappearing under a cloud of dust and rubble. I fell and rolled, barely making it to the shelter of a computer desk before a huge wooden beam smashed down where I had just been standing.

Every one of us in that room lost our bearings as the wreckage came down. You could see virtually nothing through the dust and smoke. I had no idea what had caused the explosion, just that I had to survive long enough to take Ascardi out.

The dust began to clear. I couldn't hear much, but I saw two figures approaching out of the haze. They were more of Ascardi's oversized henchmen. I felt the space around me close in while I tried to reach for some sort of weapon. The men had seen me. I was surrounded by wreckage with nowhere to go. In desperation I wrapped my hands around a heavy piece of stone—that would have to do. I raised it in the air.

"Take it easy, Rambo," said a muffled voice.

I wiped the dust from my eyes.

As the figures cleared the smoke, I could slowly make them out. They were big men, walking with purpose and aggression. As they neared, I decided I was all right with that. They came right up to where I was half-lying-half-crouching and looked down.

To anyone else they would have looked like monsters—not to me. “About freakin’ time,” I said as Jack Greatrex and Joe Santoro reached down and pulled me to my feet.

Chapter 42

I knew there was a story behind what had just happened, but there was no time to hear it.

"Sit-rep: there are four armed men plus Ascardi somewhere in this room," I said. I realized I was probably shouting the words. The effect of the explosion on my hearing made my voice sound like I was talking through a wet sponge. "We've got to find them. Until we do, Ascardi is still a danger."

"Got it," said Greatrex.

Joe Santoro was already searching the room. There was some dim light, most likely from an emergency generator, but it revealed little. Suddenly, a man appeared out of the shadows behind Joe. Unsurprisingly, the figure appeared shaky on his feet. Before I could warn the giant, the outline of a gun appeared in the shadowy figure's hand.

"Joe," I finally managed to half yell, half cough.

Joe began to turn around when the sound of a gunshot resonated around what was left of the room. Joe seemed to flinch, but he never lost his footing. He then reached toward the man who had shot at him, grabbed him by the collar, hoisted him in the air and swept the gun out of his grasp with a powerful backhander. The man continued to struggle in Joe's grip, but it was pointless. One powerful punch from

Joe's clenched fist, and he fell backward onto the rubble. He lay there in an unconscious heap.

The brief altercation had sharpened our senses. The danger was still very real.

Greatrex and Santoro searched the rubble, upending beams, furniture, and piles of stone.

It was a noisy process. The sound of crashing debris being dislodged and cast aside vibrated around the room. I was on the job but still in a daze. Pain and fatigue fought for my undivided attention.

I don't know how I heard it amid the noise, but I did hear it. It was the sound of rock scraping harshly against rock. Then a quiet thump as rubble was being gently shoved aside, but not where Greatrex and Joe were searching. The grating sounds came from behind me. I turned and squinted into the dust-filled semi-darkness. At first I saw nothing, but my senses had sprung into alert mode. Someone was there.

A second later another shadow arose hesitantly from the smokey rubble. For a moment, the figure stopped. I could make out enough body language to see him—and it was definitely a male—scan the room. He was well out of my reach, with piles of rock laying between us. As quickly as the figure rose, he disappeared again behind some rubble. A few seconds later he reappeared, this time hunched in a crawling position. I couldn't work out what he was doing until his whole body appeared above the rubble. He was climbing steadily along a heavy wooden beam that had fallen at a forty-five-degree angle to the floor. It extended up into an opening in the ceiling.

"Jack, Joe,' I yelled. "You cover whoever is alive here, and watch your backs. We've got a runaway."

By the time I had taken a single step, the figure had exited through the gap in the ceiling. Willing my own body into action, I climbed over the mess of stone, wood, equipment, and shattered furniture and reached toward the angled wooden beam. I must have grasped the top of the beam only seconds after the figure I had seen had disappeared through the hole, yet sticking my head cautiously out of the gap, I saw no one.

The shadow of the old clock tower loomed over me as I laboriously pulled myself up through the hole. My first reaction was to soak in the fresh air. My second was to fix my gaze on a room that no longer existed. Any structure that was here had been destroyed in the explosion, turning the building into an open-air ruin. Nothing but stone and concrete debris lay strewn across the space. Not knowing which way the figure had gone, I decided to head for the tower building.

Just as it was impossible to find me in the undergrowth a short time ago, it would now be impossible for me to see anyone else. I raced through the trees to the edge of the tower building. I knew my way along here from my previous search, so I made good time. Soon I was out in the open, running along the stone path between the buildings and the water. I saw no one ahead of me. The only possible plan was to circumnavigate the island on foot and try to locate the missing man. If the figure I had seen was Ascardi, I knew he would have a pre-planned escape route. It was in his innate, meticulous nature. There was a lot of ground to cover and not much time to do it.

As I rounded the southern corner of the building at a full run, a bullet flew past my ear, impacting the stone wall beside me. A geyser of shattered stone spewed into the air. Had I been moving slower, I would have certainly been shot. Crashing hard down onto the path, I heard another bullet hit the ground next to me. More shards of shattered stone flew into the back of my neck and head. I risked provoking the gunman with a brief glance ahead. By now, the fog had disappeared completely and the figure firing at me was clearly outlined in the moonlight.

I could see him, and his accuracy meant he could see me as well. I wouldn't last long in such a vulnerable position, but I was unable to move, pinned down by the gunfire.

Reaching into my pocket, I pulled out the pistol. Without aiming, I held it in front of me and fired indiscriminately. I missed, but my shot had served its purpose. The figure turned and ran down the pathway.

I jumped to my feet and ran after him. I had no idea whether I was chasing one of Ascardi's henchmen or the man himself. I just kept running.

A minute later the man ahead of me disappeared from sight as the pathway ahead veered to the right. Remembering my near-death experience as I rounded the last corner, I knew caution was warranted. Not happening.

I rounded the corner at full speed. To my relief, there was no gunshot. My comfort proved to be short-lived: the figure leaped out of the bushes on my right. His left hand was raised high above his head. In the shadows I didn't see the large piece of wood in his hand until just before he connected with the side of my head. I tried to avoid the blow, but I had no chance. Once again, my world spun out of control as any sense of balance deserted me. I collapsed onto the ground, dazed but still conscious. Pain was no longer a sensation; it was the essence of my being.

My attacker didn't hang around. One second, he was standing over me, the next he was gone. Though my vision was blurred, there was no mistaking the furious face of Antonio Ascardi.

As debilitated as I felt, the fact that Ascardi was still alive spurred me on.

I staggered to my feet and tried to run. It wasn't happening. The best I could do was an erratic limp. I tried to refocus, concentrating hard to make sure I didn't go over the edge of the path. Why hadn't Ascardi finished me off with a bullet? He probably thought there was no need and that escaping was his priority. The way I was feeling, he may well have made the right decision.

I made it to the end of the pathway, where the trail stopped at a boat shed. I was about to search the building when I glimpsed movement to my right. It was Ascardi, just past the structure's northern end, advancing along the edge of the canal that cleaved the island. The man was disappearing from view. I had to slow him down. I didn't know how many rounds I had left in my gun, and I didn't want to waste any.

To hell with it. I figured he'd be out of view within a second, so I fired twice in his direction. He was running too quickly, and my shots went wide. At least he now knew I was still behind him; that might make him more cautious.

I held back what pace I had at the far end of the boat shed. I had learned my lesson. There was no clear path along the channel at this point, just a lot of undergrowth and a few ruined buildings. This had just become a very dangerous game between Ascardi, myself, and the random slivers of light provided by the moon.

I moved as silently as I could through the bush and stone landscape. Every footstep seemed to advertise my presence as twigs and rocks snapped and rumbled under my feet. I stopped every thirty seconds or so to listen for any sign of Ascardi's location. On my third stop, I heard rustling. I pushed toward the sound and then stopped again. Nothing except the gentle breeze over the water.

I saw the flash from the muzzle at the same time I heard the shot. A bullet embedded itself in a tree trunk about an inch from my head. Without thinking, I fired back at the source. When I hit the ground and listened, there was no response to my shot. I struggled as I climbed to my feet, every muscle and tendon in my body screaming.

Ignoring the pain, I moved on quietly.

A few minutes later, the palette of shadows ahead changed. The moon must have appeared from behind a cloud as an unexpected glow was cast on a stone wall about twenty yards ahead. The light enabled me to clearly make out the shadow of Ascardi cautiously traversing the length of the wall. This was an opportunity. Ascardi must have sensed he was exposed, in the very same instant that I fired. He dove for the ground, but he had reacted too slowly. I heard his grunt of pain from where I was standing. I was certain I'd hit him, but whatever damage I'd caused hadn't been debilitating. He slithered rapidly around the end of the wall before I could get off another shot.

At the very least, I knew that injuring Ascardi would probably have slowed him. I just wasn't sure if that would be enough.

I tried to move forward, but my legs didn't respond. My lower muscles cramped and froze. There was no choice but to stop for a moment. My will was fighting a losing battle with my body. As my breathing became labored and shallow, I placed my hand over the knife wound on my side. It had started bleeding heavily again. My vision wavered as the trees and bushes around me passed in and out of focus. Whether it was from blood loss, concussion, or simply the overwhelming pain, it didn't matter. It was clear I was done. Unless my last shot was true, Ascardi would escape.

Despite my state, I attempted to lunge forward again only to find myself face down on the ground. Any iota of strength I had left abruptly abandoned me. I tried to bend my knees to help me push up to a standing position—nothing. I tried the same with my arms—same response.

Shit.

I took a long, slow breath and gritted my teeth. Using a tree as support, I hoisted myself to my knees. I paused again. I could do this. I would do this.

Unexpectedly, I heard the all-too-familiar noise of a helicopter's beating blades. Raising my head painfully upward, I couldn't see a thing through the clouds, but it was there, the sound of the blades and now the bird's engine growing louder and closer. The aircraft may as well have been a thousand miles away. For me, ten feet was out of reach. Suddenly, the shape of a small chopper was silhouetted against the night sky. It was slowly descending toward fields on the far side of the island like an apparition. There were no landing lights visible on the machine. That meant it wasn't official. It was here for Ascardi.

This madman was going to get away. He'd regroup. Every trial had been for nothing. More lives would be lost, and the world would probably never know the name of the delusory villain behind it all.

No way.

I clung to the tree next to me like it was life itself. A few agonizing seconds later I was on my feet, unsteady as a leaf in the wind but gradually pushing through what was left of the thinning greenery. I didn't bother trying to conceal myself. It was too late for that.

The scrub virtually disappeared as a half wall appeared in front of me. I fell against it and clutched the stonework for support. I looked down and across the water below. A drop led to steps down to the water's edge. They continued along the side of the channel, then veered right, just out of sight.

Just beyond the steps, an arched bridge spanned the channel across to the eastern part of the island. All Ascardi had to do was cross that bridge, rendezvous with his chopper, and disappear.

I searched but couldn't see him. I assumed he was just around the bend, out of sight but heading for the bridge. I'd wait, taking the shot when he came back into view on the bridge ... Nope, not with a handgun at this distance, and not with my level of impairment.

But I lacked the strength to scale down the wall and the time to go around it. I looked across. The grass underneath the helicopter splayed in the chopper's downdraft. The machine was only a few feet above the ground, almost at the point of landing.

I did the one thing I could do. I climbed over the wall and fell the ten feet to the steps below.

The pain as I hit the stone was like a gigantic vice had crushed my entire body, sparing no limb. I know I passed out, but it must have been only for a second, because when I looked up, I could just make out the desperate figure of Ascardi running in the distance. He was on the approach to the bridge, sprinting forward and clutching his arm.

I wasn't going to make it in time.

Again I felt the anger well inside me, consuming me. The anger overpowered the pain and exhaustion. I was half on my feet and dragging myself haphazardly down the steps before I realized what I was doing. If I could get closer to the river bend, I might have a chance of a shot. The pain fought back as my muscles spasmed erratically, sending more waves of agony through my body. Suffering versus rage: it was a pretty even match.

As I reached the bend, I saw that Ascardi had made it to the middle of the bridge. I watched as he looked over his shoulder and saw me. I raised my gun. My hand was unsteady; sweat poured into my eyes. My vision was distorted—the river, the bridge, Ascardi, they were all changing shape and focus, blurring at the edges. How could I possibly calculate the distance of the shot in this condition? I saw that he had stopped. He changed his stance, his feet apart, facing in my direction. It took me half a second to realize what he was doing as he held up his pistol with his good hand and pointed it at me.

Neither of us had anywhere to go. The moment seemed almost suspended in time. We would both die here.

All I could do was focus on staying upright and keeping my gun as steady as possible. I knew my hands were wavering as Ascardi appeared in my sights one second and then vanished the next. I heard the chopper's engine reduce power as it landed. It was now or it wasn't going to happen. I knew this would be a shot of faith rather than skill. I breathed out and squeezed the trigger.

The sound of the hammer smacking down on the firing pin in the empty chamber echoed through my head, completing my defeat.

I would die here alone, and Antonio Ascardi would get away.

Then I heard the sound of my shot, only it wasn't my shot.

Then I understood. Of course, Ascardi. I braced for the bullet.

Nothing.

I looked up and saw Antonio Ascardi doubled over, clutching his stomach. A second later he toppled forward off the bridge and into the water.

I breathed again. Relief and confusion. Another troubled soul had joined the island's previous one hundred and fifty thousand. But how?

My legs gave way for the last time, and I crashed onto the stone. I strained every aching muscle to turn behind me and look up. My vision was distorted to the point where I wasn't even sure what I was seeing. Standing at the wall at the top of the stairs was the blurred outline of a man. I concentrated on his image. He looked to be in a bad way. Bloody bandages covered parts of his face, and he swayed unsteadily on his feet. There was no doubt, however, about the rifle he held in his hands, the smoking gun. I was dimly aware that I was fading in and out of consciousness, and the disorder of my rambling thoughts told me I wasn't thinking straight. I tried to get a grip. I knew the face from somewhere. I had it, and then I didn't. I couldn't place him. The man at the wall smiled, but it was a cold smile. A cold smile—that was it. Suddenly, I knew who he was, but I didn't understand.

Then I allowed the pain to take me. Cue: exit stage.

Epilogue

Five months later ...

The crowd were on their feet and applauding wildly. The volume of their response filled the cavernous space with warmth, human warmth. Emotions were running high, and not only with the audience. Next to me, a cascade of tears was streaming down Aislinn Byrne's cheeks. They weren't tears of pain. It was not just an appreciation of our performance; it was also a declaration of defiance. This was not the first time that the population of Paris had united in their resolve to be free. The message was clear: no one is going to intimidate us; no one is going to destroy our culture and our way of life. No terrorist will ever be granted that power. Five minutes on, they were still applauding. The power of rebellion.

Aislinn, Patrick Jay, and I locked eyes with each other as we joined hands in the middle of the stage. I briefly wondered if my face mirrored their demeanor as they stood proud and impudent. I glanced back to the audience, still cheering. Their faces portrayed the same resolve. The three of us took one final bow, looked out at the audience, held our hands high, and applauded them. Their strength gave us strength.

It had been five months since that night on Poveglia Island when I had seen Antonio Ascardi die. I'd spent a good deal of that time recovering, first in hospital and then at my apartment in Venice, California. The knife wound, the gunshot wound, and the extreme concussion—my journey to back to health had been difficult. Mentally, I had not been in a good place.

None of the physical damage had been permanent, and soon I was keen to get back to work: my creative work. I was pleased when an invitation arrived for Aislinn, Patrick Jay, and I to perform at the reopening of the Palais Garnier. Standing on the stage, gazing at the splendor of the revered concert hall, alive with humanity and hope, it was like the bombing five months earlier had never happened. Box five had been rebuilt; it was pristine, and the historical venue was as magnificent as ever.

That night, we performed the finale of the show we had started several months before.

Eventually, we were allowed to leave the stage. As we walked back to our dressing rooms, the atmosphere was festive. Backstage crew were cheering, and champagne bottles were popping before we'd even cleared the performance area. When I made it to my own dressing room, I sat down and stared at the man in the mirror. Despite the adulation, he still looked weary and a little troubled. Worry lines ran like rivers across his brow, and the eyes seemed to have lost some shine. Permanent or temporary—who knew?

As had been too often the case, my mind retreated back to the events of a tour plagued by violence and deceit. Every memory led me back to that night on the 'island of death,' the night that had almost cost me my life.

"It will get easier," said the voice behind me. Jack Greatrex, sitting in a chair against the wall, was almost too smart for his own good, but I knew he spoke from experience.

"I know," I said. "Being back here has refreshed the memories ... and the questions. It makes you wonder how tragedy can turn a sane man into a killer."

"Are you talking about Ascardi or you?"

I didn't respond.

"I'm also thinking about all those who died," I said.

"And how many more would have died, if not for your actions?"

"I know," I repeated, "but Ascardi's grief spoke to the lust for revenge that lies in us all," I said.

"I would have called your role more that of a guardian. I know you punish yourself for those who were lost, but it would have been many more if Ascardi had continued unimpaired. If you hadn't stopped him that night, he would have been able to trigger all those needless deaths," said my friend.

"Elena," I said. "I don't know that I'll ever unravel the mystery of that beautiful but tortured soul."

"Perhaps that one is best left as a 'love unresolved.' It is the Italian way." I recognized the voice of Joe Santoro, although I hadn't noticed he'd entered the room.

"Enough of this morbid reflection," I announced, smiling. "This is the first time the three of us have been together without either being in a hospital or facing imminent death. We should celebrate." I indicated the bottle of expensive French champagne on my dressing room table.

Greatrex poured us each a glass.

I looked at my two friends. While I was in hospital in Italy, they had been to see me. I had been keen to fill in the blank moments of that night. They had explained how the two of them had dealt with Ascardi's guards as Greatrex's boat had arrived at Poveglia. It was sheer good luck that Ascardi's men had stored some left over C4 explosive in the bow of the boat in an attempt to keep it dry. Greatrex had taken it with them as they searched for me.

"When we heard the gunshots from the basement, we knew there were too many shots being fired for it to be going well for you, Nicholas. We couldn't get in unseen through that trapdoor, so a couple of hastily placed explosives, and there we were," Greatrex had explained.

Back to the moment.

I raised my glass. "To the two of you and your childish need to blow things up," I said. "Thank you."

They both nodded. That was as sentimental as we were going to get.

There was a knock on the door.

"Entrez," I said.

A security guard poked his head around the door. "There are two men here to see you, Monsieur Sharp. They would not give their names, but they have government credentials."

Greatrex, Joe, and I just looked at each other, our eyebrows raised. "What now?"

"Show them in please," I responded.

In walked Jasper De Vries from Europol, followed by his brother, Thomas De Vries, also in the family business. I hadn't seen the former since the Ascardi affair had ended, and the latter since I'd given him the slip on the train.

I felt myself tensing up, unsure which way this was going

to go.

"If you're here to continue your vendetta against Nicholas, you're going to have an insurmountable issue with me," said Greatrex, now on his feet.

"And me," added Joe, looming above them.

I put up my hand. Time to show a little faith. "Agent De Vries, Jasper, we are all feeling a mite grateful just to be sitting here this evening. I believe I owe you an apology for the way I manhandled you on the roof of the basilica."

The room was silent as Greatrex, Joe, and I waited for a reaction.

"Let's be clear, Sharp. You didn't manhandle me; you beat the crap out of me," he said.

A few seconds more of silence passed. You could feel the unease in the room. Both Greatrex and Joe voicelessly exuded their concern, their foreheads furrowed as they both moved forward on their chairs. Then De Vries smiled, and for the first time it didn't feel like an icicle through my heart.

"And in doing so you saved countless lives in the Piazza San Marco that day. I'm afraid it's I who owe you an apology."

I breathed out, not having realized I was holding my breath.

De Vries continued. "I think I should explain a few things. First, let me formally introduce my brother, Agent Thomas De Vries. As I believe you know, Thomas also works for Europol. What you probably don't know is that he works in our European Cybercrime Centre."

I nodded.

"After I had been patched up following our altercation on the roof that day, I had a very interesting conversation in the hospital with one Norbert Fontana. The man has the backbone of an invertebrate. After you shot that cell phone from his ear, he was in need of some serious plastic surgery. While I had nothing to officially hold him on, I felt that your protestations were so strong there was a small chance you may be telling the truth. I threatened Fontana with a life in prison and no prospect of remedial surgery. He decided to talk. In fact, he wouldn't stop."

Greatrex and I glanced across the room at each other, the traces of a grin creeping onto both our faces.

"After talking with him," the agent continued, "I spoke to my brother. Thomas was already examining reports of increased online activity by some suspected terrorist groups. Despite my earlier misgivings about your innocence, I had asked him to look at the backgrounds of the groups who claimed responsibility for the events we were blaming on you, Mr. Sharp." He paused. "Yes, despite what you may think, I am a professional who pursues all avenues to get to the truth. My brother had wanted to eyeball you; he's old-fashioned that way. This is why he volunteered for the duty of following you on the train to Venice. When I told Thomas what Fontana had told me, a picture started to form. It didn't paint Antonio Ascardi in a very favorable light."

Again, Greatrex and I looked at each other. This was all starting to make sense.

"An interesting aside to this was that Thomas also discovered that other people were looking into Ascardi's activities. He traced those enquiries and ended up having a very interesting conversation with a General Colin Devlin-Waters, retired … or maybe not so retired," he added. "Either way, it appears the General has quite a reputation, and he spoke very highly of you."

I just stared at De Vries, unwilling to interrupt.

"So," he concluded, "that is why and how I ended up on Poveglia Island, with my visit apparently timed to perfection. It's also why I decided to shoot Antonio Ascardi instead of you."

The agent smiled again, allowing a hint of his previous coldness to creep into his expression. Then he added, "It could have gone either way really."

Laughter erupted around the room. I knew it was at my expense, but I didn't really care.

"I am extremely grateful to you, Agent De Vries, but I have one question," I said.

Both agents looked at me.

"Elena Beria," I continued. "What can you tell me about her background, her story?"

Joe Santoro gave me a dismissive look, as though I should have known better.

Thomas answered. "Sometimes it is better not to know everything, Mr. Sharp. Elena Beria had a history full of contradictions. Perhaps it is better just to remember that she gave her own life to save yours."

It was obvious that no one was going to tell me anything more. I just had to inhale, exhale, and move on.

Greatrex shared the champagne with the agents, who had decided they were off duty. The atmosphere in the room lightened. We talked a while and invited the De Vries brothers to the post-show party for the reopening of the Palais Garnier.

"Sadly, we won't be able to join you," said Jasper De Vries. "We have a plane to catch. I do, however, have one most important question to ask you, Nicholas," he added.

The room went quiet. We all waited.

"Tonight I sat there in the audience, listening to the uplifting and spirited music that you, Ms. Byrne, and Mr. Olden created. I found it moving."

"Thank you," I responded, "but that's not a question."

"No," he said. "My question is this. If you can play the piano as beautifully as you do and create a sound so rich that it can either torture or calm the souls of so many, then you must surely know that you have a vocation in the arts?"

I just nodded, almost imperceptibly. I still couldn't see the question. De Vries seemed to sense my uncertainty.

"If you can do all I've just said, then why the hell do you choose to spend your time running around with guns shooting people and getting shot at?"

Again, the room erupted in raucous laughter. A minute later the laughter trickled down to silence as everyone waited for my answer.

I looked directly at Jasper De Vries. As I answered him a small amount of discomfort sidled into my voice.

"It's not a choice, De Vries. It never was."

Afterword

Get your FREE electronic copy of the NICHOLAS SHARP origins Novella PLAY OUT, the latest news about new releases and some other exciting freebies along the way by joining my mailing list at my website: https://markmannock.com

Although you can begin reading the NICHOLAS SHARP THRILLER series at any point here is my suggested order of reading:

1. **KILLSONG** (NS thriller No. 1-*available on Amazon*)
2. **BLOOD NOTE** (A NS short story-*available exclusively to my mailing list members. I'll send you the link 7 days after sign-up*)
3. **LETHAL SCORE** (NS thriller No. 2-*available on Amazon*)
4. **HELL'S CHOIR** (NS thriller No. 3-*available on Amazon*)
5. **SILENT VOICE** (NS thriller No. 4-*available on Amazon*)
6. **COUNTERPOINT** (NS thriller No. 5-*available on Amazon*)
7. **ECHO BLUE** (NS thriller No. 6-*pre-order on Amazon-out August 2023*)

PLAY OUT-an origins novella (*available exclusively to my mailing list members on sign-up*) can be read at any point. The story takes you back to when Nicholas Sharp left the U.S. Marines.

What readers are saying about the Nicholas Sharp Series:

"I had to keep reading to the end, could not put it away until I had finished."

"I love Lee Child and now have another author who is just as good."

"Jack Reacher's attitude... John Lennon's sensibilities."

"I really enjoyed the sniper-musician-reluctant warrior character..."

"I've read hundreds of books throughout the years and the pandemic has provided me with extra time to discover more reading treasures. Play Out (Nicholas Sharp Origins novella) is one of the best."

"Without a doubt this is a cracking novel... the story then keeps at you in leaps and bounds! Full of action all the way. Just brilliant!"

Reviews are life's blood to an author. If you've enjoyed LETHAL SCORE please consider leaving a review on the book's Amazon page.

Acknowledgements

My heartfelt thanks and love to Sarah, Anisha and Jack for your love, tolerance and support. Lachlan, your counsel and wisdom has always been appreciated. Tony Ryan, editor extraordinaire. Thank you so much.

Cover by Anisha Mannock

About the Author

Mark Mannock was born in Melbourne, Australia. He has had an extensive career in the music industry including supporting, recording with or writing for Tina Turner, Joni Mitchell, The Eurythmics, Irene Cara and David Hudson. His recorded work with Lia Scallon has twice been long-listed for Grammy Awards. As a composer/songwriter Mark's music has been used across the world in countless television and theatre contexts, including the 'American Survivor' TV series and 'Sleuth' playwright Anthony Shaffer's later productions.

Mark is presently writing the successful 'Nicholas Sharp' thriller series about a disillusioned former US sniper whose past plagues him as he makes his way in the contemporary music industry. Sharp is a man whose insatiable curiosity and embedded moral compass lead him to places he ought not go. The series is currently read in over 50 countries.

Mark lives in Kettering, Tasmania with his family. His travels around the globe act as inspirations for his writing.

Mark enjoys hearing from his readers, so please feel free to contact him.

You can connect with me on:

https://markmannock.com

https://www.facebook.com/markmannockbooks

Subscribe to my newsletter:

https://markmannock.com

Also by Mark Mannock

PLAY OUT
A Nicholas Sharp Origin Novella

Sign up to my mailing list and receive this book for free!

Set five years before **KILLSONG**

A Terrorist attack on the London Underground. Nicholas Sharp doesn't think so.

While on leave from Iraq, the U.S. Marine Sniper finds himself intervening when innocent lives are threatened. He walks away, but for Sharp it's never that easy. Something doesn't feel right. Twenty-four hours later everything is wrong.

The brief solace he finds in his beloved piano is shattered when Sharp becomes the attacker's next target. Step up or step away. Nicholas Sharp doesn't like to kill, but he sure as hell knows how to.

Somewhere between Clancy's *Jack Ryan* and Ludlum's *Jason Bourne,* Nicholas Sharp may be a flawed and reluctant hero, but you certainly want him on your side.

***"I've read hundreds of books throughout the years and the pandemic has provided me with extra time to discover more reading treasures. Play Out is one of the best."* Goodreads Reviewer-5 STARS**

The Nicholas Sharp origins novella PLAY OUT is sent to you FREE when you join my mailing list at
https://markmannock.com

KILLSONG
Nicholas Sharp Thriller #1

Reluctant, determined, lethal. Nicholas Sharp is a killer musician... literally!

Nicholas Sharp knew there would be blood on his hands. It was just a question of how much.

The death of a child and her mother, or the loss of countless thousands. Sharp is ordered to choose, but the former Marine Sniper gave up following orders long ago.

Sharp's newfound refuge as a musician is suddenly blasted apart. While he is preparing to back well-known singer Robbie West on a USO tour of Iraq, a close friend and her daughter disappear.

Trapped in a deadly maze of colliding worlds and dark agendas as competing forces race to locate discarded biological weapons, Sharp is compelled to act.

One wrong decision, one misstep... and the consequences could be disastrous.

"I had to keep reading to the end, could not put it away until I had finished." **Amazon Reader- 5 STARS**

Available on Amazon:

http://www.amazon.com/dp/B08CT1FHF5
http://www.amazon.co.uk/dp/B08CT1FHF5
http://www.amazon.com.au/dp/B08CT1FHF5
https://www.amazon.ca/dp/B08CT1FHF5

HELL'S CHOIR
Nicholas Sharp Thriller #3

A goodwill visit to Sudan, what could possibly go wrong?

Nicholas Sharp is performing as part of a political and cultural group representing the US. Suddenly caught up in the middle of a political coup, the leader of the American contingent goes missing and his security staff murdered.

Communication with the outside world is cut off. It falls to Sharp and Greatrex to track their missing leader down.

But then things get really complicated…

"The story then keeps at you in leaps and bounds! Full of action all the way. Just brilliant!" **Amazon Reader-5 STARS**

"Great read and a fun ride." **Amazon Reader-5 STARS**

Available on Amazon:

http://www.amazon.com/dp/B08LRB8CWN
http://www.amazon.co.uk/dp/B08LRB8CWN
http://www.amazon.com.au/dp/B08LRB8CWN
https://www.amazon.ca/dp/B08LRB8CWN

SILENT VOICE
Nicholas Sharp Thriller #4

It's dangerous to be right when the government is wrong...

Hunted down by their government's secret service, the members of protest band Kha Cring flee to Los Angeles to begin a new life. After an unexpected attack, the musicians' safe exile in LA is jeopardized. The desire to fight for their country's freedom undiminished, the band find their soaring popularity and politically messaged music no longer enough to protect them from the evil they escaped.

A deadlier weapon is needed. Nicholas Sharp.

In an instant things go terribly wrong as Sharp finds himself the focus of a network of international conspirators intent on wiping both he and the members of Kha Cring from the face of the planet.

Available on Amazon:

http://www.amazon.com/dp/B08W1V9FWS
http://www.amazon.co.uk/dp/B08W1V9FWS
http://www.amazon.com.au/dp/B08W1V9FWS
https://www.amazon.ca/dp/B08W1V9FWS

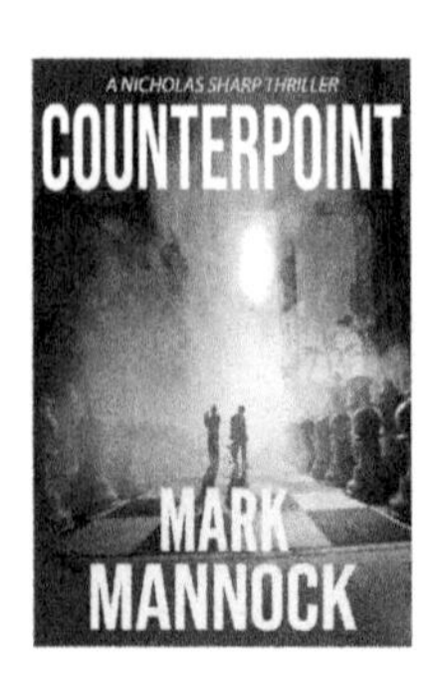

COUNTERPOINT
Nicholas Sharp Thriller #5

Looking in the mirror, he saw only death...

Pursued by one of the world's most efficient and ruthless assassins, Nicholas Sharp almost admires the deadly operator's meticulous talents, until the assassin starts coming after Sharp through his friends. Sharp's investigations reveal that the killer also has another target in sight: the US Secretary of Defense. Is there a dark connection?

Face to face with a past he'd considered banished from his memory, Nicholas Sharp questions not only his own moral compass but also his slim chance of survival.

Available on Amazon:

http://www.amazon.com/dp/B0BVTVWZ6N
http://www.amazon.co.uk/dp/B0BVTVWZ6N
http://www.amazon.com.au/dp/B0BVTVWZ6N
https://www.amazon.ca/dp/B0BVTVWZ6N

ECHO BLUE
Nicholas Sharp Thriller #6

Are you safe?...

Nicholas Sharp receives a mysterious phone call from Jack Greatrex... then Greatrex disappears.

In a hunt that takes him through South America, Texas, the mountains of Northern Spain and eventually the Middle East, Sharp encounters world renowned environmental activist Dr Deagan Jones from the notorious Crimson Wave. As Sharp uncovers a chain of complex deceptions, Jones' teenage son is kidnapped. The stakes never higher, the ex-Marine sniper turned musician fights to prevent an environmental and humanitarian catastrophe with unimaginable consequences.

Available on Amazon: (August 2023, pre-order now)

http://www.amazon.com/dp/B0BVV25R2F
http://www.amazon.co.uk/dp/B0BVV25R2F
http://www.amazon.com.au/dp/B0BVV25R2F
https://www.amazon.ca/dp/B0BVV25R2F

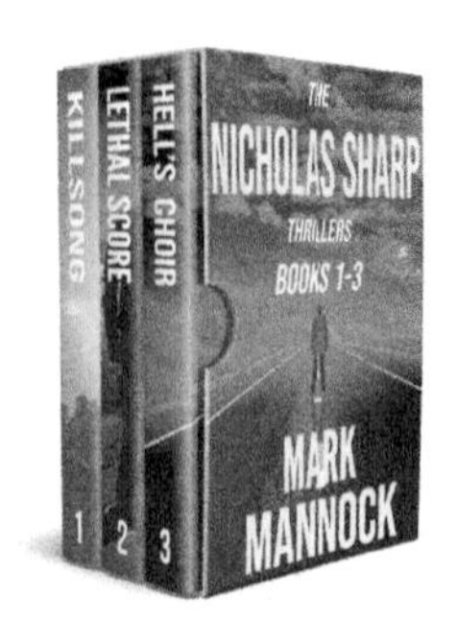

The NICHOLAS SHARP THRILLERS BOOKS 1-3 BOXSET

KILLSONG

LETHAL SCORE

HELL'S CHOIR

Three great Nicholas Sharp Novels in one Box Set

http://www.amazon.com/dp/B08NYLGW1G http://www.amazon.co.uk/dp/B08NYLGW1G http://www.amazon.com.au/dp/B08NYLGW1G https://www.amazon.ca/dp/B08NYLGW1G

BLOOD NOTE

A Short Story Prequel to the Thriller KILLSONG *(should be read after KILLSONG-available FREE to mailing list subscribers 7 days after sign-up)*

Just turn around and walk away. That was all Nicholas Sharp had to do when the mysterious and intoxicating Elena approached him for help.

She knew far too much about him. The warning signs were all there.

Sharp didn't listen to them.

What followed for the former Marine Sniper turned musician, was a harrowing night of violence, deceit and intrigue.

When the sunrise ushered in a new day, Sharp thought it was all over...but it was really just beginning.

Printed in Great Britain
by Amazon